# The Mud Woman

## The Mud Chronicles, Volume II

**by**

**ROB ERRERA**


Riverdale, NJ
USA

The Mud Woman

**roberrera.com**

Bad Hound Press
A Division of Giant Dog Books
**BadHoundPress.com**

This is a work of fiction. All of the characters, organizations, and events portrayed in this story are either products of the author's imagination or are used fictionally.

Editorial guidance by Dominic Wilde and Ken Kimmel

Cover design by Dominic Wilde


ISBN: 978-1-949043-34-1
First Edition Trade Paperback

## *... a scrap of research ...*

*From* America 2222: Year of Change, A Collection Of Images, Words and Music, *compiled by Tinja Richter, Green Giraffe Press, 2251.*

In 2222
  We didn't know what to do
  Our leaders lied
  People died
  We were animals in a zoo

From the forest, the Mud Man came
  To save us all from Sudukocane
  Our poisoned water, poisoned air
  Did not give him any care
  His righteous walk could not be tamed

He fought to free his lady fair,
  Mother Maggie, from her metal lair
  One shot killed a little girl
  One shot changed the whole wide world
  Maggie, Oh Maggie! The fences have fallen! Beware!

The bullets bounced right off him
  Like little drops of rain
  They say they he is driven
  By our sorrow and our pain

He freed our Blessed Mother
  Saved the world for you and me
  Then he and Blessed Mother
  Walked into the sea

# 1

## *First Final Report*

*From Military.Mail.Box, private account, General X____X, March 7, 2301.*

To: Lt Commander Thomas McDougal

From: General X____X

RE: MSE Report

Thom,

A boisterous and slightly tipsy Second Lt named Tina Lumpa (sic) cornered me at the Governor's Ball and started spouting a bunch of shit about the mobile stone entities. WTF? I thought that shit was classified. How could some newbie LT know about the MSEs?

I politely asked her to deliver a report about the MSEs and this is what she gave me—a bunch of folklore, press releases, and KnowNet articles. She doesn't even mention Ghee Dorfhouse, even though she probably crossed the Dorfhouse Memorial Bridge on her way into DC! And Missy Polly? Clearly Lt. Lumpy is a dunce—and a sloppy, lazy one at that. Christ, the shit that oozes out of the officer academy these days.

But what if a non-dunce gets the bug to investigate the

MSEs further? What's out there if you dig around? The lid's been screwed down tight on this shit for sixty years, but the smell is leaking from somewhere, Thom. I need you track this down. I need to know what information's out there related to the MSEs and how to cloud it if necessary. Tamp it down for another sixty years—if the truth floats up then, you and I will both be long gone and it won't matter.

General X____X

Attached: Mobile Stone Entities Final Report from Second Lt. Tima Lampu, PPC

*From Military.Mail.Box, private account, General X____X, March 5, 2301.*

To: General X__X

From: Second Lt. Tima Lampu, PPC

Re: Mobile Stone Entities Final Report

Dear General X__X,

It was a pleasure meeting you at the Governor's Gala and briefly discussing the history of the Mobile Stone Entities. I can't fully express how honored I am you asked me to compile a report on the MSEs. Your approval of my security clearance allowed me to dive deep into the subject matter. I hope this report sheds more light on the "walking stones." Please contact me at your convenience if you have any questions or would like to discuss the matter further.

*What Are Mobile Stone Entities (MSEs)?*

Though shrouded in mystery and folklore, the Mobile Stone Entities (MSEs) are generally believed to be two rogue soldiers in modified Talos Combat Suits who were last sighted in 2242 along the Aleutian Islands between Russia and Alaska. Prior to that, the MSE were last spotted off the coast of Iceland in November 2222. Both the MSE sightings in Iceland and the Aleutian Islands coincided with American Presidential elections, leading some to believe the MSEs were part of a campaign hoax. No charges were proven however, though Maggot-backed candidates prevailed in both the 2222 and 2242 elections. If the MSEs were a political strategy to get a Maggot elected POTUS, it worked.

A large, crudely modified MSE—referred to as the "Rock God"—was used by rebel terrorists during the Sixty Mile March and Battle of Newark Bay, May 1-3, 2222. Some folklorists and deep-seated religious faithful still believe the Rock God and Maggie are *actual* mobile stone entities, but most accept the more practical and logical notion that MSEs are soldiers wearing combat armor that mimics the appearance of stone.

*Aleutian Islands Sightings of 2242*

MSEs were sighted sitting atop an unnamed Aleutian Island outcrop on May 6, 2242 by military drones. The sighting followed several weeks of intensive military training exercises in and around the Bering Strait, leading most to assume the MSEs were soldiers, possibly robotic navy divers, testing new Talos armor. The lack of an official statement by either the United States or Russia fueled rumors that the Rock God and Maggie had returned, leading to an overwhelming Presidential victory for Maggot-backed Senator Cara Lewis on November 7, 2242.

*The Iceland Incident of 2222*

MSEs were spotted along Iceland's eastern coastline on October 26, 2222, prompting the assembly of a multi-nation task force led by American Naval Commander J. Daniel Moore. The task force engaged the MSEs on November 1, 2222, resulting in the famous "snowball fight" photograph. It is presumed modifications to Talos Combat Armor allowed the MSEs to breathe underwater for extended periods. They were tracked walking off the northern coast of Iceland on November 7, 2222, but an unseasonably intense Arctic storm sunk Commander Moore's vessel and ended pursuit of the

MSEs.

*Battle Of Newark Bay, 2222*

An MSE known as the Rock God was used to attack a military storage facility in Newark, New Jersey on May 3, 2222. It is unclear which rebel faction employed the Talos suit used in the Battle of Newark Bay, but most believe it was funded by the Maggot Revolutionary Force.

As I'm sure you're aware, the Maggie statue was destroyed during the Battle of Newark Bay, along with the MRF's MSE. Later sightings of Maggie and the Rock God in Iceland (Oct/ Nov 2222) and the Aleutian Islands (May 2242) are replica Talos suits designed to mimic the MSE used in the Battle of Newark Bay and a "vandalized" version of Maggie with missing hands. (Talos engineer Ross Juliano later confirmed the truncated forearms were likely weapon ports.) These post-Battle of Newark Bay sightings are generally considered political propaganda utilized by Maggots to influence American elections.

*Origin of Maggie*

Regardless of religious belief, the story behind the Maggie statue is extraordinary. It was made by New Jersey sculptor and folk artist George Ottomeyer as a headstone for his wife sometime in the early-2000s. Reports of alleged "miracles" (healing the sick, crying blood, etc.) led to the growth and spread of Maggie worshipers ("Maggots") over the next two hundred years. Fighting among Maggot factions resulted in the statue being vandalized in 2221. Concerns for public safety led President Loren Ipson to order government confiscation of the statue. Maggie was stored at a government facility in Newark and destroyed in the Battle of Newark Bay. Support for Mother Maggie and the Maggots waned in the late 2220s, partly due to the statue's destruction, and partly because the Maggot Revolutionary Force was blamed for the August 2222 national power grid failure. (The grid failure was later identified as being caused by a seaquake.)

*Origin of Rock God*

The legend of the Rock God (AKA Mud Man) is part of Northern New Jersey folklore. Rock God sightings were a phenomena in the early 2000s, but faded with time. Some claim the Rock God was an early prototype of the Maggie statue, made and abandoned by the same sculptor. There is no evidence linking the Rock God with George Ottomeyer other than geographical proximity and few old (fictional) books and movies.

*Origin of Missy Polly*

This report wouldn't be complete without the inclusion of Missy Polly, the alleged "stone dog" seen alongside the rebel MSE employed in the Newark Bay attacks. Though clearly a small dog in Talos K9 armor, Maggot faithful insist Missy Polly was actually a stone dog sculpted by George Ottomeyer to sit at Maggie's feet. (Maggie's canine statue was stolen by vandals more than a century ago.) The dog in Talos K9 armor seen during the Sixty Mile March was also destroyed during the Battle of Newark Bay.

*Conclusion*

The MSEs are one of the most interesting facets of "secret" military history. The confusion between camouflaged combat suits and actual walking statues is as fascinating as it is hilarious and showcases the gullibility of civilians. I hope this report helps clear up the confusion about Mobile Stone Entities and the military's response to them.

Sincerely,

Second Lt. Tima Lampu, PPC

Attached Files:

- KnowNet - "Maggie (Sculpture)"
- KnowNet - "Legend of The Stone Man (New Jersey, USA)"

*From KnowNet, "Maggie (Sculpture)," last updated, March 4, 2301.*

The sculpture known as Maggie once resided in Franz Rock Memorial Gardens cemetery (now Gallomart Gardens) in the early 2000s where it was revered by several religious sects, the largest of which was the Maggots. The statue originally held a baby, but it was vandalized by Stone Earth Extremists Lucas and Jasmin Dorfhouse in 2220. The stone infant was destroyed along with the statue's hands. Safety concerns led to government seizure of the statue in December 2221, which historians cite as an inciting incident leading to the 2222 revolutionary movements known as the Sixty Mile March and the subsequent Battle of Newark Bay. Historians widely believe the Maggie statue was destroyed in the Battle of Newark Bay, though no official remains were recovered. (See "Maggie Ash Hoax / Concrete Swindle.")

<u>Table Of Contents</u>

- Statue Origins
- Location in Franz Rock Memorial Gardens 2000
- Growth As A Religious Icon 2069-2200
- Vandalism 2221
- Government Seizure 2222
- Connection with Stone Man of New Jersey folklore.

See "Maggot (Religon)"

See "Sixty Mile March"

See "Legend of The Stone Man (New Jersey, USA)"

*From KnowNet, "Legend of The Stone Man (New Jersey, USA)," last updated, March 4, 2301.*

("Mud Man of North Jersey" redirects here.)

The legend of the Stone Man of New Jersey (aka Mud Man, Franz Rock Monster, Rock God) is an example of modern folklore/urban myth borne of a real-life event, in this case, an attack on a rural law office on November 8, 2016 near what is now Gallomart, NJ, (then Franz Rock). The attacker, who remains unidentified, wore prototype combat armor presenting as mud or stone, giving rise to the legend of a creature made of stone.

Table Of Contents

- 2016 Cashman and Clarke Law Office attack
- Connection to Maggie Statue of Gallomart Gardens (formerly Franz Rock Memorial Gardens)
- Sixty Mile March and Battle Of Newark
- Iceland Incident 2222
- Aleutian Islands Sighting 2242
- Golem / Frankenstein Connection
- Man of Stone In Pop Culture

*From Military.Mail.Box, private account, General X____X, March 7, 2301.*

To: General X____X

From: Lt Commander Thomas McDougal

RE: New MSE report

I'm on it. To be frank, I wasn't aware of the MSEs. Rather, I'm aware of Ghee Dorfhouse and the Talos Combat Armor used by rebels at the Battle of Newark Bay, but I wasn't aware of the backstory (or after-story). I'll get to work compiling a thorough report. In the meantime, I've attached an interview snippet with Lee Knutt and Marsha Dillon, creators of the original Talos military suit, which may have some bearing on the subject.

Also, Second Lt. Tima Lampu, PPC has been reassigned to a supervisory role at the new Oahu Military Center. You'll get no more questions from her.

Lt. Commander Thomas McDougal

*Attachment: Interview excerpt with Army Corp Of Engineers, Lee Knutt and Marsha Dillon, creators of the original Talos Combat suit, 2049.*

DILLON: Yeah, we were definitely influenced by the old *Man of Stone* movie.

KNUTT: I love that film! I used to watch it with my grandmother.

DILLON: I didn't discover it until I joined a film cult in college, but I loved the idea of an indestructible stone man.

KNUTT: The idea is much older than the *Man of Stone*. You see it in The Thing from the old Fantastic Four comic books and the golem in Jewish folklore. Stone is strong. We both struck upon that theme while designing the software for Talos.

DILLON: Yeah, from there it was all about getting the camouflage engineered to render the look and texture of stone…

To: Lt Commander Thomas McDougal

From: General X____X

RE:RE: MSE Report

You sent that bitch to Hawaii? Not much of a punishment. Should've put her on the lunar base. I've got a unit reserved at OMC. Another five and I'm hanging up my brass for good. Hope Lampu learns to keep her trap shut by the time I get there.

*Man Of Stone?* Really? That old stinkbomb? Interesting…I always wondered where the idea for the Talos suits came from. I'm curious to see what else you come up with on this, Thom.

General X____X

# 2

## *Second Final Report I*

*From Military.Mail.Box, private account, General X____X, November 5, 2301.*

To: General X___X,
From: Brigadier General Jayden Gamble
RE: MSE: Final Classified Report

Dear General X_____X

It is with great pleasure that I present this complete, in-depth investigation into the MSEs (Mobile Stone Entities).

We were all shocked by the sudden and unexpected passing of Lt Thomas McDougal. What a terrible loss for the entire military. My team and I submit this report in honor of Lt McDougal's memory.

We have literally worked day and night on this project for seven months, expanding on Lt Lampu's original report and launching several new, in-depth investigations. I hope this expanded look at the MSEs and their role in the revolutionary events of 2222 meets with your satisfaction. Please do not hesitate to contact me with your questions or concerns.

Sincerely,

Brigadier General Jayden Gamble

*Sussex County College lecture, "Revolt! 2222 In Review," adjunct Professor Kent Larkie, May 7, 2289.*

Like the universe itself, today's lesson starts with an explosion. A sudden violent outburst, in this case, a terrorist attack inside of a house of worship in Paterson, NJ. This was 2221, a year of religious oppression and revolt. These turbulent, violent times were primarily caused by pollutants pumped into the air and water by a global BizGov collective aimed at keeping the populace calm and controlled.

But it was the worst kept secret on the planet. People caught wind of it—no pun intended—and began to revolt—sometimes violently. In some cases, the removal of government-sponsored air and water filtration systems had disastrous results, like the return of famine and disease to Sub-Saharan Africa. People demanded change without having a viable alternative first and things began to collapse.

Our humble little corner of New Jersey played a starring role in this global revolution. As the home-base of Maggie, Franz Rock was considered a holy place by Maggots. People came from all over the world to touch and be healed by the Maggie statue. Ownership of the statue was widely contested by various religious sects during the early 21st century. Some tried to promote their agenda through acts of violence toward other religions, even the Old Religions, which were traditionally considered beyond rebuke.

*From News12 New Jersey, Headline News, March 9, 2221, 3pm EST.*

A suicide bomber detonated a powerful explosive during a multi-denominational Old Orders service in Paterson today, leveling the New Shalom Baptist Churchagogue on Washington Avenue, killing 14 people and seriously injuring

64 others. Three men, Brother Robert Franks, Rabbi Solomon Jacobson, and Caliph Mustafa Ba-Lin, were trapped under debris for several hours before rescuers freed them…

*From "The New Revised Modern King James Bible: Uni-denominational Edition," Catholic University Press, May 2267.*

Angels spoke to Brother Robert while he was trapped beneath the wreckage and said: "Be not afraid, for we are with you always. The Lord has spared you this day so that you can fulfill his holy mission. There is a Savior of Stone who will lead the righteous to justice…

*From "The Living Torah: The Word Of Maggie," Synagogue of Honor Press, copyright February 2254.*

Rabbi Solomon had nearly lost faith when he heard scratching in the rubble around him. It was a faint sound, but it gave him hope. Someone was coming to save him at last! Godly strength flowed through Rabbi Solomon's body and he dug and clawed toward the sound until he was free and in the company of his rescuer. It was a stone dog carrying a tattered book in its mouth. Rabbi Solomon took the book and thus, *Still Stone* by the Prophet Jeremy Haines, with its promise of a living golem, became our beacon of light during the Dark Time of ignorance and persecution.

*From "Modern Surahs, Timeless Wisdom," Seven Pillars Press, October 2239.*

Caliph Mustafa knew he could not dig out of the ruined house of worship, so instead he dug down, deep into the basement, into a labyrinth of half-buried, forgotten hallways, deeper still, to a sub-basement where ancient relics were held. Caliph Mustafa discovered a forbidden text written by the Prophet Jeremy that foretold of a living statue that dwelt in a haunted forest.

*From "The Gospel According To Maggie: Modern Prayers For Maggots," Digital Disciples Media, last updated March 14, 2226.*

*The Rockman Cometh (Hear Us, Stone Savior)*
All is not lost, Great Mother.
No shame, no degradation
Can mar your beauty
At the hands of the wicked and the damned
Your child has found eternal peace
Your sorrow knows no bounds
Chained and imprisoned
You wait with the patience of rock
For the Savior of Stone to rise

*Cease and desist request from Tom Brath Esq. (Finnigan & Moore) to Digital Disciples Media, et.al., sent January 18, 2227, received January 19, 2227.*

As the executor of the estate of the late Tom Sholz, I must inform you that "RockMan" and "The Rockman" are registered trademarks of Tom Sholz, Inc., Boston Music, Inc., and More Than A Feeling Enterprises LLC, and should not be used to promote or endorse any product or purpose without the sole written consent of Tom Sholz, Inc., Boston Music, Inc., and More Than A Feeling Enterprises LLC…

*Tinja Richter, performance artist, Modern Speakers series, GAP College, BabyGAP Auditorium, March 4, 2244.*

Think about it…three men survive this terrible explosion that kills 14, wounds 64, and levels the Churchagogue. They pull these guys out of three different spots in the rubble, yet they all tell the same story. They all say they heard the voice of God, or angels…maybe space aliens living under the North Pole. Who knows, right? Whomever spoke, they all got the same message: a savior of stone awaits in the woods. And they all saw a stone dog...a beagle. As far as religious parables go, this one is pretty whacky, even by biblical standards! I mean, Dog Is My Co-Pilot, am I right?

*From "TXT presents Your World Today hosted by Bridget Pine," streamed Monday, April 23, 2221, 9:42am, EST.*

*Footage: Groups of protesters holding signs and shouting. Signs read, "Give us back our air! Give us back our water!" and "No False Idols" with a scripture reference in the lower corner.*

*Bridget Pine V/O*: After weeks of violent clashes between Maggots, Old Order religious disciples, and various anti-religion organizations, federal officials today removed the statue of Maggie from its location in Franz Rock Memorial Gardens in the incorporated township of Quiet Pines by TargMart, to a secure, federally-protected facility.

*Footage: Overhead shot of square hole in the earth where Maggie statue once stood. Uniformed national guardsmen stand in a circle around the area, holding back protesters.*

*BP V/O*: Mark Plank, spokesman for the Unified Enforcement Division, said the statue was moved in the interest of public safety.

*Footage: Mark Plank.* We understand the statue is a holy relic to many, many individuals around the world and we are sensitive to that. But until we restore order to the community it is best we move Maggie to a secure location both for the public's safety and the safety of the statue.

*Footage: Maggie with hands broken off, her baby chiseled away.*

*BP V/O:* Earlier this month, two individuals carrying hammers attacked the Maggie statue. The statue's arms were broken off and the child Maggie held was destroyed. President Loren Ipson supported the UED's decision to relocate the statue and condemned acts of lawlessness and the destruction of public property. Violent clashes between the Maggot Revolutionary Force and Stone Earth Extremist, left four people dead last Friday.

*Footage: President Loren Ipson:* Personally, I think it is nonsense that people are killing each other over a statue. This is why I introduced the religion ban last year. This is a new age, an era of clear thinking. Advances in science and medicine have finally lifted millennia of religious mind fog. We're no longer slaves to superstition. This is a period of unification, unified thought, unified action, and religion divides us, turns people against one other. It always has. Unfortunately our Constitution still protects religious freedom and as President I'm bound to uphold that right. However, this nation will no longer tolerate terrorism in the name of any god, nor will we tolerate acts of vandalism, violence, or public unrest by any religious group or organization. Behave yourselves, people!

*BP V/O*: Over the past century, followers of the Maggie statue have grown exponentially. Maggots now outnumber Jews and Christians worldwide, but radicalized factions of the Maggots, like the Maggot Revolutionary Force, have splintered off…

*Professor Sum-Te Hua, "America in Turnabout," New Academic Online Lecture, Summer 2278.*

Contrary to popular belief, the American Revolution of 2222 was never about religion. The social upheaval of the late-22nd and early-23rd centuries was about a political power exchange. The Freedom Party in America was transitioning to a unified world government and the Maggot movement was the face of that change. But I don't think the people behind the scenes, the decision-makers, had any real interest in the Maggot belief system other than as a mechanism to organize and mobilize large numbers of people. Think about it, BizGov was forced to take opiates out of air and water filtration, so they created an "opiate for the masses"—a pseudo-religion—

to fill its place. It's as genius as it is insidious.

*VoiceRant: Comment for Sum-Te Hua*

Fool! The Maggie statue was created as a memorial by local New Jersey artist George Ottomeyer for his deceased wife, Margaret. The statue is rumored to have Margaret Ottomeyer's ashes inside (and possibly the remains of their unborn grandchild). George Ottomeyer made a stone dog too. Maggie could heal the sick and predict the future, and she spoke to Brother Eli during his pilgrimage to Franz Rock in 2059, telling him the Edicts Of Action that all Fly orders follow to this day. Do your research, Sum!

*VoiceRant: Comment for Sum-Te Hua*

I don't know who's a bigger moron: Sum-Te or that last caller. The Maggie Statue was nothing but a graveyard headstone that everyone got delusional over. Didn't you see the "Mystery Of Faith" documentary? The whole Maggot religion was a hoax. That's why it fell apart once the statue was destroyed in the Battle Of Newark Bay.

*VoiceRant: Comment for Sum-Te Hua*

Sum-Te is correct. Maggie was developed by covert government operatives to control the masses. The statue emitted odorless, colorless gas that made everybody who got close to it high as fuck. That's how the legend of its power spread. Stoned chatter.

*VoiceRant: Comment for Sum-Te Hua*

Maggie emerged whole from a rock, as the Rock God and Mithras did before her. Blessed be, Mother Maggie! Miss Polly too!

*VoiceRant: Comment for Sum-Te Hua*

I just find the whole history of the statue so fascinating. Even if the statue never existed, it's still a good story.

*VoiceRant: Comment for Sum-Te Hua*

The Maggie statue is real. Her dog, Miss Polly was killed at the Battle of Newark Bay, but Mother Maggie walked into the ocean alongside the Rock God.

*Tinja Richter, performance artist, Modern Speakers series, GAP College, BabyGAP Auditorium, March 4, 2244.*

Don't forget Miss Polly. This little faithful dog was built as a protector and companion for Maggie. When Maggie was put into storage by the government, it was Miss Polly who sprang into action, leading Ghee Dorfhouse to the Rock God.

*From "Mr. KnowItAll's Truthcast," hosted by Perci Downs, November 2292.*

Here's what happened.

Once upon a time, shortly after the dawn of the 21st Century, there was a sculptor named George, who could bring statues to life by mixing the ashes of the dead into his vat of clay and mud.

The first statue he made was a reincarnation of the family dog, a beagle named Miss Polly. Polly pretty much acted like a normal dog, except she hardly made a sound, except for a hellacious howl that cut right down to the bone.

Then George's son-in-law, a guy named David Lawrence, died unexpectedly. Some say he was murdered…some hush-hush stuff at the law firm where he worked. George didn't like David, but his daughter, Sarah, begged her father to bring David back to life.

So he did. That's how the Man of Stone was born.

But the Man of Stone woke up angry. Murderous angry. He returned to the law office where he worked and tore the place to pieces. Killed ten people. Police shot him a bunch of times, but the bullets bounced off, and Old Stoner escaped into the woods of North Jersey, never to be seen again…until 2222.

Now, old George's wife, Maggie, died the same day as the law office attack. No, the Man of Stone didn't kill her—cancer'd been eating away at Maggie for years. David had no beef with his mother-in-law that I'm aware of. Just a strange coincidence she died when she did.

Old George poured his wife's ashes into his mud mix and created what is considered by many to be one of the world's greatest sculptures— the statue of Mother Maggie and her baby. Some say he worked for ten years straight, day and night, no breaks. At some point George's workshop burnt down and George's daughter moved Mother Maggie to Franz Rock Memorial Gardens where the Maggot movement took root. People barely remember the Maggots now—almost like they're drugged into forgetting—but the Maggots changed America in 2222. Of course, they had Mother Maggie's help. And The Man of Stone. And Ghee Dorfhouse…God bless that poor, dear girl.

*Mr. KnowItAll welcomes your feedback! Please leave a comment below!*

*Boris wrote:* It's true, there was an attack on November 8, 2016 at the law office of Cashman & Clarke, a legal firm based in Pottsville, New Jersey. Ten people died. The attacker wore an early prototype of Talos combat armor.

Cashman & Clarke held several classified military contracts and also represented Downing Pharmaceuticals during the early days of the Sukodom drug trials. It's quite possible the firm had powerful enemies.

Several survivors said the attacker resembled former employee David Lawrence, even though Lawrence died of heart failure a week prior to the attack. Although the attacker was never identified, it's generally believed to be a lone act of terrorism conducted by a highly trained soldier in a modified ghillie suit.

David Lawrence, however, *was* the son-in-law of George Ottomeyer, the artist believed to have sculpted the "Maggie statue" as a tribute to his late wife. Ottomeyer lived in Franz Rock, a neighboring community to Pottsville.

All of this is true. Everything else is fairy tales, folklore, and myth.

*Mary Pat wrote:* This is bullshit. The Mother Maggie and Man of Stone sightings of 2222 were part of a massive political hoax to oust President Ipson and put a Maggot candidate in office. Look at what they got—Grant Layton was a shithead president. He was such an embarrassment, the entire Maggot movement dissolved just to distance itself from him. Don't fall for Maggot campaign manipulation again! We're smarter than that, people!

*Dave wrote:* With all due respect, I've seen no evidence people are smarter than anything…even rocks.

*New York State Federal Detention Center, Syracuse, NY, August 15, 2221.*

*VisComm Transcript*

*Inmate: Jasmine Dorfhouse # F633890*

*Inmate: Lucas Dorfhouse #M556233*

*Visitor: Margaret "Ghee" Dorfhouse (daughter)*

LUCAS: Hello, Ghee.

JASMINE: Hello, sweetheart.

GHEE: Hi.

LUCAS: Gosh, honey, you look so grown up. We've missed you.

GHEE: I was here two weeks ago. Do you think I'm getting fat?

LUCAS: No…no, honey…I-I just…

JASMINE: Your father misses you, Ghee. We both do.

GHEE: Thanks.

JASMINE: How's Grandma?

GHEE: Fine.

LUCAS: How was school this week? Still working on the play?

GHEE: Yes. Fine.

JASMINE: Don't hate us, Ghee. We did what we thought was right.

LUCAS: It *was* right! We righted a wrong! Mother Maggie shouldn't be with child! It's blasphemy!

GHEE: You sound stupid.

JASMINE: Just because we're separated by plastiglass doesn't give you the right to disrespect your father, Ghee. When I was your age, I didn't always agree with everything my parents did, but I didn't disrespect them.

GHEE: Did your parents ever attack a public statue? A piece of art? A holy relic? Talk about disrespect!

LUCAS: Disrespect is how the Maggots made a circus freak out of Mother Maggie! Her child was unclean! It says so in the scriptures! 'The broken child…the child of sand…' Maggie is the mother of us all! *Not* an unclean child! *Not* a dirty dog! The Freemasons took care of Miss Polly a hundred years ago. It was time for your mother and I to rid Maggie of her unholy spawn in the name of the Stone Earth and all who cherish truth!

JASMINE: Lucas! Chillax! The VisComm…

LUCAS: I don't care who hears, Jas! Our religious freedom is protected under the American Constitution!

JASMINE: Okay. Well…admissible in court is all I'm saying. Anyway, we get fifteen minutes a week to parent our daughter. Can we stay focused?

LUCAS: You're right. I'm sorry. I'm sorry, Ghee.

GHEE: Is it any wonder I'm fucked up?

JASMINE: Language, young lady! I know Grandma Aria doesn't let you talk like that. Your father and I have made some mistakes. I admit that. We could be better parents. I know that. But we acted in accordance to our faith, following the message of our scripture. The Stone Earthers have disavowed Mother Maggie's child for decades. There are people out there who support what we've done. They'll support you too, Ghee, if you let them.

GHEE: I don't want the support of your freak Stone Earth cult or the Maggot Revolutionary Force or anyone! I just…I just want my parents back. I wish you hadn't vandalized Maggie. She was good…so many people loved her…

JASMINE: Like I said, Gheely Girl. I didn't always believe in what my parents did when I was your age. But I think differently now. Some day you will too.

LUCAS: Mother Maggie *is* good. Trust in her love and purity, Ghee. Pray to her for guidance. And read the scriptures. The answers you seek are there. In time you will understand that what your mother and I did was right and you will find forgiveness in your heart.

GHEE: I believe *you* think chipping a stone baby off a statue was a good idea, Dad. But the police classify vandalizing a religious statue as a hate crime, and the President—the freaking President of the United States—has confiscated the statue, so *nobody* gets to enjoy Mother Maggie anymore. Is that what you wanted?

LUCAS: They use us as an excuse to further their own agenda! Ipson's cronies have been trying to lock Maggie away for years!

JASMINE: Lucas, shut up. Ghee, I'm sorry—truly sorry—for the position our actions have put you in. I hope some day you can forgive us.

GHEE: I wish I could make things right again.

LUCAS: We took a big step towards making things right. That baby—

JASMINE: *Shh*! Dad's right about reading the scripture, Ghee. You'll find strength there. Answers.

GHEE: I've read the scriptures. It's all crap. Is that what I'm dealing with?

LUCAS: Read them again with an open heart, sweetheart. Pray to Mother Maggie for guidance.

JASMINE: We love you, Gheely Girl. Be strong.
GHEE: Yeah. Thanks.

*From BigEar Surveillance, transcript, Aria Trotman (AT), Ghee Dorfhouse (GD), living room, September 3, 2221.*

GD: You're a badass, Grandma Aria.

AT: Hardly. I'm am old woman whose head is still filled with the silly dreams of a girl.

GD: You may have the dreams of a girl, but you're a woman of action. You make things happen. Speaking before the World Counsel. Organizing the Peace March.

AT: That was just me and a few friends deciding to walk to the government office in Trenton and a bunch of people joined us along the way. I really didn't organize anything.

GD: Why don't you like to talk about it? Why are you so modest? I think it's, like, the coolest thing ever. I'm proud you're my Grandma.

AT: Thank you, Ghee. You're my sweet angel and I'm proud of you too. But I sacrificed a lot to do the things I did. I neglected people. Hurt people. I was a lousy mother to your mother, Ghee. That's why I'm asking you to forgive her... again.

GD: I always do, don't I?

AT: Don't say it like that. Say it with a soft heart, Ghee.

GD: How many times did *your* mother get arrested, Grandma Aria?

AT: Don't be fresh. You know your Grandma and I spent every day in my father's pizzeria. My mother had her hands full with my sister and I. But *her* grandfather was a total screw-up, pardon my language. I'm sure you've seen the KnowNet entry about the Unified Maggot Front scandal.

GD: Yeah. So Jasmine is following in Grandpa Larry's footsteps and running on the wrong side of the law?

AT: I didn't say that. Your mother doesn't believe she's on

the wrong side. She's fighting for what she thinks is right.

GD: By defacing a holy statue? Isn't our family allegedly *related* to Mother Maggie?

AT: Don't get nutty, Ghee. I have a hard enough time dealing with your mother's nonsense. The statue is a statue, and it *is* a holy relic. Your Great-Grandmother Bernadette, God bless her soul, *she* was an activist who fought hard to get the Maggie statue properly preserved and secured.

GD: Wouldn't she be disappointed to see her granddaughter destroying Maggie's baby.

AT: Yes...(*sigh*)...yes, I'm sure she would be. It's...it's a terrible thing your mother has done. But don't be so sure it was all her idea. Your father had his hands in this.

GD: I think Mom runs the show. Dad's her lapdog.

AT: Don't be so sure. Lucas Dorfhouse always worked behind the scenes, scheming in the shadows.

GD: It's the other way around, Gram. Either way, they're both going to prison.

AT: Well, yes...after the trial.

GD: Good riddance. My parents are shit!

AT: Hey! I don't like that kind of talk, Ghee. Everybody makes mistakes. When it's family you have to get it right in your heart to forgive them. No matter how bad. Even if it's something awful.

GD: This is pretty awful. Everybody at school will know who I am and what Mom and Dad did. It's mortifying.

AT: I know, Gheely Girl, but the state wants you in a public high school where they can keep an eye on you. You need a break from home schooling anyway. You got nothing to worry about. You're a smart girl, probably a lot smarter than those public school kids.

GD: I'm scared, Grandma. I haven't been to a public school since, I don't know...what was I? Seven? Eight? I'll be the new kid...the freak whose mother killed Maggie's baby!

AT: Hush! Nobody killed nobody! That thing was made of stone! Plus, the baby is still around…the Federal Parks Commission has the pieces…

GD: It's nothing but dust and rubble. People *worship* that fucking statue! I'm so…fucking *fucked*!

AT: Quiet now, Ghee. You're not so big I can't wash your nasty mouth out! For starters, everybody's scared starting freshman year. It's going to be a new experience for everybody, so you'll fit right in. Plus, if teenagers are still teenagers, they all think their parents are terrible. You're in the same boat as everybody else, I'm telling you.

GD: I hope so, Grandma. I'm going to bed.

AT: Now you're thinking right. A great day starts with a good night's sleep.

GD: Speaking of which, did you hear a dog howling outside last night?

AT: No. You know I sleep like a stone.

GD: It was so loud and strange…I thought it might be a coyote. Or a pack of them. But there was only a little gray dog sitting up on the path behind the house. Howling like hell.

AT: Hunters abandon dogs in these woods all the time. It's sad. You worried about Muffin?

GD: No. Muffin can take care of herself. Plus, she always comes in at night.

AT: Well, you get some rest now and don't let any howling dogs keep you awake. Think happy thoughts, my love. High school is going to be fine.

*From Franz Rock High School, EduGuide Transcript, Counselor Ripple, January 13, 2222.*

"Hello, Margaret. Please sit down."

"Hello, Counselor Ripple."

"Do you know why you're here today, Margaret?"

"I'm here every day."

"Do you know why you were sent to my office today?"

"I'm sent here every day."

"Not every day. Twenty-two out of the forty days so far this term. Do you know why you were sent to my office today, Margaret?"

"You look very handsome today, Counselor Ripple. Have you done something different with your hair?"

"I...I am hairless, Margaret. Thank you for your kind words. They are very meaningful to me. Do you know why you were sent to my office today, Margaret?"

"To chat about hairlessness?"

"No, Margaret. Are you aware of the academy's rules against contraband, and the associated penalties for bringing contraband into this institution?"

"What's contraband? I'm not enrolled in the music program."

"Chapter 11, Heading 14 of the student handbook defines contraband as any material not sanctioned by the academy as part of your educational training. This includes, but is not limited to, stolen property, medication not sanctioned by the academy medical staff, or any other materials or items deemed unlawful, banned, or forbidden by the academy. Do you know why you were sent to my office today, Margaret?"

"Gee, Counselor Ripple, are you asking me to join the academy band? I'm honored."

"No. You have misunderstood my statement, and I apologize if the misunderstanding is a result of my words or actions. You have been charged with bringing contraband into this academy and exposing your fellow classmates to potentially dangerous materials and concepts—

"Counselor Ripple, what time does the academy band practice?"

"The academy music program is held each morning before

school and three days a week after school for private instruction. Please consult Instructor Whittock for individual student schedules. You have misunderstood my statement, and I apologize if the misunderstanding is a result of my words or actions. You have been charged with bringing contraband into this academy—"

"Good morning, Counselor Ripple!"

"Good morning, Margaret. Do you know why…You have been charged—"

"Good morning, Counselor Ripple!"

"Good morning, Margaret. You have been charged—"

"Good morning, Counselor Ripple!"

"Good morning, Margaret."

"Counselor Ripple, I'm here because I'd like to drop band from my schedule.

"Please wait…you have misunderstood…please wait…"

"Good morning, Counselor Ripple! Have you done something different with your hair?"

"Good morning…please wait…please wait…"

"Good morning, Counselor Ripple. Triple. Dipple. Good morning Counselor Meatpole. Counselor Toilet."

"Please wait…please wait… I'm sorry I can't assist you on your quest for educational excellence at this time. Your case has been re-assigned to Educational Prefect Wickerson."

*From Franz Rock High School, EduGuide Transcript, Prefect Wickerson, January 13, 2222.*

"Good morning, Ghee. Have fun messing with Counselor Ripple this morning?"

"I only mess with them when they mess with me."

"You know it takes hours to reprogram the Counselors. Drives the IT department crazy. Doesn't help your standing at the academy either. You're already on thin ice here."

"Whatever."

"The state is running out of educational options for you, Ghee. Expulsion from the academy would probably mean a transfer to a federal educational program. You don't want that, Margaret. There's no leniency there, only surgical and pharmaceutical solutions to student problems."

"Student problems or problem students?"

"If you won't behave like a good student, Ghee, the Feds will carve you into one. I'm not kidding you, kiddo."

"Machine-speaking the counselors isn't an expellable offense. The student handbook—"

"Failure to complete assignments and adhere to the academy's code of conduct *are* expellable offenses, Maggie. So is bringing contraband to school. Do you know what this is?"

"No."

"Really? You brought it to school, yet you have no idea what it is?"

"No. I don't. I thought it might be an old machine disk. A game or something.

"Yeah? Based on this picture on the cover, you thought it was a game?"

"I don't know…old video games used to be violent, right?"

"Where did you get this?"

"I-I found it."

"Where?"

"I don't remember."

"Come on, Maggie, that's bullshit and you know it. Where did you get this?"

"Are…are the recorders on?"

"Yes, Maggie. They're on. They're always on. Wondering why I called bullshit on your bullshit? Because nobody is ever going to listen back to this conversation, Maggie. It'll be archived and never heard again. The only way our conversation will become an issue is if you make it one. Do you understand?"

"I-I guess."

"Ripple logged your contraband. Once I approve the report, it goes up the ladder...Principal McKnight... Superintendent Donner... The investigation will widen, Ghee, and whomever this belongs to will face serious consequences. Do you understand?"

"Yes."

"But I'm not going to approve Ripple's contraband report. I'm giving this back to you. Take it back to wherever you got it, and never bring it to the academy again. I'm putting myself at personal and professional risk by doing this for you, Ghee, because I feel bad for you. I know about your parents...I'm sure this is a difficult time. But this isn't helping. This is a relic from a time best forgotten. I don't know what you're looking for, Maggie, but you won't find any answers here. This is just nonsense. Trash. This isn't what you or your family is about."

"(*Inaudible*). Thank you, Prefect Wickerson."

"We're giving you every chance, Maggie, but it's up to you to turn it around. Bringing items like this into the academy is a direct ticket to a federal facility. Don't (*inaudible*)...

"I understand."

"(*Inaudible*)"

"Basement. There's a trunk with stuff in the back. I think it's my grandmother's."

"Probably your great-grandmother's. This is really old."

"What is it?"

"You really don't know?"

"No."

"Then why did you bring it to the academy?"

"I thought there might be some way to play it here."

"Ha! You'd be better off bringing it to a museum...I doubt you'd even find a working player there."

"So it *is* a game?"

"It's not a game. Don't treat it as such. Put it back where you got it and forget about it. I don't know what you're looking for, Ghee, but you won't find any answers here. This is an old fairy tale."

"Fairy tale? It doesn't look like it's for kids."

"It's not. And it's not for young ladies like yourself, either. This is your grandmother's private property. I don't know why she has this, but she could get into trouble if people knew. Put it back, Ghee. Discreetly. Then forget about it."

"But…the guy on the cover…I thought, like, the prophecy of the stone savior…"

"Really, Ghee? You believe Old Religion prophecies now? Well, if The Man Jesus or a rock with legs helps improve your behavior at school, I'm all for it. How's the school play going?"

"It's stupid."

"You've been showing up at rehearsals?"

"Mostly."

"Stage crew is just as important as the acting roles. Maybe more so. You should've tried out for a role, Ghee. You've got a pretty face and a nice speaking voice…when you're not using it to mess with edubots."

"Only when they mess with me."

"The hope is that involvement in the school musical will have a positive effect on your behavior and grades. Let's make that happen, Ghee. Have fun with it. Make some friends."

"Sure."

"Open your heart and mind to new social experiences, Ghee. Life isn't about going off and doing your own thing. It's about working on a team. Be part of the team, Ghee! Go Franz Rock High!"

"I see your point. My parents went off and did their own thing. Look where it got them."

"Well…not to make light of it, but since you brought it up, you're right, Ghee. These are dangerous times. You need to toe the line before you can even think about stepping over it, understand? You need to play well with others. It's not right that you should have to walk in your parents' shadow. Defacing Mother Maggie…it struck a nerve with the faithful."

"They should dump that dumb statue in the ocean."

"Perhaps you should look at things from other people's perspective, Ghee. Be more tolerant. Even if you're not a Maggot, you should respect the icons other religions hold dear. Would you burn the Koran, or smash a crucifix, or disrespect other Old Religion relics? Think about it, Ghee."

"Religion…it just divides people. President Ipson is right."

"It helps people too, Ghee. Heals them. Unifies them. You don't have to agree with *everything* about *everyone* in order to be part of the team, Ghee. Tolerance…other people's perspectives…remember?"

"Yes."

"I read an article the other day that claims atheism is making a comeback, so maybe you're on the cutting edge here."

"I feel like I'm on the edge of something."

"Listen, Ghee, I'm scheduling you for a visit to the academy's Therapy Center. You can get talky-talky there… pills…patches… You can get the help you need."

"Don't bother. I've been there three times already. The guided meditation is okay, but the Psychbot keeps trying to prescribe me asperxenomoxitine."

"They've got a new Psychbot with expanded therapies. Reiki energy healing…sonic bowl therapy…the works. She's fantastic. Hypnotized me two months ago and I'm down fifteen pounds! It really works."

"Okay. You look trim, Prefect Wickerson."

"Thank you very much, Ms. Dorfhouse. See, a little

manners and polite conversation works wonders! Now, I'll be there opening night to witness all your hard work behind the scenes of the high school musical."

"High School Musical."

"Yes."

"We're All In This Together, Prefect Wickerson."

"I like that! That's the spirit!"

"'Get'cha Head In The Game.'"

"Good advice."

"'Bop To The Top.'"

"Okay, Ghee. I'm not a damn robot. Knock it off."

*Collected Contraband Evidence, Franz Rock High School, Ripple.R., January 13, 2222.*

ITEM: Digital Video Disc, *MAN OF STONE, Deluxe Director's Cut,* Lifetime Original Movie, written by Martha Rhymes, directed by Arthur Dalage, copyright 2023.

STATUS: DRAFT / ITEM NOT LOGGED

*Excerpt from* CARA & GHEE: A LOVE STORY, *written and directed by Oliver Jones, LoveStream Networks, Inc., January, 2243.*

MARSHA: Cara, have you met Ghee Dorfhouse?

CARA (*smiles, shy, coy*) : Hello, Ghee. I'm Cara Lewis. I play Sharpay.

GHEE (*smiles back, shy, interested*): I know who you are. Your great-great-grandfather pulled my great-great-grandfather out of the woods.

CARA (*confused*): What?

GHEE: The Legend of Rock God? I'm named after the Maggie statue.

CARA: I…I'm not familiar with it.

GHEE: You never saw that old movie, 'Man Of Stone'?

CARA: No.

GHEE: It's part of Franz Rock's history, for Christ's sake!

*Cara is taken aback. Marsha steps in.*

MARSHA: Ghee, Cara's not a Maggot.

GHEE: I never said she was! Neither am I. But you should know your local history. At least know your *movie* history if you're a theater major.

CARA: How can you not be a Maggot if your great-great-grandmother is, like, Mother Maggie?

GHEE: Just because I grew up around that crap doesn't mean I believe it. Do you believe everything you were taught growing up?

CARA: N-no.

GHEE: Maggie's not a queen. She's just a lump of stone… with tits.

*Marsha gasps, but Cara smiles.*

CARA: Lovely tits.

*Ghee and Cara laugh. Marsha looks on, horrified.*

*My Family Tree Chart for Ghee Dorfhouse, Maternal Branch, range: ~300 years, summary, prepared March 2222.*

Hello, Ghee! This is your family tree for the maternal branch of the Dorfhouse family.

Maggie Brennan wed George Ottomeyer, and they had a girl named Sarah, born in 1990. Sarah Ottomeyer married attorney David Lawrence, who died. Sarah later married Steven Stickler, and gave birth to her daughter, Margaret, in 2026. Margaret was named after her grandmother.

Margaret Stickler was a nurse. She married Boris Cavella. They had two children: Brian born in 2050, and Margaret born in 2053.

Margaret Cavella married Elmo Bisset, and bore him three children: Lawrence born in 2069, William born in 2075, and Peter born in 2079. Maggie Bisset is best known for her involvement with the Maggot Virtual Church.

Lawrence Bisset married Mary Rees. They had two children: Lawrence born in 2095, and Bernadette born in 2100. Lawrence became the head of the Unified Congregation of Maggots, but the Unified Maggot Front scandal divided the megachurch in 2148.

Bernadette Bisset married Clinton Neumann. They had two children: Sean born in 2119, and Dwayne born in 2122. Bernadette advocated for the preservation of the Maggie statue, located in what was then Franz Rock Memorial Gardens in northwest New Jersey.

Dwayne Neumann married Amanda McCurr. They had two children: Aria born in 2147, and Elizabeth born in 2150. Dwayne Neumann owned a pizzeria restaurant.

Aria Neumann married Alan Trotman, and gave birth to a daughter, Jasmine, in 2175. Aria Trotman is recognized for her clean air and water activism.

Jasmine Trotman married Lucas Dorfhouse, and gave birth to a daughter, Margaret "Ghee" Dorfhouse in 2205.

That's you!

*My Family Tree Chart for Cara Lewis, Paternal Branch, range: ~300 years, summary, prepared March 2222.*

Hello Cara! Welcome to your family tree, the paternal branch of the Lewis family. Police detective Walter Lewis gave birth to a son, Walter, who married Alison Mayer. They had two children: Walter born in 2020, and Alice born in 2022.

Walter became a police officer, like his father. He married Tamara Holtz and had three children: Walter born in 2037, Barth born in 2040, and Albert born in 2044.

Walter Lewis the third was an Army major. He married Laura Appleton and they had three children: Laura born in 2054, Wendy born in 2057, and Olaf born in 2060.

Wendy Lewis (I) married Vladimir Morris and had three children: David in 2175, Wendy (II) in 2180, and Bug in 2183.

Wendy Lewis (I) was a dentist.

Wendy Lewis-Morris (II) married Barry Baja and give birth to Valter in 2207 and Cara in 2203.

That's you!

*Excerpt from* CARA & GHEE: A LOVE STORY, *written and directed by Oliver Jones, LoveStream Networks, Inc, January 2243.*

*Ghee and Cara kiss passionately in the upstairs loft backstage. They are surrounded by lighting rigs and costume props: a dress dummy with a wide-brimmed hat, cardboard boulders, a thin palm tree cut from plywood. Ghee is the aggressor, sliding her hand beneath Cara's shirt as they kiss. Cara pushes her hand away.*

CARA: Did your great-great-grandfather really make the Man of Stone?

GHEE: What? You been reading KnowNet? Don't tell me you buy into that Mud Man crap like the Stone Earth Extremists.

CARA: SEE and know, baby.

GHEE: Yuck! You're quoting SEE propaganda, now? I grew up with that crap! You really know how to kill a romantic mood.

*Ghee sits up and crosses her arms. Cara massages her shoulders.*

CARA: Will you relax? I'm just teasing you! Why are you so tense?

GHEE: You know why.

CARA: The play will be over this weekend. We won't be cooped up in this moldy theater all the time. We can go out, get some fresh air! It's springtime!

GHEE: You know I don't dig on fresh air…unless it's really fresh.

CARA: I know. We'll go out past the grassland, where the filters can't reach.

GHEE: You don't have to do that for me.

CARA: I want to, Ghee. I care for you so much. I-I…

GHEE: But what's going to happen after the play ends, Cara? And after school ends, and the summer's gone, what then? You'll be off to college, probably at the Lunar Science Center, and I'll be stuck here at Franz Rock High for another three years. It might as well be forever.

CARA: (*laughing*) I'm not going to school on the moon, you crazy bitch! I'll be here too. I can commute to Chemolco College.

GHEE: Don't do that. You can go anywhere and do anything. Get out of this shit town.

CARA: I-I don't want to go anywhere without you. I don't have to.

GHEE: Yes, you do.

CARA: Baby, there's no rush.

GHEE: There might be. (*Sighs*) Listen, Cara, I have to tell you something.

CARA: Are you breaking up with me?

*Cara pulls away, but Ghee turns and takes her hands.*

GHEE: No, it's not like that, baby. It's my mother…she has a plan to get the Maggie statue back.

CARA: From jail? How? Is she part of the Maggot Revolutionary Force?

GHEE: (*looking around, even though they're alone) Shhh*! No… not exactly. But three men came to our house last night and they sat down with my grandmother and I…I can't tell you what they talked about. The less you know, the better.

CARA: Christ, Ghee! Were they Flies? Suicide bombers?

GHEE: No, no. They were…holy men. From the Old Religions.

CARA: The Old Religions?

GHEE: Christianity, Judaism, Islam…

CARA: I know what they are, fool! It's just…nobody practices them anymore.

GHEE: Some of the Stone Earthers do. There's a lot of

crossover between SEE's rites and Old Religion practices. Back to nature, tree-hugger, hippy-dippy shit.

CARA: Who were these men?

GHEE: A priest, a rabbi, and a calliph.

CARA: Is this a joke?

GHEE: It sounds like one, believe me. I haven't even told about the stone dog yet.

CARA: A stone dog? Are you serious? (*whispered*) What are you up to, Ghee?

GHEE: You…you wouldn't believe me if I told you.

*From LunarVibe action widget, "What To Watch On Your Next Lunar Expedition!"* Cara & Ghee: A Critical Review, *February 2243.*

If Cara Lewis wasn't a rising star in the Freedom Party [*update: Lewis was elected President of the United States in November* 2242] this film never would have been made. Add it to the list of things to blame on Cara Lewis.

In this terrible film, written and directed by Oliver Jones (following the fallout/firing of directors Sarah Burke and Emilio Rosamilia), Hilja Carlson plays a scene-chewing Cara Lewis to Sharon Milling's understated Ghee Dorfhouse. Milling's performance hits all the right notes—we feel for this lonely, teenage outcast, her awkward relationship with Lewis, and her yearning to redeem her family's name at all costs. But, just as Ghee Dorfhouse's time on Earth was cut short, so too is Milling's screen-time. The bulk of this movie erroneously paints Lewis as a public savior, feeding the hungry, housing the homeless, and single-handedly transforming a cranky government into a smooth-running machine. I'm surprised this film didn't end with the tag-line, "Paid for By People For President Lewis." Surely, Senator Lewis must approve this message. This movie is nothing more than thinly veiled political propaganda.

Perhaps the greatest sin of *Cara and Ghee: A Love Story,* is the way they take the political complexities behind the Sixty Mile March and the Battle Of Newark Bay and reduce them to a simple parable—Ghee freeing the "family" statue to atone for her parents' crimes. The film ignores known factors like the international uprising of Maggots, the instability of the global economy, and the history of struggle between Clean Earth activists and the BizGov pharmaceutical forces behind the Sukudom scandals of the late 21st century. Instead it makes it seem like Ghee Dorfhouse did things "all on her own…for love" without the support of an organized anti-government force. Does anyone believe the "Man of Stone" soldier that accompanied Ghee during the march and subsequent battle was simply "a friend wearing combat armor"? We all saw the Rock God beat down the US military during the Battle of Newark Bay. Such advanced tactical skills belies the film's "a buddy in armor" concept. Additionally, the casting of Clap Sapperstein as "Chip," the man inside the monster suit, is ludicrous to the point of distraction. It makes you wonder if the producers of *Cara & Ghee* considered marketing this film as a comedy or a cut-rate action thriller; how else can you explain the presence of the cinematic black hole that is Clap Sapperstein in this film?

*Comments on this review:*

*BenjiRR wrote:* Clap Sapperstein aside, I didn't think the movie was too bad. Sharon Milling is captivating to watch… but you're right, there's not enough of her in the movie. The fight scenes were good. I liked when the soldier got his arm ripped off.

*HairyTom wrote:* Hot lesbo scenes! I used to spank to this movie when I was a teenager. Still do.

*MarryS wrote:* The Man of Stone is real! He's really made of stone. He walks around North Jersey all the time.

*JerzyGrrl wrote:* I saw the Man of Stone in Walmart in

Franklin, NJ!

*DiddyPUFF wrote:* I am the Man of Stoned! 420!

*FosterMom wrote:* This movie may gloss over many of the factors behind the Battle of Newark, but I think it captures the relationship between Ghee Dorfhouse and Cara Lewis nicely. The loss of innocence is quite affecting. Remember, Ghee was barely 17 when she marched on Newark. Today's youth could learn a thing or two from that girl's drive and moxie!

*BO-red wrote:* There WAS no relationship between Ghee and Cara, you old coot! They didn't even know each other in high school. The entire story is made-up fiction. Take a dirt nap, Grandpa.

*VentriliJim Wrote:* That's not true! I went to Franz Rock High School and I was in that production of *High School Musical*. Ghee and Cara were always making out in the loft backstage, just like in the movie! I was also in Franz Rock High's production of *Twelve Angry Jurors, Mama Mia,* and *Equus,* and I played Tiny Tim in *A Christmas Carol* at West Caldwell Community Theater.

*Tinja Richter, performance artist, Modern Speakers series, GAP College, BabyGAP Auditorium, March 4, 2244.*

The mystical journey into the woods is my favorite part of the whole story. Three holy men, all from different Old Religions, come together with a shared vision of a stone savior hidden in the woods of North Jersey, like the three wise men following the star of Bethlehem to find Baby Jesus. It's sweet, and it gives the whole gruesome story a rather happy, wholesome start.

*FloxiMax Digital Lecture Series, Carolyn Wales, "Portrait of Two Women, The Daughters of the Revolution and the Mothers of Tomorrow," November 2260.*

Show of hands, how many people in the auditorium

tonight believe Ghee Dorfhouse was led into the protected woodlands of North Jersey by a trio of religious figures?

Wow, nearly half of you. A lot of true believers in the room tonight!

(*Chuckles*)

How many believe Ghee Dorfhouse was led into the woods by an organized revolutionary group, like the Clean Air Coalition or the Maggot Revolutionary Force?

Okay, there's the other half of the room. Anyone believe Ghee Dorfhouse acted alone, that she found a stone golem in the forest and convinced the creature to march with her to Newark to free the Mother Maggie statue all by herself?

Ah, good! It's always nice to see a few out-and-out fabulists in the crowd! Welcome! I hope the three of you will find something interesting in tonight's discussion! If not, there's a Lord Of The Thrones fan convention across town. Maybe you'll find something more fitting your belief system there!

(*Laughs. Chuckles.*)

All kidding aside, you can see how even an informal poll of the people in this auditorium tonight reveals the division that exists over Ghee Dorfhouse's march on Newark. We can all agree—well, most of us, anyway—that 2222 was a year of great social and political upheaval. Religious in-fighting among the Maggot sects was intense and often violent. When President Loren Ipson made the decision to impound the Maggie statue in a Newark warehouse, Maggot tensions boiled over and found a new focus. The United States government inadvertently ended the Maggot civil war by making itself a unified target for the divided Maggot factions. It also gave the Maggots a singular mission: free Mother Maggie.

You'd think, even in 2222, there'd be ways to accurately track and investigate Ghee Dorfhouse. But, even in 2222, there were people who found ways to live off the grid. Protected woodlands are one of those places. There are robo-sentries at the park entrances and flyover drones, but they can't tell the complete story of what's happening inside the woods. What happens in the forest, stays in the forest to a certain extent.

We know for certain the last time Ghee Dorfhouse used her com device was on the morning of May 2, 2222 to plot a GPS route from North Jersey to Newark Bay. We don't know exactly when she entered the woods, nor when she emerged. She is seen at 10:59 am on a traffic light surveillance camera, crossing Route 94 with the so-called Rock God and a group of approximately one-dozen citizens. Are the three holy men in that group? It is impossible to know. We do know, however, that over the years, thousands upon thousands of individuals claim to have marched with Ghee Dorfhouse from Sussex County to Newark, but, as you can see, barely a dozen individuals were there at the start of the Sixty Mile March.

Ghee Dorfhouse is seen again at 11:15 am, when a drone media camera captures the first interaction between marchers and police at a roadblock on Route 23 South in Newton. The armored "Rock God" pushes a police cruiser off the road and the marchers continue south. Historians consider this moment the un-official start of the Sixty Mile March. After this, it's impossible to know exactly who joined the march, even though media coverage of the event is continuous. The complexities of the political, social, and religious groups who joined the Sixty Mile March make it impossible to determine the exact level of Ghee Dorfhouse's involvement. She's become an iconic symbol of the Revolution of 2222, but, other than leading the march and dying in battle, Ghee Dorfhouse's true motivations may never be known.

*From Everybody's a Critic, "Cara & Ghee: A Love Story Film*

*Analysis," cast October 3, 2277.*

The story behind the production of this film is arguably just as interesting (and some would say more-so) than the fantastic tale it tells on screen. An examination of early scripts and deleted scenes shows how the troubled production veered from a film about religious folklore to a political film with a clear campaign-driven agenda.

*Excerpt from* CARA & GHEE: A LOVE STORY, *written and directed by Oliver Jones, LoveStream Networks, Inc, January 2243.*

[ORIGINAL SCENE (written by Emilio Rosamilia, directed by Sarah Burke.)]

*Ghee in woods with three men. They stand before something we cannot see, but look astonished.*

BROTHER ROBERT: Praise Man-Jesus! It's the Rock God!

RABBI SOLOMON: It's true! It's true! Dear God!

CALIPH MUSTAFA: What the great prophets predicted has come to pass. Praise Allah!

*The three men drop to their knees and bow their heads, but Ghee remains on her feet, studying the Man of Stone.*

GHEE: Is it really you?

MAN OF STONE (*deep voice OFF CAMERA*): What do you want?

GHEE: The world needs your help.

MAN OF STONE (*deep voice OFF CAMERA*): Fuck the world.

GHEE: Maggie needs your help.

*The Man of Stone grumbles and growls. Ghee steps back and looks up. Dust billows toward her and there is a great creaking of wood and the sound of branches breaking. Several tree limbs, some quite large, fall to the ground and Ghee takes another step back. The three wise men look up, slowly rising to their feet, looking ready to run, their expressions a mix of awe and terror.*

*Excerpt from* CARA & GHEE: A LOVE STORY, *written and directed by Oliver Jones, LoveStream Networks, Inc, January 2243.*

[REVISED SCENE (re-written and directed by Oliver Jones)]

*Ghee in the woods, helping Chip buckle into his combat armor. The armor makes him look like a massive gray statue with glowing red eyes. Ghee stands on a stump, fitting the helmet over Chip's head. Cara runs into frame.*

*Cara and Ghee look at each other for a long moment, and then Ghee returns to buckling Chip in. When she's finished, she slaps Chip on the shoulder. He turns around slowly, in a robotic fashion.*

CARA: Who's in the suit?

GHEE: Chip.

CARA: Looking good, Chip.

*Chip waves a massive stone arm.*

CARA: Where did you get combat armor?

GHEE: How did you find me here?

CARA: I tortured Tasha until she told me.

GHEE (*surprised*): Are you serious?

CARA: I know what you're planning, Ghee. I'm begging you to stop. You'll get yourself killed.

GHEE: I'm sorry, Cara. Mother Maggie is family.

CARA: I thought *we* were starting our *own* family.

GHEE: Cara…

CARA: Are you giving up on us? Running out?

GHEE: You know I'm…yes. That's what I'm doing. I'm giving up. Running out.

CARA: Don't try that reverse psych trip on me.

GHEE: You should go, Cara.

CARA: I'm going with you, Ghee. Whatever you're going to face, we'll face it together. As a couple. As a team.

GHEE: I can't let you do that. I…I can't let you get hurt.

CARA: It's my choice. I want to be with you. We'll rescue Maggie together. We'll face down the police or the army or whatever together. And if we die, we die together.

GHEE: No. This is something I need to do alone.

CARA: Alone? With Chip?

*They both look at Chip. Chip shrugs.*

GHEE: I don't want you with me, Cara.

CARA: You don't think we belong together?

GHEE: No.

CARA: You're breaking up with me?

GHEE: Yes.

CARA: This is bullshit! I'm coming with you! I love you!

GHEE (*shouting*): I don't love you! It's over, okay? Just go.

CARA (*through tears*): You're a liar, Ghee Dorfhouse. Either you lied to get me into bed, or you're lying to me now. Maybe you're lying to yourself. Either way, you're not doing what's true here, Ghee. I love you more than anyone, and I want to stand beside you. Can't you see that? Can't you let me love you?

GHEE: I don't want you here, Cara.

*Cara sobs once, loudly, then lunges and slaps Ghee across the face. Ghee instinctively slaps her back. Cara clutches her cheek, gives Ghee a final, teary look, and runs away.*

*Ghee stands with her shoulders slumped, head down. Her shoulders begin to shake, as she cries silently. Her knees buckle but she catches herself before she collapses, slowly standing straight again and wiping her face clean. She looks at Chip. Chip shrugs.*

GHEE: Let's go get Maggie.

*Ghee and Chip exit into the darkness.*

*From "The New True Word: One World, One Faith, The Book Of Clifton, Chapter 3, Verse 40," Digital Disciples Media, last updated November 24, 2244.*

And Caliph Mustafa said to the Rock God, "Forgive us, oh Lord, for we know not what we do. We have forgotten the face of our fathers and your promise of healing love. We have allowed your enemies to kidnap and desecrate your wife and daughter."

And Brother Robert said to the Rock God, "We have failed you by letting wicked men lead us astray and steal our minds."

And Rabbi Solomon said to the Rock God, "Forgive us, mighty Father, the trespass of forgetting. Truly you are the clay protector created by Rabbi Loew centuries ago to save us from our enemies."

"Rise and show us your glory!" they cried as one, and the stone hound unleashed an unearthly howl that drove the Wise Men to their knees.

The Rock God stood and the mountain shook with his footsteps. Mighty trees fell with his every stride. He emerged from the haunted wood with the stone hound and the Wise Men, and all who saw him fell to their knees and sang, "Shalom! Glory to God in the Highest! Allah Akbar! Jai Guru Deva! Mother Maggie, He has risen!"

They saw in Him the One True God, a bridge between the Old Orders and the New, a God born of honest Earth, not man-made lies, a Stone Savior to free The Loving Queen Who Heals.

*From "The Polly Cast: An Inside Look At The Legendary Stone Dog Of North Jersey," November, 2298.*

If you look at the still image of Ghee and the Rock God crossing Route 94, you can see Miss Polly in the lower right corner. She's pixilated and blurry, but clearly there is a tiny four-legged creature leading the pack across the road. There are other dogs in the group—a German Shepherd and a pit mix—but those animals are on leash. Miss Polly is free, out front, leading the Sixty Mile March.

*From "Rabbi Barry's Letter To America, The Living Torah: The*

*Word Of Maggie," Synagogue of Honor Press, February 2226.*

I can't tell you where we entered the woods. I'm not being coy or mysterious here. Brother Robert drove and I'm not familiar with that part of New Jersey. We all packed into Bob's Camry—me, Mustafa, Ghee, and the stone dog, Miss Polly. I rode shotgun because of my bad knee, and Polly stood on my lap and stuck her head out the window while we drove. Good God, was she heavy! She turned my thighs black-and-blue! The dog wasn't breathing but she seemed to enjoy the scent of the morning air anyway.

Brother Robert drove us deep into the woods, following a rutted path that may have been passable in a pickup truck but was punishing to Bob's Camry. His auto-pilot switched off, refusing to go further, but Bob switched to manual and drove us another mile or so deeper into the woods. A fallen tree blocked the path so we all got out. Miss Polly took it from there. She scooted beneath the tree and waited for us to catch up. Ghee climbed over the tree while Bob, Mustafa, and I walked around. It went on like that for some time, the girl and the dog going ahead, waiting for the old men to catch up. It got more difficult the hotter the day grew and the higher we climbed. My knee screamed with pain, but I prayed to the Lord for strength and he answered my prayers, as my pain subsided.

The dog took us up the rutted road and then onto a narrow footpath which led to an even narrower deer path. Stickers and branches tore at us, whipped us, but we pressed on into the thickening forest. Miss Polly slowed only long enough for us to keep up. She knew exactly where she was going.

Sometime later we came to a clearing. It didn't look any different from the surrounding forest, but it felt different, the air was different, charged by some unnamable force. Polly sat in the middle of the clearing and stared at a wall of stone. A thin waterfall—perhaps from a tiny feeder stream or late spring snow melt—cascaded down the wall into a small pond.

I followed Polly's gaze and saw him sitting there among the rocks, a stone cut and shaped like a massive man, covered in green moss and vegetation like the other stones, tree vines wrapped around his legs, fusing him to the earth, weeds growing up between his splayed fingers, head bowed, a foot of soil and debris piled at the nape of his neck.

He was there and he was real.

Miss Polly howled and it sounded like the rusty gates of Hell being pried open. We all covered our ears, and, I'm not ashamed to say, I started to cry. I was frightened in the presence of so great a being, humbled to my core. My lifetime of faith and devotion to God had led me to this place, this forgotten spot in the woods the Stone Savior called his home.

# 3

## *Mudspeak I*

Want to hear a joke?

A Muslim, a Jew, and a Christian go for a walk in the woods.

Can you guess the punchline?

They came looking for me.

I am made of mud and river clay. Twigs and sticks, sand and crushed stone. My father-in-law, George Ottomeyer made me out of hate, revenge, and spite. Well, some—a lot—of the hate and revenge were all mine. I was murdered, for Christ's sake! You'd feel hateful too! Revenge is tasty served cold, but it leaves a shitty aftertaste. I killed people by mistake and others by design. I didn't feel good about any of it. Plus, I couldn't be with the woman I loved. How could I? I was stone and she was flesh and bone. It wasn't right. Sarah deserved to live a full, happy life with a man who could be a true companion to her. I didn't deserve anything.

So I sat in the woods.

I mean, I creep-stalked Sarah Ottomeyer-Lawrence-Stickler for many, many years. Decades, really. I made sure her husband was a good man who treated Sarah well. I stuck around and watched when Sarah came to visit her parents' graves with her husband and daughter, hid among the trees like a Peeping Tom while the family knelt before Maggie, paying respect to the family matriarch. Maggie Ottomeyer deserved respect. That woman was a saint for a lot of reasons, surviving a marriage to George Ottomeyer not the least among them. I watched Sarah and her family visit Franz Rock Memorial Gardens many times, until Sarah's little girl had grown into a woman herself. I figured it was safe to stop watching by then, but I kept on a little while longer anyway.

*Then* I sat in the woods.

It took a while, but I finally realized one of the great things about living forever is that you don't have to. You can sit and rot, weather away, erode to nothing. It's okay. Nobody judges you. Eroding is what stones do. So I found a cozy spot in Highpoint State Forest, a stone ledge with a tiny waterfall, and I sat.

Miss Polly came to visit from time to time. She's a good dog. She never stayed for very long and once she saw how I sunk into the earth and let the vines grow over me, she stopped coming altogether. I didn't blame her. Rocks are no fun to hang out with. Even though she was made of stone herself, Miss Polly was still a dog, a canine at home running around the woods. I was…well, let's say I fully embraced my stone side.

How many summers since an adventurous hiker or group of thrill-seeking teens came looking for me? A hundred or more? I saw plenty of hikers but they didn't see me, and if they did, they pretended they didn't. When people stop believing in you, you become invisible.

I figured Miss Polly had deserted me forever, but I should have known better. Forever is a long time, even for stone. I heard footsteps following her, but I knew Polly wouldn't lead anyone untrustworthy to me. It's like that old saying, "I only trust people my dog likes." Miss Polly got my attention, but it was Ghee who got me on my feet and got me moving.

Ghee and Maggie.

Two women connected through time by blood and bone, gossamer strings of DNA, and more, much more, a shared purpose, a shared spirit. Ghee inherited Sarah's chin and cheekbones and Maggie's inner glow. It shone through her eyes and the warmth of her touch. She lay her hand on mine, pulling away the vines, brushing off dead leaves.

"Are you real?" she asked.

I nodded. The dirt and leaves that had accumulated atop my head rained down on us both.

"I need help," she said. "It's Maggie."

Those were the magic words needed to free me from my self-imposed, self-centered exile. The three holy men were embarrassingly respectful, kneeling before me with genuine humility. They wanted to help Ghee and Maggie. They didn't have their facts straight, but when I tried to explain their mistakes, they grew frightened and the priest, Brother Robert, pissed himself. My voice was still pretty rough. It didn't really matter. Maggie was in trouble and it angered me, got me moving.

Why would anyone hurt Maggie? All she'd ever done—both in life and in death—was bring beauty and light into the world. She brought Sarah into the world. That alone was reason enough to help Ghee.

I stood, which I hadn't done in a long time. The vines and weeds growing around my body snapped away easily, except for the roots of a maple sapling that I needed to tug off my ankle. I was stiff from sitting for so long, but after following Ghee, Miss Polly, and the holy men out of the woods, I loosened up, ready to rock 'n' roll.

# 4

## *Second Final Report II*

*From "The Sixty Mile March, New Songs Of Maggot Worship," words and music by Bessie Johannson, Maggot Music Inc, copyright 2237.*

The Sixty-Mile March
Come on, children, on the sixty-mile march
Follow the big stone man down the great highway
Join us all, come one and all
The One True God gonna set things right
Gonna make a stand with his big stone hands
Gonna make things right with his holy might
Come on, children, on the sixty-mile march
From the woods up north to Newark Bay
Marching man gonna save the day
Marching man gonna save his bride
Marching man don't skip a stride
Come on, children, on the sixty-mile march to justice

*From KnowNet,* "Sixty Mile March," *last updated July, 2301 [Note: Some sources require citations.]*

The Sixty Mile March was a protest march against the

United States government's use of mood- and DNA- altering additives in air and water filtration systems, as well as against the seizure of the iconic Maggie statue by government forces in 2221. It is named for the approximately 60-mile span between where the march began in northwestern New Jersey and where it ended near Newark Bay.

Beginning in remote Sussex, NJ shortly before 10am on May 2, 2222, the Sixty Mile March was led by young American revolutionary Ghee Dorfhouse. The year before this incident, Dorfhouse's parents, Lucas and Jasmine Dorfhouse, were found guilty of vandalizing the Maggie statue. Dorfhouse may have been attempting to right her parents' wrongs by freeing the Maggie statue. [*Citation needed.*]

A traffic camera in Hamburg, New Jersey, captured the first image of the Sixty Mile March. Ghee Dorfhouse, an armored soldier, and approximately one-dozen followers crossed Route 94 toward Route 23 south. By the time the March concluded at Newark, New Jersey—approximately 30 hours later—it had swelled to an estimated 150,000 protesters.

The Sixty Mile March was immediately followed by The Battle of Newark Bay, where American rebels attacked and destroyed a government storage facility on the Newark Bay docks. The Maggie statue was destroyed in the battle. One hundred and fifty-four civilians were killed, along with eight US soldiers. Injury totals grew to nearly 1,000 American citizens.

*Sub-Topic:* The Early Hours
*Sub-Topic:* Showdown at Rt 287
*Sub-Topic:* Overnight, May 2
*Sub-Topic:* Morning, May 3
*Sub-Topic:* Afternoon, May 3
(See also, "The Battle Of Newark Bay")

*Interview with Peter McCloud, resident, Hamburg, NJ, NEWS 12*

*NJ, 12:33 pm, May 2, 2222.*

I'm heading to work this morning and state troopers have the exit to Route 23 blocked. Traffic's all backed up, with people pulled over and everything. So I pulled over too and got out of the car to take a look.

I seen 'em walking down the middle of the highway, a whole group of people with the big stone guy out front. He's hard to miss. They even had a couple of dogs running around with 'em. I didn't know what was goin' on, 'cause they weren't chanting or holding signs or anything. It was just a dozen people walking down the middle of Route 23. Two police cars were parked sideways, blocking the highway. The police shouted through a bullhorn to stop, but the stone guy kept right on walking. You could feel everybody getting nervous. A hush fell over everything.

Then the stone guy grabs the front bumper of the police car and flips it into the ditch beside the highway. I mean, just tosses it aside like it was a toy, or something, and everybody watching—even the state troopers—let out this collective gasp, you know, like a sound of pure disbelief. I think that's the moment we all realized we were witnessing something big.

*Audio transcript, New Jersey Governor's Office, 12:42 pm, May 2, 2222. Attendees:*

*GOVERNOR MAUREEN SUTTON /STATE POLICE COMMISSIONER ROGER BERGER / FEDERAL HOMELAND SECURITY AGENT ISABELLE JESSOP*

GOV. SUTTON: What the fuck? What the fucking fuck?

COMM. BERGER: Well said, Governor.

GOV. SUTTON: We can't let these people stroll down the middle of a state highway in the middle of the goddamn day, Roger. It's a public safety hazard.

COMM. BERGER: Aside from minor damage to one of our

cruisers, they haven't hurt anyone or damaged any property, public or private.

GOV. SUTTON: They flipped over a police car and shut down a major traffic artery traversing the northwest corner of our state! They've disregarded the orders of law enforcement and showed willful aggression toward a phalanx of state troopers. What is *your plan* to contain this *threat,* Commissioner Berger?

COMM. BERGER: I'd like Agent Jessop to answer that question, Governor.

GOV. SUTTON: Well?

AGT. JESSOP: The Department of Homeland Security believes it's in the best interest of public safety to allow these vagrants to continue their journey along the Route 23 corridor. If necessary, we have the ability to take out the female leader and the armored soldier.

GOV. SUTTON: The Feds are willing to put a SWAT sniper on that little girl?

AGT. JESSOP: Only as a last resort. We don't think it will come to that. We're confident we can bring this situation to a peaceful resolve.

GOV. SUTTON: How?

AGT. JESSOP: The vagrants have been marching for over two hours already. They'll tire out eventually, certainly by nightfall if not before. This movement cannot sustain itself. It'll peter out soon enough. But, in the meantime, HSA would like to follow along, see where they're going.

COMM. BERGER: You *know* where they're going!

AGT. JESSOP: We don't know *for certain* where they're going, Commissioner Berger.

GOV. SUTTON: Where are they going?

COMM. BERGER: To Newark! To wherever you all are holding Maggie!

AGT. JESSOP: The Parks and Rec Commission made the

call to remove the Maggie statue and the Department of Defense is keeping watch over it. HSA has no involvement with the Maggie statue. We're interested in this particular Maggot faction and what it has planned...particularly the soldier in combat armor.

GOV. SUTTON: Is that what that thing is? Christ, it looks like it's made of mud.

AGT. JESSOP: Talos combat armor can be camouflaged to mimic earth and stone. We believe the armor we're seeing may be modified with actual soil or clay in order to appear more stone-like, probably as an homage to the Maggie statue.

GOV. SUTTON: Who the hell is behind this and where did they get military-grade combat armor?

AGT. JESSOP: That's one of the things we hope to learn, Governor. A group called the Maggot Revolutionary Force may be behind this, but it has yet to claim responsibility. We're hoping it will if we let this play out a little longer. If this soldier is wearing the combat armor we think, it's a very rare, very dangerous, and very expensive piece of weaponry. We are investigating possible theft from a military facility, but so far nothing has come up. If combat armor like this was purchased on the black market, then this group is far more organized and better financed than previously thought. They may be backed by a large-scale terrorist organization or possibly a foreign government.

GOV. SUTTON: Christ!

COMM. BERGER: I thought you expected this to peter out quickly?

AGT. JESSOP: We do. But we'd like to gather as much information as possible first. The girl walking beside the soldier is Ghee Dorfhouse. Her parents are currently in a federal prison for vandalizing the Maggie statue.

GOV. SUTTON: The ones who chipped off her baby?

AGT. JESSOP: Yes. So you see why her appearing at the

head of a protest march alongside a large, expensive military weapon is giving us some concern. She may be trying to continue her parents' mission on a larger, more aggressive scale.

GOV. SUTTON: You think she wants to destroy the Maggie statue?

AGT. JESSOP: It's one possibility.

COMM. BERGER: Ghee Dorfhouse is a 17-year-old girl! There's no way a schoolgirl masterminded this grand coup!

GOV. SUTTON: I'm sure Agent Jessop will back me when I say young ladies are capable of quite a lot, Roger. Perhaps more than you'd expect.

COMM. BERGER: Listen, Maureen…Isabella…I meant no offense. Women can do anything. Girl power, okay? But Ghee Dorfhouse has no prior arrests, not even juvvies. She's a bad student and gets into trouble at school, but so what? So did I. She's been raised and homeschooled by her grandmother, Aria Trotman, most of her life, and you *know* Aria Trotman commands respect among a large block of your constituents.

GOV. SUTTON: What's your point, Roger?

COMM. BERGER: Ghee's parents, Jasmine and Lucas Dorfhouse, have a long history of fucked-up behavior as Stone Earthers, but their daughter doesn't. It appears Trotman tried to keep her granddaughter shielded from the extreme religious stuff. Whatever Ghee Dorfhouse is up to, I don't think she's planning to continue her parents' mission of destruction.

AGT. JESSOP: Can you take that chance when she's got advanced weaponry beside her?

COMM. BERGER: So you'll take them both out with, what…a guided missile? How much collateral damage have you factored in? How many civilians will get hurt?

AGT. JESSOP: You're getting ahead of yourself, Commissioner. In all likelihood this alleged protest march will run its course in a matter of hours. If, by some off-chance they make it down Route 23 as far as the Route 287 interchange, they will be met by the National Guard. They have orders to disperse any remaining crowd with tear gas and capture both the girl and the armored soldier.

GOV. SUTTON: Alive?

AGT. JESSOP: Yes.

GOV. SUTTON: You're not slaughtering that girl on my watch, Isabella.

AGT. JESSOP: It won't come to that. Let it play out for a few more hours and see where it goes.

COMM. BERGER: Fingers crossed.

*From "The Tribulation of Caliph Mustafa Ba-Lin, Modern Surahs, Timeless Wisdom," Seven Pillars Press, October 2224.*

We walked and walked, the sun beating down on us, the pavement hard and unforgiving beneath our feet. It was punishing. But believers came to our aid. That afternoon, a woman and her daughter brought us bottled water and sandwiches, bologna and mustard, I think. She thanked me, and said we were doing the Lord's work. She wasn't Muslim, but I called her sister and we hugged. "Free her! Free Mother Maggie!" she asked and I promised I would, or die trying.

But our flesh was weak. We'd walked all day and our legs were tired. Rabbi Solomon fell first, knees buckling and dropping to the pavement. The Rock God lifted Rabbi Solomon to his feet but the crowd of people following us scooped him from the Rock God's grasp and lifted the rabbi over their heads. I hadn't turned around since the march began, so I didn't realize how many people had joined us. There were hundreds...thousands...stretching as far as I could see. They lined the road ahead of us and packed the highway behind us. Cheering, crying, holding signs, giving us their love and energy. I felt it in my bones, a renewed sense of strength and purpose that propelled my tired body onward.

The faithful swept me up too, hoisted me onto a pair of shoulders. Brother Robert, Rabbi Solomon, and I rode atop the crowd, as tall as the Rock God, overlooking the sea of heads, highway unfurled like a black ribbon before us. The crowd chanted as one—"Free Mother Maggie! Free! Free!" Maybe they shouted the girl's name—"Ghee! Ghee!" The crowd hoisted her up, too. We had told no one about our mission, yet word spread quickly. They all knew where we were going, what we were doing. They even lifted the little stone dog over their heads; it howled at the sky and it sounded like a rockslide.

The crowd didn't lift the Stone Savior. Instead, the Stone Savior led our march, each mighty footstep making the earth quake. Praise Allah!

*From Action News Live, hosted by Jane Curry and Matt Gorman, Wednesday, May 2, 2222, 7:33 p.m. EST.*

CURRY: We are looking at a live helicopter shot right now of what appears to be a man—possibly a man wearing a costume or perhaps military armor—leading a march of people down Route 23 in New Jersey. If you're just tuning in, News 12 has had continuous coverage of this march since it began around 10:30 this morning. Evidently this figure emerged from a wooded area in Quiet Pines by TargMart in northwest New Jersey this morning, and has been walking southeast along Route 23 throughout the day. As you can see, there are a large number of people following the figure, as well as a police escort leading the crowd, making sure nobody gets hurt. The marchers are chanting "Free Maggie," leading us to believe this march is related to the confiscation of the Maggot statue from Franz Rock Memorial Gardens, which is also located in the TargMart area. According to some reports this may not be a man at all, but a military robot. If so, it seems rather foolish for those civilians to be following it so closely, Matt.

GORMAN: Jane, people are following this man because he is *made of stone* and he is obviously the husband or father of Mother Maggie.

CURRY: Those are unverified reports, Matt.

GORMAN: That's what people on the street are saying! I've personally interviewed several people who have been marching since early this morning.

CURRY: Matt, those reports are not sanctioned and as a professional news organization, I suggest we stick to sanctioned media briefs only. At this time we do not know if the figure leading the march is a rogue soldier in combat armor or a military robot.

GORMAN: He's neither! He's made of stone! We're witnessing a real-life miracle on live television, Jane!

CURRY: Matt, I think you need to check yourself. All we know so far is that late this morning state police in Sussex County, New Jersey, put up roadblocks on Route 94 that the marchers broke through. The National Guard has a barricade erected at the junction of Route 287 in Riverdale, which the marchers will reach very soon. We don't know if the marchers intend to challenge this barricade as well, but it certainly seems impassable.

GORMAN: You can't stop a god with police barricades! (*Touching his earpiece and speaking to an off-camera producer)* What? Yes, I took them…you can't make me take them! Listen, I don't see how my dietary choices are any of your business!

CURRY: (*looking into the camera*) Commercial? No? OK, we are going live now to Route 287 in Riverdale where what appears to be an armored soldier is approaching a National Guard barricade. Oh! Okay! Look at that! It appears the National Guard is using smoke or gas to disperse the marchers. Whatever it is, it doesn't seem to have an effect on the armored soldier. Does he have air filters in his helmet, maybe? Does anybody know? Oh! He appears to have just shoved a National Guard vehicle off the roadway. Good... *gosh*! Did you see that? What is that thing?

GORMAN: It's the Stone God come to save Mother Maggie!

CURRY: This is the last time, Matt! Leave that crazy religious nonsense at the door and act like a professional journalist!

*From "The New Revised Modern King James Bible: Unidenominational Edition," Catholic University Press, May 2227.*

Brother Robert threw himself over Ghee Dorfhouse, tried to shield her from the tear gas. He knew it was a wasted effort, but it was all he had left to give. They had walked all day in the heat and sun and, though night had fallen, a thick blanket of humidity clung to the earth. Brother Robert was weary, they all were, and they still had so far to go. He could not carry on, even with the strength of the Lord filling his veins, his body had nothing left to give. The army's poison filled Brother Robert's lungs, and Ghee Dorfhouse's lungs, and the lungs of Rabbi Solomon and Caliph Mustafa, and the freedom marchers, and the truth seekers, and the believers, and the victims. The warriors of justice were felled alike, gasping for air and getting only poison.

Brother Robert breathed his last. He died protecting the life of another, his final breath a gasp of justice, his last heartbeat the victory drum of the American revolution.

On a lonely New Jersey highway, Brother Robert went home to meet our Lord.

Brother Robert, we remember.

Brother Robert, we speak your name.

Forever and ever. Amen.

*Audio transcript, New Jersey Governor's Office, 8:22 pm, May 2, 2222. Attendees:*

*GOVERNOR MAUREEN SUTTON /*

*STATE POLICE COMMISSIONER ROGER BERGER /*

*FEDERAL HOMELAND SECURITY AGENT ISABELLE JESSOP*

GOV. SUTTON: What the fucking fuck, Roger? You let them stroll right through a National Guard blockade and then you have the audacity to open fire on that thing while it's holding the girl! I *told* you I don't want that girl killed on my watch!

COMM. BERGER: The Guard was Isabelle's call, not mine, Maureen.

AGT. JESSOP: I mistakenly assumed the New Jersey National Guard could safely dispel a crowd of under fifty unarmed citizens.

COMM. BERGER: Unarmed? That Talos suit is a walking weapon. You said so yourself.

AGT. JESSOP: Yes, but except for pushing stuff out of the way, it hasn't been utilized as such. Still, we expected the assailant to succumb to the tear gas. Talos suits aren't equipped with air filtration systems, but perhaps there's been internal modifications.

COMM. BERGER: Perhaps? Can I get my sharpshooters in there now? I will end this very quickly.

AGT. JESSOP: Conventional ammunition won't penetrate Talos armor.

COMM. BERGER: A sharpshooter with a fifty-cal will drop anything. There are dozens of overpasses along Route 287 that offer a clear shot.

GOV. SUTTON: You kill that girl, Roger, and I'll kill you.

AGT. JESSOP: Sounds like too much of a gamble,

Commissioner. Now that it's just the Stone Man and Ghee Dorfhouse I'd advise an overhead net or a road trap.

COMM. BERGER: My men can bring them both in. Alive. Keep the highway closed all the way to Route 78 if you have to. We'll wait for the right moment, away from prying eyes and looky-loos.

GOV. SUTTON: Looky-loos? It's hard for me to support you when you use stupid words, Roger.

COMM. BERGER: Give me another chance, Maureen. I'll bring them in.

AGT. JESSOP: Hope it works out better than your National Guard blockade.

*Transcript: HelmetComm, Marine Sniper Mark Taft/Marine Commander Louis Wahl. 9:04 pm, May 2, 2222.*

TAFT: Shit! Shit! Shit!

WAHL: Status, Oh-Two.

TAFT: Fucking rounds are bouncing right off him!

WAHL: Confirm fifty-cal ammo, Oh-Two.

TAFT: Head shots! Torso shots! Nothing's taking him down! Even the fucking dog is getting back up!

WAHL: Confirm fifty-cal ammo, Oh-Two!

TAFT: Yes! Yes, I'm using the fifty-cal armor-piercers, but they ain't piercing shit!

WAHL: Collateral damage?

TAFT: No. The girl's okay. She took cover beneath the overpass. The dog, too.

*Audio transcript, New Jersey Governor's Office, 12:05 am, May 3, 2222. Attendees:*

*GOVERNOR MAUREEN SUTTON /*

*STATE POLICE COMMISSIONER ROGER BERGER /*

*FEDERAL HOMELAND SECURITY AGENT ISABELLE JESSOP*

GOV. SUTTON: You're a fucking asshole, Roger! A real fuck-up!

COMM. BERGER: I am sorry the sharpshooter didn't work out. We were afraid using a heavier caliber weapon might harm the girl.

GOV. SUTTON: You're sorry? Do you realize what a colossal public relations disaster this is? How many times are you going to fail to capture these assholes?

COMM. BERGER: Honestly governor, I think Agent Jessop's plan for a netted capture may be in order at this time.

GOV. SUTTON: Thanks for telling me I should've gone with her plan in the first place, Roger. Sit there and shut up and wait for me to fire you.

COMM. BERGER: Yes, Maureen.

GOV. SUTTON: Agent Jessop, you're prepared to move forward with a plan to capture these assailants?

AGT. JESSOP: I am.

GOV. SUTTON: Then do it. And don't fuck up like Roger.

*HelmetComm transcript: Pilot FC Holly Sellwood, Private Arthur Wells, Marine helicopter BG 13-A. 12:44am, May 3, 2222.*

WELLS: No way! No way!

SELLWOOD: Shit, Wells! Did you miss?

WELLS: No! The dog pulled the net off!

SELLWOOD: Repeat, Wells.

WELLS: The dog lifted the net! The girl got out. The big fucker is still in there…wait, now he's out too!

SELLWOOD: Goddamnit!

*Audio transcript, New Jersey Governor's Office, 2:15 am, May 3, 2222. Attendees:*

*GOVERNOR MAUREEN SUTTON /*

*STATE POLICE COMMISSIONER ROGER BERGER /*

*FEDERAL HOMELAND SECURITY AGENT ISABELLE*

*JESSOP*

GOV. SUTTON: Goddamnit!

AGT. JESSOP: Let them come. Let them come. We'll take them in Newark. Clear a path and let them come.

COMM. BERGER: It'd be easier to act during daylight…in a controlled environment.

GOV. SUTTON: Shut up, Roger! When I want your opinion, I'll ask for it. You are both on my shit list. Come on, Isabelle, the Feds need a better plan than drop a cheap net on these bastards. A fucking dog tore it up! A little dog!

AGT. JESSOP: Just to clarify, the net was neither cheap nor flimsy. It's made of steel mesh and weighs nearly a ton. There's no way any man or animal should have escaped it, even with Talos suits. We're looking into possible mechanical failure.

GOV. SUTTON: Spare me the details of your investigation into *utter failure,* Agent Jessop. Just give me a peaceful end to this march.

AGT. JESSOP: We believe our best chances of that happening is to halt all aggression toward the marchers. Welcome them with open arms. Let them come.

GOV. SUTTON: Let them come…Christ, Isabelle, couldn't you have figured that out two failed captures and a dead priest ago?

*From Action News Live, hosted by Jane Curry, Wednesday, May 3, 2222, 12:33 p.m. EST.*

CURRY: Law enforcement officers line the protest route, but are making no effort to stop the marchers, nor disperse the crowd of onlookers. I'm not even sure they could at this point. The streets east of I-95 are clogged…latest estimates put the number close to 50,000 people packed into a very tight area along the Newark docks.

The young lady leading the march is identified as Franz

Rock High School student Ghee Dorfhouse, the same girl who began this march in Hamburg yesterday morning. Her remarkable journey has captivated viewers around the globe. She's accompanied by what looks like an armored—and most likely robotic—soldier as well as several marchers carrying hunting rifles and pistols. This peaceful protest is looking more and more like an armed militia.

There are unconfirmed reports Dorfhouse evaded capture *twice* overnight. This followed yesterday's march that saw protesters break through two police roadblocks, as well as a teargas attack that left Jesuit priest Brother Robert Franks dead and more than a dozen citizens injured.

It's unknown why law enforcement has let this march escalate to this point. It's going to take military intervention to bring this march to a peaceful conclusion and you have to wonder how much longer President Ipson is going to wait before ordering…

*Audio transcript, New Jersey Governor's Office, 2:11 pm, May 3, 2222. Attendees:*

*GOVERNOR MAUREEN SUTTON /*

*PRESIDENT LOREN IPSON / (via phone)*

GOV. SUTTON: Excuse me, Ms. President, but time is of the essence here. My police commissioner's troops are *not* able to maintain a secure perimeter within the city of Newark. The warehouse on McLester Street is surrounded on all sides by civilian protesters, some of them armed. The Talos rebel is less than two miles away, also followed by armed protesters. We need help.

PRESIDENT IPSON: (*on phone*) You're getting it, Maureen. The infantry's on its way from Fort Dix. They're coming.

GOV. SUTTON: So is Christmas, Loren. I've got a serious public safety issue brewing. Turn on the tube…it's live on every stream!

PRESIDENT IPSON: (*on phone*) I've seen the streams, Mo. I'm fully apprised of the situation. There are two M-4 battle tanks outside the warehouse and three Talos troops inside. I've been assured the facility is secure.

GOV. SUTTON: With all due respect, Ms. President, I disagree. The warehouse is *not* secure. The situation outside the warehouse is not secure. If we don't get some help here *immediately,* things are going to get violent...on live stream, Ms. President.

PRESIDENT IPSON: (*on phone*) I'm doing the best I can, Maureen. Hang in there. The cavalry is on its way.

GOV. SUTTON: They should have been here yesterday, Ms. President. We need help now. Shit's about to get ugly.

*Excerpt from* CARA & GHEE: A LOVE STORY, *written and directed by Oliver Jones, LoveStream Networks, Inc, January 2243.*

*Cara stands in a crowded student union at Chemloco College, watching a live widescreen news stream. Everyone in the student union is transfixed by the images of the Sixty Mile March. Ghee and the Man of Stone (Chip) walk down the middle of a two lane highway—Route 23 in northern New Jersey. It is after sunset, but the group is lit from overhead by choppy helicopter spotlights and media floodlights on the roadside. The camera cuts to a close-up of Ghee's face looking fierce, determined. Cara gasps and covers her mouth with her hands. Tasha puts her hands on Cara's shoulders, but Cara doesn't seem to notice.*

*CUT to TV screen. Picture-in-picture shows events from earlier that morning—Man of Stone pushing police cruiser off the highway. Live images switch from marchers—a crowd of 20-30 people, some carrying homemade protest signs—lit in harsh searchlight white, and a National Guard barricade further up the highway, flashing red and blue.*

TASHA: Where is she going?

*Cara answers, turning and shouting her response above the*

*crowd in the student union.*

CARA: Ghee Dorfhouse is marching to Newark to free Maggie! I'm going to meet her there. Who's coming with me?

*The student union erupts into cheers.*

*Excerpt from* CARA & GHEE: A LOVE STORY, *written and directed by Oliver Jones, LoveStream Networks, Inc, January 2243.*

SHOT IN SLOW MOTION

MID-SHOT: Cara pressed against a chain link fence, pushed from behind by the surging crowd. Behind her, protesters hold signs—"Free Maggie!" and "Fresh Air & Water Is A Basic Human Right." A group of protesters to Cara's right wear purple and white robes, like members of a religious order. A woman on Cara's left, wearing a hat made of crinkled tin foil, films the crowd behind her.

CLOSE-SHOT: Cara looks around, but doesn't see any of her classmates. Tears streak her face. She looks up and to the left. Her eyes widen with fear.

CUT TO MID-SHOT of Ghee scaling the chain-link fence. She stands on the upraised palms of the Man of Stone. She steps on the strands of barbed wire atop the fence, pressing it flat. Before swinging her other leg over the fence, Ghee looks around, scanning the crowd below her.

CLOSE-SHOT: Ghee sees Cara pressed against the fence and smiles.

CLOSE-SHOT: Cara smiles back, crying, yet beaming with pride.

MID-SHOT: Ghee swings her leg over the fence. A loud gunshot rings out and Ghee's head explodes in a spray of red. Her headless body is silhouetted against blue sky for a moment before slumping forward and falling over the fence, out of frame.

CLOSE-SHOT: Cara's mouth and eyes wide with terror. She screams. Gunfire erupts.

WIDE-SHOT: Tanks firing machine guns. The fence falls. Cara is crushed beneath the stampeding crowd.

# 5

## *Mudspeak II*

I didn't care for our fellow marchers. Ghee's supporters terrified me; eyes wide and crazy, manic, mad energy flowing off them in waves. They all wanted to touch me with their dead-fish hands. It gave me the creeps. Humans were weak but plentiful and I had a flash of envy for the casual ease with which they reproduced. I kept waiting for the crowd to break out torches and pitchforks. Didn't they know I was a monster? Did they see me as a hero now? The world must have gone ass-over-teakettle since I'd checked out.

They tried to touch Ghee, but I couldn't allow that, so I swung my arms wide until we had a clear space around us. People challenged us often. Fortunately Caliph Mustafa knew how to throw a punch and Brother Robert and Rabbi Solomon grew proficient at shoving bodies out of our way as the afternoon wore on and the crowd grew thicker and more frenzied. After dark the helicopters thumped overhead, following us with unsteady spotlights, bouncing flashlight beams cutting criss-cross patterns into the darkness before us. The crowd pressed in...somebody was going to get hurt. Ghee huddled beside me, trembling. I put my hand out and

Ghee pressed her palm against mine, lookin up with soft eyes.

"This is our exit," she said.

Two enormous tanks blocked the Route 287 off-ramp. (However, once I got a look at *real* tanks in Newark, I realized these National Guard vehicles were simply heavily armored box trucks.) They looked heavier than the police cruisers we'd encountered earlier.

A canister hit the asphalt with a soft clink about ten yards from us and the night filled with thick orange smoke. Ghee gagged and clutched her throat. She tried to duck beneath the gas cloud but it was everywhere. I heard another canister hit the ground somewhere off to the left, but couldn't see it. Bodies dropped all around—Ghee, the priest, the rabbi, along with dozens of marchers, all falling to the highway and writhing in agony, curling into fetal shapes, or worse yet, lying stone-still. The rest of the marchers retreated like a wave, running from the tear gas. Good riddance, weirdos.

Miss Polly ran among the fallen, her hellish howl joining the wail of police sirens. She dashed around the back of the National Guard truck and down the off-ramp. The police and guardsmen didn't try to stop her. Maybe they were so focused on Ghee and I, they hadn't noticed Polly. But that little dog showed me the way out.

Brother Robert was dead when I pulled him off Ghee. At least he felt that way. I didn't have time to give him a thorough exam. Ghee looked dead, too, her skin pale. I couldn't tell if she was breathing when I lifted her off the roadway. I didn't even stop to check. I tucked my head and ran toward the back of the National Guard truck, hoping to exploit the same narrow gap as Miss Polly.

I closed to within two strides when the driver threw the truck in reverse and blocked our escape. It didn't matter; I had weight and momentum behind me. I stiff-armed the back corner of the truck and it slid away easily, popping two tires on the far side. The vehicle started to tip, so I gave it a hard shove, sending it all the way over. It landed on its side with a crash of metal and breaking glass, followed by a shouted curse from the driver's compartment. I dashed around the truck and down the off-ramp. Miss Polly paced nervously at the bottom.

A rifle slug hit me square in the middle of the back and I dropped to one knee, trying to cover Ghee's body with my own. She was unconscious but I felt her heart beating against my fingertips. Another rifle crack followed, the bullet sparking off the asphalt six feet to my right. Damn, if they opened fire on us now we'd be finished.

But somebody blew a whistle and no more shots were fired. I stood and ran down Route 287 with Ghee in my arms and Miss Polly at my heels.

The highway was empty, apparently closed by the military. Helicopter spotlights found us a few minutes later, but they stayed well elevated, too far away for a sniper to take a shot. I looked around for more police cars but none came. Maybe the helicopters would swoop in for an aerial assault. They weren't going to let us run away from their tear gas party, were they?

I ran anyway, sticking to the shoulder of the highway, hoping the trees offered some cover. It was a dumb plan, I'll admit. Why bother hiding? They knew exactly where we were. But it felt good to stretch my legs, it felt good to run. Polly seemed to like it too. Was she smiling? Can dogs smile?

Polly and I ran beneath an overpass, empty except for swirling police lights. But a few miles later we passed beneath an overpass packed with cheering spectators (fans?) and adorned with a "Save Mother Maggie!!!" message crudely spray-painted on a bedsheet and hung from the security fence. How could word of our march spread so fast?

Maybe everybody was on the same group chat, or whatever wireless garbage they used now. Maggie had many followers…now Ghee did too. People chanted her name as we passed.

As if in response to the crowd's gushing adoration, Ghee suddenly sat upright in my arms and vomited hot liquid all over my chest. She turned her head, spat on the roadway, and vomited again, this time onto the asphalt. She turned her face to mine.

"Sorry about that," she said. "Put me down."

I stopped running and did as she asked.

Ghee stood by the side of the road, hands on her knees, retching. I stripped a handful of green leaves off a nearby branch and wiped vomit off my chest. Miss Polly paced a few yards down the road, eager to get moving again. She liked to run.

"Sorry I puked on you," Ghee said, wiping her eyes.

I shook my head. No worries. Hopefully the tear gas would be out of her system soon.

She looked back down the highway.

"We lost the caliph," she said. "The priest…the rabbi…"

I nodded.

Ghee shook her head.

"They were good men."

I nodded. Now wasn't a good time to mention Brother Robert's death.

She stared at her feet for a moment before lifting her face.

"I still can't believe you're real," she said.

I couldn't believe she was real either. Yet here she was, a direct link to Sarah and Maggie. And she came looking for *me*. How could she still believe in me? How could she know? Maybe desperate hope compelled Ghee to search the woods of North Jersey, or maybe it was Miss Polly's insistence. The stone beagle still paced the road ahead, eager to get moving.

"I love you," I blurted out, but it came out sounding like a rockslide.

Instead of recoiling in terror, Ghee looked at me and cocked her head to the side.

"Huh," she said. "I wish we had more time so we could figure out how to communicate."

Oh, Ghee. Dear child. From your lips to God's ears. More time and the desire to understand one another is something we all need.

I nodded.

"Are you ready?" she asked, pointing up the road to Polly. "Looks like he's raring to go."

Miss Polly was obviously a girl, but I saw no need to correct Ghee. I nodded and extended my arms to pick her up again. She shook her head.

"No. I want to walk," she said. She started down the road and I fell into step beside her. Polly seemed happy to be moving again. But Ghee was slow, tentative. After half a mile, she stopped.

"Okay. Maybe you should carry me," she said. "I'm weak..."

I held my arms out again and she climbed into my embrace. She was small enough for me to tuck into the crook of my arm and carry like an oversized infant. Ghee wrapped her slender arms around my neck and rested her face against my shoulder.

"Okay. Thank you," she said. "We can go. But no running."

Polly and I walked for several miles. I thought Ghee had fallen asleep when she muttered, "Okay, this is taking forever. You can jog."

Polly and I broke into a trot and the next time I checked, Ghee was asleep, her breath soft against my neck, her features smooth save for a tiny crease running the length of her forehead. God, she was just a kid, barely more than a child.

I should have turned around. Or taken the next exit and hidden in Boonton or Parsippany, anyplace but where Ghee wanted to go. Nothing good waited for us at the end of the road. I suppose that goes for all of us, but most definitely for Ghee and I. I wanted to run away, plain and simple.

Memories of Maggie kept me going, along with Ghee's soft, sleeping breath on my neck. My footfalls kept time with her breathing as Polly and I trotted down the highway.

Just before dawn, the helicopter came back, swooping low twice. On its third pass, it dropped a net that spread open into a wide, mesh circle above us. Polly leapt to the side of the road to avoid the falling net. I tried too, but wasn't quick enough. When I realized the net was going to trap us, I dropped to one knee, wrapped my arms around Ghee and hunched over her body. Ghee awoke with a startled scream just as the net fell over us. It felt like it was made of iron, the weight of it pushing me down further. Ghee climbed out of my arms and sat on the asphalt between my feet.

"What should I do?" she asked.

"Polly," I said and Ghee seemed to understand. Polly whined like a rusty gate and clawed at the edge of the net until it lifted and she was able to shimmy beneath. I held the steel net aloft, clearing a path for Ghee to crawl to Polly. Meanwhile, the helicopter circled back, laying down a strafe of machine gun fire that torn up a strip of roadway nearby.

"Oh, God!" Ghee screamed and crawled faster. The helicopter circled to the south and came back around for another pass. I lifted my arms high enough so Ghee and Polly could scurry from beneath the net and climb partway down the embankment on the side of the highway. The helicopter laid down another line of machine gun fire off to my right. A few of the shells bounced off the pavement and hit me in the face. Were these clowns trying kill us or frighten us? Lord, their aim was terrible! This was their big chance to take us out and they were blowing it.

I peeled the net off my head like an ill-fitting shirt. When the helicopter swooped low on its next pass, I tossed the net at it before it could start firing again. I didn't hit the helicopter, but came close enough to make it fly away.

"Fuckers!" I roared, shaking with rage. I stood in the middle of Route 287, waiting for the helicopter to return. It didn't. After a few minutes, Polly and Ghee climbed back up onto the road.

"Do you think they're gone?" Ghee asked.

I shrugged.

"They wouldn't try this if we still had people marching with us," Ghee said. She was right. A maniacal mob had its advantages.

We caught a break at the Route 78 exit. People lined the overpass ahead of us, chanting Ghee's name and waving signs. A state police cruiser blocked the top of the exit ramp, but the driver was kind enough to pull aside and allow us onto Route 78. The trooper probably didn't want his car tossed into a ditch like the others.

Route 78 was also closed to traffic. The right lane was packed with parked cars and people. A barricade ran down the center of the road, giving Ghee, Polly, and I a clear run all the way from Chatham to Newark. The helicopters returned, but stayed up high and out of range.

Ghee's supporters scared me, but their presence made the trip safer. I put Ghee down and she walked a few steps ahead of me. She waved and the people lining the road roared back their approval, like she was a celebrity, royalty. State troopers parked every 500 yards along the route made no effort to stop us, only to contain the crowd along the roadside. A few brave souls jumped the wooden barricades and fell into step behind us. The police didn't stop them either. More joined and we had our march back. Ghee smiled, people cheered, and the sun shone brightly, but it chilled me to consider what waited for us at the end of the highway.

There were more people than I'd ever seen in my life packed along McCarter Highway, and the crowd grew thicker the deeper into Newark we traveled. This was bigger than anything a city police force or the National Guard could contain. Maybe, after the tear gas incident last night, the Powers That Be had decided it was simpler, safer, and better public relations, to let us take Maggie back. I wondered if Maggie would be waiting in the doorway when we got there, bags packed and ready to go, like a proper mother-in-law ready to join the family vacation.

We crossed a series of service roads and flyovers that took us out near the water behind the airport, back where it was all warehouses and nondescript office parks. Faces filled every window and the crowd pressed in close on both sides. A group of five guys who looked like me climbed over the police barricade and I drew up, worried I was in for a scrap. But one of the men gave me a high-five and I could tell he was wearing an inflatable plastic suit. Is this what I'd been reduced to? A fragment of folklore and a tacky Halloween costume? Ah, so be it. People will see you how they want to see you, I suppose, truth be damned. The truth is usually a pack of lies, anyway. At least I was remembered in some small way, if only as a Halloween costume.

People packed shoulder-to-shoulder nearly a mile deep around the warehouse where Maggie was held. The police barricades disappeared the closer we got, the troopers having abandoned their posts. The path was barely wide enough for Ghee and I. Polly skirted nervously about our feet. Everybody wanted to touch us, a sea of dead-fish hands. Ghee reached out, brushing the outstretched fingertips of her faithful. Several swooned and fainted dead away. I made a wide semi-circle with my arms and kept Ghee inside as we waded through the crowd. People screamed in our faces.

"Ghee! Ghee! Ghee!"

"Save Mother Maggie!"

"Free our air! Free our water!

"Stop South American deforestation!"

"Save the whales!"

"Come to our house for dinner!

"We love you, Ghee!"

"Where did you buy those jeans?"

"Please, God! Help us!"

"Save us, Ghee-Ghee!"

"We love you, Gheely Girl!"

"We demand chemical-free air!"

"Chemical-free water!"

"Save us! Save us from ourselves!"

"Deliver us, Stone Savior!"

Stone Savior? That one amused and appalled me in equal measure. Who can live up to *that* expectation? Part of me wished I'd stayed hidden in the woods, ignored Polly's howl and the touch of Ghee's hand. Forget about Maggie and her worshippers, forget about family and what it means to be part of something bigger than yourself, the responsibility, the honor, the glory of connection. Being human is an obligation to both the past and the future, and I suppose I was still human enough to care, to want to do my part, however strange it might be. My temper, drive, and ambition was my undoing with Sarah. I couldn't let Maggie down. I couldn't let Ghee down.

We were close enough to see the top of the barbed wire fence surrounding the warehouse. The crowd parted before us like a biblical sea, clearing the way to a gate secured with a padlock and a chain. Ghee and I stepped up to the gate, the ground beneath us trembling from countless stomping feet. Ghee placed her palms against the fence. Two tanks—*real* tanks, with long, sleek canon barrels and black, domed machine gun turrets—sat less than twenty feet away on the other side of the fence. Behind the tanks stood half-a-dozen soldiers in riot gear, holding glowing metallic shields, faces tight with fear.

Nervous, frenzied energy radiated from both sides of the fence, springs coiling tighter and tighter, bad vibes boiled to a breaking point. There were too many dissenting views here, too much anger, too much hate, and no clear target in sight.

"Pick me up," Ghee said.

I looked down into her brown eyes, ancient eyes, incongruent with her young features. *She's just a girl.*

I shook my head. No. It's too dangerous.

"I have to talk to them!" She had to shout to be heard over the roaring crowd.

No. I shook my head more intently. This was too much. Too many people. Not enough space. I should grab Ghee and pull her into me, curl into a ball around her until everyone left us alone. But it was too late for such foolish notions. I'd let a good-hearted little girl lead us into an inescapable trap, caught between military tanks and an angry mob.

"I need to talk to them," Ghee repeated. She placed her hands on my forearm and relief flooded through me, a sudden and startling sense of calm. Even if this was a trap, it was exactly where we were supposed to be.

"Don't be scared," Ghee said, but my fear was already gone. Her touch dispelled my panic and adrenaline filled the void left in its place. Ghee no longer needed to shout in order for me to hear her. "Pick me up."

Still, I hesitated. Lifting her above the crowd meant exposing her to all sorts of dangers I couldn't protect her from. What could she do up there? What could she change? But we both knew that was where she belonged.

She put her arms out and I lifted her up. I tried to get her to sit on my shoulders but she planted her feet and stood on them instead. A deafening cry rose all around us as the faithful caught sight of Ghee rising from their midst. Here was the true savior.

Ghee lifted her right foot and looked down at me, the smile on her face full of childish mischief. She wanted to go higher, of course. I lifted both arms as high as my shoulders and Ghee stepped into my palms, right foot, left foot, and I lifted her up and up, higher and higher, the late afternoon sun setting her hair ablaze. I was her pedestal and she, a work of art.

Then a shot rang out. I looked up and Ghee's head was gone.

It rained blood.

# 6

## *Second Final Report III*

*Private transcription, President Loren Ipson, conference call, May 3, 2222, 5:22 p.m.*

Who fired that shot? I want to know who gave the order to fire that fucking shot! Yeah, well I don't care if he's dead, heads are going to fucking roll for this! Yes. Yes. Of course, I understand. But all of this could have been avoided if your fucking people hadn't blown that girl's goddamn head off! Fuck me! Fuck *you*! You've destroyed me! You've *destroyed* me!

*Presidential news conference, President Loren Ipson, delivered live, May 3, 2222, 9 p.m. EST.*

Today is a sad, terrible day in our nation's history. Today we saw what began as a peaceful protest turned violent. This afternoon, a government storage facility in Newark, New Jersey, holding the iconic religious statue known as 'Maggie' was attacked by a highly organized group of homegrown terrorists who used the guise of a non-violent protest to breach the facility's defenses and launch an attack on the building. One of these terrorists, wearing tactical combat armor, was able to enter the warehouse and detonate an explosive that destroyed the warehouse and the statue of Maggie inside. Our nation's forces were able to eliminate and contain the remaining terrorist attackers. I want to assure everyone watching and listening to me right now that you are safe, your families are safe, and America is safe.

But the defense of our nation came at a terrible price—154 civilian lives were lost, with another 330 injured. Innocent citizens who simply found themselves in the wrong place at the wrong time and paid an agonizing price.

In addition, four brave American soldiers sacrificed their lives today, and another four were injured, some gravely. Sergeant Janet Baxter, who has been with Special Forces for over a decade; tactical vehicle specialist Ensign Dennis DeForge, who served six years; Lieutenant Lucas Wallace, who has been with us for eight years; and Sergeant Ethan Reed, who has defended our country for the last five. These soldiers gave their lives defending a global symbol of peace and healing. While it personally sickens me that these brave individuals died defending a statue, I recognize the cultural and spiritual importance of Maggie and fully embrace the Maggot message of love, forgiveness, and reconciliation. Despite what I've said in the past, I truly hope Maggie's healing message spreads to everyone in America and that today's tragic events mark an end to civil unrest and the dawn of a new age of national unity. Good night and God bless America.

*Democratic candidate Grant Layton, InstaMessage rebuttal, May 4, 2222, 9 am.*

President Ipson's message to the American people shows how out-of-touch and secretive her administration has become. The Ipson Administration confiscated Maggie, which prompted the protest march, then completely failed to keep

Maggie safe. Yet the President refuses to take any responsibility for the massacre of American citizens we saw yesterday. She didn't even mention the public execution of Ghee Dorfhouse! We all saw that young woman murdered in horrific fashion. Until President Ipson addresses the murder of Ghee Dorfhouse, I don't know how we can trust anything she says.

*Presidential news conference, President Loren Ipson, delivered live, May 4, 2222, 8 pm.*

This is a time of healing, but I want to expound on some of the things I said during my public address last night. I too was shocked and horrified by the murder of Ghee Dorfhouse yesterday. Though I never met her personally, Ghee's determination and spirit were an inspiration to us all over the last couple of days and to see it end so tragically…

Ghee Dorfhouse will not be forgotten. In a little over 24 hours Ghee has become a symbol of yesterday's tragedy. I want to assure the American people that my administration will find whomever is responsible for the murder of Ghee Dorfhouse, even if that person is a member of the American military, and we will bring the responsible parties to justice.

As our investigation continues, I implore you to remain calm and patient. There have been disturbing reports of violence over the last 24 hours. I assure you this behavior doesn't solve anything…it only causes more problems. This should be a time of national healing, not division.

*Public comments on President Ipson's statement: May 5, 1:22 a.m*

*BarryInTx:* "Disturbing reports of violence…" The Maggot Revolutionary Force took over two military bases near Amarillo yesterday morning. Is that disturbing enough, Ms Prez?

*77Johnny451:* I heard the Air Force base near Albany, NY

fell as well, but the media isn't reporting it.

*RevoltingMae:* Albany and Amarillo both true. White House is next. Maggot Power!

*TheDrgonLrd44:* Fuck the White House and fuck Ipson! The shot that killed Ghee clearly came from the tank positioned on the left. Ipson is a liar and her "investigation" a farce.

*NancyBr33m:* Guess I'm voting Freedom Party in November...Layton?

*GeeGheeGee1:* Best man for the job.

*MillwoodOgre:* Layton is backed by Maggots and the Rock God. He's unstoppable.

*HouseFrown2202:* The Rock God rules!

*GayGamer:* Fuck Loren Ipson in the cunt!

*Mustachio2277:* President Ipson has nice lips. She can blow me.

*HHHBomb:* Ugh! You wouldn't say such disgusting, filthy things if a man were President!

*Mustachio2277:* Grant Layton can blow me too.

*Mggts4VR:* Avenge Ghee Dorfhouse! Don't let her die in vain! Take down the government killers!

*YYNOt:* Long live Miss Polly!

*Teacher's Edition of* Heidi in the Tippy-Top Wayback, *by Karen Price-Walters, Learning Story Press, 2290.*

1.

Magic the Unicorn lived in Ms. Goodall's kindergarten classroom at Happy Valley Elementary School.

Magic was very happy there and the students all loved him.

Year after year, kindergarten students in Ms. Goodall's class enjoyed Magic.

Former students grew up and had children of their own.

And Magic made a whole new generation of friends in Ms. Goodall's class!

Generation after generation.

Year after year.

Everybody loved Magic.

<u>*Section 1 Questions:*</u>

*Did any of your parents/family go to school here? (Teaching Target: "Generations.")*

*What was the last magical thing that you saw, read, or heard about?*

2.

But Heidi's class was different.

The kids in Heidi's class loved Magic too, but they all had different beliefs about how Magic should be treated.

Caroline Hawkridge wanted Magic to stand near the window so he could soak in the sunshine.

Elizabeth Mohammed wanted Magic in the shade so he wouldn't get too hot.

Lucas Looper wanted to hang Magic from the ceiling in the middle of the room!

Holly Halfbrite wanted Magic to stay on Ms. Goodall's desk, because that's where he'd be safest.

And Holly Halfbrite was all right, because Evil Earl Corpland broke off Magic's horn!

"I thought it'd look better as a horse," Earl said.

Oh, Earl! How could you?

<u>*Section 2 Questions:*</u>

*What's the difference between a unicorn and a horse? (Teaching Target: "Animal Classifications.")*

*Where do you think the best place to store Magic would be?*

3.

This infuriated Heidi.

Heidi was convinced Magic was her own special unicorn.

Heidi's parents and grandparents and all her aunts and uncles told her Magic belonged in their family.

A distant relative of Heidi's brought Magic into the world a long, long time ago.

No one was quite sure how.

But Heidi knew Magic belonged to her.

She didn't mind sharing Magic with her classmates, as long as they were respectful.

But her classmates were not respectful, especially Earl Corpland.

Now Heidi was so angry, she couldn't speak and her eyes filled with tears.

It wasn't fair.

*Section 3 Questions:*

*What's the right way to share Magic? (Teaching Target: "Sharing")*

*Do you think Heidi and Earl will ever be friends again?*

4.

"Something very sad has happened to Magic," Ms. Goodall said. She stood in front of the class holding Magic in one hand and his broken horn in the other. "Very sad, indeed. Because of what's happened, I'll have to put Magic away, in the tippy-top wayback of the storage closet where I keep old chalk and dusty, forgotten things I've taken from misbehaved students over the years. The tippy-top wayback is the deepest, darkest part of the closet, where things go and are never seen again."

Earl Corpland raised his hand.

"What have you taken from students over the years, Ms. Goodall?" he asked.

"Naughty books and dirty looks, filthy minds and hopeful futures, chewing gum, umbrellas, braces and crosses, old sports equipment, happiness, and pencils top the list. But there are many, many things, on a very long list. Have no doubt, Earl. Things go in, but they don't come out."

Ms. Goodall put Magic and his broken horn in the tippy-top wayback of the closet and shut the door.

She read the class a story from a square, brown book about old men taming wild horses, but it was hard for Heidi to pay attention.

Earl Corpland raised his hand and asked to go to the nurse and Ms. Goodall excused him from class. He went home sick and didn't come to school the next day. At recess, after lunch, Caroline Hawkridge told Elizabeth Mohammed who told Lucas Looper who told Holly Halfbrite who told Heidi that Earl Corpland was sent to the tippy-top wayback by Ms. Goodall as a punishment for harming Magic.

Heidi hoped it was true.

<u>*Section 4 Questions:*</u>

*Was Ms. Goodall right to put Magic in the closet? (Teaching Target: "Rules")*

*What else do you think Ms. Goodall might keep in the tippy-top wayback?*

5.

Heidi did not go home after school that day. She told the bus driver she had another ride and hid in the girl's locker-room. It was scary in there—all the sounds echoed—but she told herself to be brave for Magic's sake. She heard her gym teacher talking with someone in her office, laughing loud and long. After a while, the gym teacher turned off the lights and left. Heidi waited a little while longer before creeping out into the Happy Valley Elementary School hallway.

The hallway was dark too—not completely, plenty of outside light spilled in from the windows—but shadows pooled in every doorway. Nothing was bright and happy the way it looked during the school day.

Ms. Goodall left her classroom door unlocked and Heidi walked right in, closing the door softly behind her. She left the lights off, keeping the classroom dark. All the chairs were upside down on the desks and Heidi felt like tight clusters of thin-headed adults were looking down on her. She did not like it, so she crossed the room quickly to the storage closet behind Ms. Goodall's desk.

Heidi opened the closet door. She pulled Ms. Goodall's chair over and stood on it so she could reach deep into the tippy-top wayback. She reached as far as she could, but felt nothing. What about all the things Ms. Goodall said she put there? What about Earl Corpland? What about Magic? Heidi has *seen* Ms. Goodall put Magic on the closet shelf. It *must* still be in there. She stood on the back of Ms. Goodall's chair, even though she knew it was a very dangerous thing to do, something you should never do. But Heidi thought if she could only stretch a bit further, she could grasp Magic, maybe his horn too. She'd take Magic home and fix him up. Her family would be happy and proud and her classmates would be happy and proud and Ms. Goodall would be happy and proud.

Ms. Goodall's chair slipped out from beneath Heidi's feet and clattered to the ground. The sound was very loud in the empty classroom. Heidi dangled from the closet shelf. Half of her was already wedged into the tippy-top wayback. Without the chair to stand on, Heidi had no choice but to crawl deeper and deeper into the tippy-top wayback. Surely Magic must be here somewhere. There was must be *something* up here. Ms. Goodall said…

Heidi crawled so far into the tippy-top wayback, she didn't even hear the closet door close behind her.

<u>Section 5 Questions:</u>

*Why is it important to follow the instructions of a parent, teacher, or other childcare-certified adult? (Teaching Target: "Consequences")*

*How else could Heidi have handled the missing Magic?*

6.

The next morning, Ms. Goodall stood before the class alongside a handsome man with a friendly smile.

"Students, this is your new teacher, Mr. McCash. I want to thank you all for letting me be your teacher and I hope to see some of you again in high school or even college. You're all big boys and girls now, on your way to being grown-ups. You've outgrown me. Mr. McCash will lead you the rest of the way. Good luck, children!"

Ms. Goodall smiled, waved, and left the classroom.

Mr. McCash clapped his hands together and smiled.

"I'm eager to get started, students!" he said.

Elizabeth Mohammed raised her hand.

"Where are Heidi and Earl?" she asked.

"They've been promoted. Qualified students graduate and move on to advanced levels. Teaching everybody, all at once, in the same classroom, isn't practical anymore. There are better ways to teach. If you're really good at something, we'll give you more time to practice it. Heidi was a really talented artist, so she's in a different class creating wonderful artwork. Earl was very, very good at math, so we moved him to a mathematics and technology lab where he can focus on those skills. Before long, we'll find out what all of you are good at!"

Lucas Looper raised his hand.

"What if I'm not good at anything?" Lucas asked. He sounded worried.

"Everybody's good at something," Mr. McCash said. "You don't have to worry. Take time to explore and learn, and together we'll figure out a plan for what's best."

Lucas nodded, but he suspected Mr. McCash might be lying. Heidi wasn't that good at art.

At recess, after lunch, Caroline Hawkridge told Elizabeth Mohammed who told Holly Halfbrite who told Lucas that Heidi and Earl had been sent to the tippy-top wayback together.

Lucas decided to hide in the boys' locker room after school and wait until Mr. McCash left. He needed to explore the tippy-top wayback for himself.

<u>*Section 6 Questions:*</u>
*What do you think Lucas is going to do next? (Teaching Target: "Story Forecasting")*
*What do you think he'll find there?*
*What can go wrong when you don't follow rules, rituals, and routines?*

*From Books4U comments on:* Heidi in the Tippy-Top Wayback, *by Karen Price-Walters, Bedtime Story Press, 2290.*

*Post(g)al wrote:* This story scared the hell out of me as a kid! It's really a twisted story when you think about it. So creepy. I'm not sure why it was marketed as a kid's book.

*Haroldo wrote:* Because it is government propaganda, that's why.

*Glarry Gal wrote:* Warning! Conspiro-Nut Alert!

*BBMilkk wrote:* It's supposed to be scary. It's a parable about how Ghee Dorfhouse was murdered by the military and the government covered it up.

*MrsBKupp wrote:* I know Ghee/Heidi, Maggie/Magic is a popular theory, but I always thought this book was about going through puberty and emerging a fully aware sexual being.

*BBMilkk wrote:* MrsBKupp is a freak!

*MrsBKupp wrote:* (Blush)

*JJSmokEE wrote:* I want to fuck Ms. Goodall's fat tits!

*69Markus wrote:* Until they fall off and bounce across the classroom floor!

*PeterII wrote:* You're sick. Nobody wants to fuck Ms. Goodall. She's like 50 years old! McCash maybe. He's got such a bright, white smile.

*MeLovePolly wrote:* All of these movies, plays, and books suck because they cut out Miss Polly. That dog was the TRUE hero!

*MasterPEE wrote:* I'd fuck Mr. McCash until his bones broke!

*VeronicaJK wrote:* I love the illustrations in this book. They make the story.

*LitFannie wrote:* I don't know what book y'all just read, but this is clearly a message about the failure of capitalism and the spread of socialism/communism in the Western Hemisphere. "Before long, we'll find out what all of you are good at!" There hasn't been Marxist propaganda like this since the Cold War!

*JHB wrote:* Fuck's a cold war?

*VeronicaJK wrote:* We are all doomed.

*RemembranceOnline: How Do You Remember Ghee Dorfhouse? (10.4K comments)*

*Statement from Aria Trotman, grandmother, posted on June 3, 2222.*

Good Lord, people, what's our world coming to? People fighting over power—political and electrical—while my poor baby Gheely Girl gets her head blown off in some Newark slum. That's not a protest. That's a mob. That's slaughter of innocents and innocence simultaneously. I tell you, people, you've gone blind, deaf, and dumb. Can't you hear the cries of the helpless and needy? Couldn't you hear my little Gheely Girl crying out for justice? The poor child wanted to right wrongs and free Maggie for all of us. Now Maggie's gone. Ghee's gone. I feel like my insides are gone too. My heart. My lungs. I feel scooped out like a Jack-O-Lantern, a hollow husk of an old woman, an old woman whose time has passed, an old woman confused about what's happening, about where this country is going. See, I fought for you, all of you. Back in '87 we challenged BizGov, we got the Sukodic Prohibition Act signed in '90, and the Clean Air Initiative in '91. I stood alongside Stone Earthers, Flies, Old Religion delegates, BizGov attorneys, and elected officials, and we all worked TOGETHER to make change happen. We didn't lose our heads and raid government buildings. We didn't vandalize. We didn't slaughter little girls. Good God, how you massacred my Gheely. Shame on you. Shame on all of you.

*PieCENick replied:* Sorry for your loss, Ms. Trotman. We all owe you a debt of gratitude for the work you've done bringing the problem of Sukol/Benzil-ring poisoning to the forefront of public consciousness. While the CAI and SPA were a good start, the struggle for clean air and water continues. Sukol/Benzil-rings can be easily disguised with the addition or subtraction of sub-atomic chemicals. The war isn't over.

*BobbiKite replied:* It's the same shit with a different name. Sukodol isn't going away.

*BrrrMI replied:* That stuff gives me a terrible rash. I can't believe they still use it.

*McLeanPSA replied:* Benzil-ring poisoning doesn't produce a skin rash. It turns you into a zombie by altering your DNA. Get your facts str8!

*Ainikki54 replied:* Thank you, Aria. I'm sorry for your loss. Ghee was an inspiration to us all.

*DharmaDuck replied:* Justice for Ghee!

*Statement from Jasmin Dorfhouse, mother, posted on June 6, 2222.*

My name is Jasmin Dorfhouse. I'm Ghee's mother. I'm currently serving a twenty year sentence in Tagment Detention Facility for defacing the Maggie statue in 2221. My husband and I chiseled away Maggie's baby. We did this because it conflicted with our religious beliefs at the time. The Stone Earthers believe Maggie should be pure, without adornment. The sect my husband and I belonged to found Maggie's child offensive. So my husband and I took her child away.

Now I've had my own child taken away, blown to bits the way we chipped away Maggie's child. My prison term will eventually end, but my daughter will always be gone. I understand this is my punishment and I accept it. May Mother Maggie forgive me my trespass.

But what was Ghee's crime? All she wanted was to right her parents' mistakes. Yes, it was foolish and idealistic, but she was a teenager! Did you have to kill her for trying to make the world better? My daughter wanted to free Maggie and unite the Maggots. Now we are more divided than ever. May Mother Maggie have mercy on us all.

*ThomYen replied:* Maggots are weird.

*MeghanN replied:* I'm sorry for your loss.

*JanniB replied:* I hate your politics and I don't understand why you attacked Mother Maggie, but I'm sorry your daughter was murdered by President Ipson.

*DeannaDDD replied:* I'm not sure who's a bigger asshole: you or your husband. Shame on both of you. RIP Ghee.

*555head replied:* Ghee will never be forgotten! Maggot pride! Maggot power! Stone Earth Forever!

*LaraHope replied:* How can you feel pride or powerful about the murder of a little girl? I hope this incident brings down the entire Maggot religion. Mother Maggie spread great wisdom but she's gone. Time to take her teachings and move on. Look to the Torah for guidance.

*MikeyO replied:* The Torah…ok, I'll fire up my time machine. Maybe we can pick up the Bible and the Koran too while we're visiting the Dark Ages.

*HHHH565 replied:* All religions suck, old and new. The murder of Ghee Dorfhouse sickens me. That's what religion gets you.

*RobertBEAN replied:* Ghee Dorfhouse was murdered by OUR OWN military! Her murder was funded by

TAXPAYERS! Demand answers. Don't let Ghee die in vain.

*DanaDeni replied:* I'm sorry for your loss. I know Ghee wanted to help us all. I wish everyone would stop fighting. That's not what Ghee would have wanted.

*Statement from Lucas Dorfhouse, father, posted on Jan 6, 2249.*

Fuck you. You all murdered my little girl. You murdered her. I wish I hadn't stopped at Maggie's baby. I wished I smashed the entire statue to dust back in 2221. At least Ghee would have lived. You killed her over a fucking statue! A goddamn carved rock! Then you went and destroyed the statue anyway! You're fools...murdering fools. You slaughtered my baby. Fuck all you all.

*LauraRemi replied:* No, FUCK YOU for defacing Mother Maggie! Your scumbag daughter burns in hell and you will too!

*JesusCheeses replied:* I'm sorry for your loss.

*BartM replied:* I'm sorry for your loss.

*MaSpa44 replied:* I'm NOT sorry for your loss. Maggots get what they deserve.

*EliQu replied:* I wouldn't mess with the MRF. They'll knock out your power and lights. Make you light a candle and read a dead-tree book!

*JackieL7l replied:* I couldn't charge my com, VRstream, or anything for almost a week after the MDF attacked the power grid. Fuck the Maggots and fuck President Layton.

*PPPete replied:* Layton. Worse. President. Ever.

*WalterT replied:* Weird, though, how the Maggots totally fell apart after the 2222 elections. I think the MRF scared everybody away.

*RubySlipperz replied:* Maggots become Flies. Flies fly away.

*JeffB replied:* Or get swatted!

*LeeSato replied:* I'm sorry for your loss. Ghee will be missed.

*JAMEz replied:* Maggie lives! The Rock God lives!

Remember Iceland!

*ElliMayve replied: [RVL ImageMeme: President Ipson hanging her head following 2222 Election loss.]*

*From "Forenstream Investigates: The Death Of Ghee Dorfhouse," cast March 18, 2223.*

(*Images of Dorfhouse morgue photos. VO by Essex County Coroner John Davis*). Subject is a teenage female, between 16 and 19 years old. Cause of death is a gunshot wound to the head. Judging from the amount of tissue loss and cranial damage, I'd say we're looking at a high caliber rifle—a .50-cal or higher, possibly with explodojacket loads. An initial visual inspection shows a total loss of the eyes, optic nerves, front cortex, occipital lobe…as stated, a vast, *vast* amount of bone and tissue loss to this girl's head. She also appears to have a broken wrist, but I believe that injury occurred post-mortem, possibly from falling after being shot. Judging from the severity of the wound, her death was likely instantaneous. But make no mistake about it—this young woman was savagely murdered.

*Bedtime story, traditional, circa 2295.*

Once upon a time, Wicked Men poisoned all the air and water with sleeping potion, and, while everyone's mind was in a fog, they kidnapped Queen Maggie, crushed her baby into powder and locked her away in a fortress by the bay.

Queen Maggie was very clever. She knew not all of her disciples were sleeping, so she sent her dog, Miss Polly, to get help and find King Rockman. Wicked Men had erased King Rockman from history, so Queen Maggie gave Miss Polly an ancient relic, a forbidden book, to convince her disciples King Rockman was real.

*Q: Why did King Rockman wait until Queen Maggie was kidnapped to help her?*

*A: King Rockman was made of stone, just like Queen Maggie, so time moves differently for him. King Rockman didn't know Queen Maggie was in trouble until the Wise Men told him.*

*Q: Who are the Wise Men?*

*A: I'm getting to that.*

The Three Wise Men followed Miss Polly into the haunted woods to find King Rockman and plead with him to save Queen Maggie.

*Q: Why did they plead with him? Wouldn't he just help her?*

*A: He did help her. Once he knew she was in trouble.*

*Q: But what was he doing sitting in the woods so long by himself? Why wasn't he out healing people like Mother Maggie?*

*A: Well, he was very broken-hearted. He was grieving.*

*Q: What does that mean?*

*A: He was sad because he lost something.*

*Q: What did his lose?*

*A: His wife.*

*Q: Did she die?*

*A: No. Well…yes. But not then. That's not how he lost her.*

*Q: Did they get a divorce?*

*A: In a way. They had changed as people and couldn't stay together. But that's a tale for another day. What's important is that King Rockman agreed to go with Polly and The Wise Men to free Queen Maggie from the fortress by the bay.*

King Rockman walked sixty miles to where Queen Maggie was held captive. Thousands of people walked alongside King Rockman, cheering as he approached the evil fortress.

*Q: King Rockman walked sixty miles? How long did it take him?*

*A: More than a full day. Almost two. He had thousands of people following him by the time he got there.*

*Q: Nobody tried to stop him?*

*A: Oh, they did. Several times. But he was unstoppable.*

*Q: What does this have to do with poisoned air and water and sleepy people?*

*A: It's coming.*

King Rockman didn't stop until he reached the fortress by the bay and there he faced a deadly adversary.

*Q: Wicked Men?*

*A: A tank!*

*Q: A tank? One of those old army vehicles?*

*A: Yes. It was a very deadly vehicle made of strong steel and equipped with guns and rockets. The tank guarded the fortress by the bay. All who followed King Rockman stood behind him as he faced off against the tank. King Rockman tried to walk past the tank, but the tank opened fire. The bullets bounced off King Rockman but many, many people were killed. That was the moment Wicked Men lost the power to poison the air and water.*

*Q: Because they killed a bunch of people?*

*A: On live stream. That woke up a lot of people who had been asleep. Soon after, Wicked Men were driven from the positions that controlled the air and water…at least for a while.*

*Q: Then King Rockman rescued Queen Maggie?*

*A: King Rockman tied the long gun of the tank into a bow. Then he pulled the driver out of the tank and tied him into a bow too. King Rockman tossed both the tank and its driver into the bay.*

*Q: And* then *he saved Queen Maggie?*

*A: Yes, but not before there was a terrible battle. The Wicked Men had powerful secret weapons inside the fortress. King Rockman was attacked and gravely injured.*

*Q: What's gravely?*

*A: He was hurt so badly, he nearly died.*

*Q: Oh. Gravely. Like, ready to "lie in the grave."*

*A: Shhh. Listen.*

King Rockman and Queen Maggie were both seriously injured in the battle. Poor Miss Polly was killed. But, working together, the King and Queen defeated the Wicked Men's soldiers. They walked into the bay together and were never seen again.

*Q: They committed suicide?*

*A: No. They don't breathe air. They're rocks. They went to live under the sea.*

*Q: Like* The Little Mermaid*?*

*A: Sort of.*

*Q: Why do people kill themselves at the spot where the King and Queen walked into the bay?*

*A: Well, they put up fences to stop people from doing that. But I guess some people…want to follow the King and Queen into the water.*

*Q: This story stinks like bullshit.*

*Debriefing of Donatello Ott PSE—Lt tactical vehicle specialist, Spot One—by Alexandra Hall, May 3, 2222, 4:55 pm.*

*Hall*: Don, take a drink of water. Swallow. Now, take a deep breath. Just breathe. That's it. That's good. Great. You're safe, Don. Nothing can hurt you and you're not in any trouble. But you need to tell us who fired the round that killed Ghee Dorfhouse.

*Ott*: I told you three times already! Please, I need to call my wife…my mother…

*Hall*: Did you discuss your assignment with your family, Don?

*Ott*: No. No, of course not. But they knew I was working in Newark. They'll see it on the news. They'll be worried.

*Hall*: One more time and then we're all done, okay?

*Ott*: (*sighs*) Ensign DeForge was in the turret with the .14 millimeter. He probably took the shot. He was nervous. Jumpy. We all were.

*Hall*: DeForge *probably* took the shot or *definitely* took the shot?

*Ott*: I don't know! Sgt. Reed's weapon was also pointed out the port slot but I don't think he fired…he *didn't* fire.

*Hall*: Was Sgt. Reed's weapon locked and loaded, as far as

you know?

*Ott*: I-I guess…it happened so fast. The shot rang out and the fences fell, and then that thing…that thing destroyed the turret…and DeForge…Jesus, did you see what it did to Dennis?

*Hall*: I have. What happened next?

*Ott*: Ethan…Sgt. Reed wanted to exit out the main hatch, but I said we should sit tight. Our vehicle was damaged. Spot Two should have taken the lead. Ethan…Reed thought we should disembark and engage, but I-I thought he was crazy to go outside and attempt close combat after what that thing did to the tank. It…smashed right right through six inches of glass and steel like it was nothing!

*Hall*: I saw. You and Sgt. Reed argued about leaving the vehicle?

*Ott*: I wouldn't call it an argument…we were both scared.

*Hall*: Did you radio Spot Two?

*Ott*: I think Ethan…Sgt. Reed did, but I'm not sure if Spot Two responded?

*Hall*: Then Sgt. Reed chose to exit the tank?

*Ott*: Christ, I told you! That fucking monster ripped the hatch off! Ethan was standing beneath the ladder when it happened, but he didn't open the door.

*Hall*: Sgt. Reed did not open the hatch.

*Ott*: No! Fuck! That thing tore the hatch off and tossed it away like a frisbee. A reinforced steel door! Then he punched…Ethan…oh, God…oh shit…I think I'm going to be sick…

*Hall*: Come on, Don. Another sip of water. Another deep breath. Almost done. After Sgt. Reed died, did you try to engage the attacker?

*Ott*: No. Its arm came through the open hatch, felt around, but I…I didn't engage.

*Hall*: Why not?

*Ott*: Ethan…I had Ethan all over me…

*Hall*: Okay. Did you make any attempt to exit the tank once the attack stopped?

*Ott*: There was no time. It…the attacker moved away from the hatch but half-a-minute later the tank was skidding across the parking lot. I got tossed into the driver's compartment. Then the tank struck something and flipped on its side…I'm guessing Spot Two.

*Hall*: That's correct.

*Ott*: The crew in Spot Two okay?

*Hall*: Shaken up, obviously, but they'll be okay.

*Ott*: What about the troops in the warehouse. Janet? William?

*Hall*: Not so good. Lost two. Bill Poole will live but he lost an arm.

*Ott*: Jesus Christ! Oh, that's awful! What the hell was HQ thinking, sticking a skeleton crew on warehouse security? They saw the marchers coming…we all did. Why didn't they send help? You can't expect ten men to defend against ten thousand!

*Hall*: Not our place to question decisions, Don, just clean up the mess when it's over.

*Ott*: Christ…the mess…

*Debriefing of Lt William Poole—Talos T4 Armor Specialist—by Alexandra Hall, May 3, 2222, 11:55 pm.*

*Hall*: How are you feeling, Lieutenant?

*Poole*: Like I'm going to vomit.

*Hall*: That's the anesthesia wearing off. You should feel better soon. Would you like some water?

*Poole*: No.

*Hall*: Can you tell me what you remember about today, Lieutenant Poole?

*Poole*: A monster ripped my arm off.

*Hall*: I'm sure it appeared that way. But you were attacked by a terrorist soldier in Talos combat tactile armor.

*Poole*: Bullshit. Wallace, Baxter, and I wore Talos suits. Whatever attacked us was solid stone.

*Hall*: Perhaps it was prototype MF4 combat armor.

*Poole*: It wasn't armor! Its body was made of stone!

*Hall*: Unlikely, but let's not get hung up on specifics. You're the sole survivor of the warehouse attack, Bill. I need you to run me through what happened.

*Poole*: Spot Two told us the Man of Stone was heading our way, that it had flipped the tanks, so we took up position inside the bay door; Wallace, Baxter and I. Christ, why were there only three of us defending the entire warehouse? Whose fucking call was that?

*Hall*: Not mine. Not yours. Nobody's blaming anybody, Bill. I just need to know what happened next.

*Poole*: The man of stone ripped the door off and tossed it behind him into the parking lot.

*Hall*: Did the attacker use an explosive device on the door?

*Poole*: He ripped it off with his bare hands and tossed it away like it was tin foil. How could he do that?

*Hall*: Maybe a prototype MF4…

*Poole*: I'm telling you it *wasn't* combat armor. He was made of actual stone, like a statue, like Maggie. So was his dog.

*Hall*: Dog?

*Poole*: A stone beagle. It attacked first. Bit Wallace's balls. Wallace fired on it but he blew his dick off and bled out.

*Hall*: Wallace…self-injured?

*Poole*: By mistake.

*Hall*: How did Wallace get the skull injury?

*Poole*: The Man of Stone kicked him in the head when he was down. But Baxter was able to fire a clean shot. That stone sonofabitch dropped and we had him! We had him…

*Hall*: And?

*Poole*: You're not going to believe me.

*Hall*: I don't need to believe you, but I need to hear your side of the story.

*Poole*: I think I should have an attorney present.

*Hall*: Christ, Bill! I'm not interrogating you! This is a standard de-briefing. I'm fact-finding. It's my job.

*Poole*: There's nothing standard about this, Alex. I got my goddamn arm torn off. Nothing is going to be the same again.

*Hall*: I know. I'm sorry. But the military has deep pockets and access to the best tech in the world. They'll get you a new arm ten times better than the last.

*Poole*: I was pretty attached to that arm.

*Hall*: That's funny, Bill. Glad you haven't lost your sense of humor.

*Poole*: I…I don't know what's left of me anymore…

*Hall*: Listen, Bill, you've been through a serious trauma. That Talos T4 suit saved your life today by sterilizing and sealing your wounds. We could have lost you. Be grateful.

*Poole*: The armor didn't save Wallace.

*Hall*: Well, that's true…or Baxter.

*Poole*: (*sigh*) I killed Janet.

*Hall*: What?

*Poole*: I killed her. She attacked me and I killed her. God, help me.

*Hall*: Wait…Wallace killed himself and Baxter…

*Poole*: Wallace killed himself by accident…after the dog attacked him.

*Hall*: The dog. Right. But you and Baxter had the attacker subdued.

*Poole*: We did. But Maggie showed up and shouted for us to stop. Baxter…obeyed Mother Maggie.

*Hall*: The Maggie statue walked? And spoke?

*Poole*: It did. It told…It told Janet to attack me and she listened. She would have killed me. I had to defend myself!

*Hall*: Of course, Bill. Nobody's blaming anybody. We're just talking here. I need you to help me understand.

*Poole*: I don't understand it myself…

*Hall*: Baxter attacked you…why?

*Poole*: Mother Maggie told her to.

*Hall*: The statue spoke to Baxter and she obeyed its commands?

*Poole*: It spoke to both of us, but yes, she obeyed.

*Hall*: What did the statue say?

*Poole*: She told us to kneel. Baxter did. I didn't. Then she told Janet to kill me.

*Hall*: She spoke…aloud…and ordered Baxter to attack you?

*Poole*: I think she said, "Defend your queen."

*Hall*: Oh, come on, Bill!

*Poole*: See! This is why I need a lawyer!

*Hall*: Okay, okay…Janet attacked and you defended yourself. Then you were attacked by the armored soldier?

*Poole*: I don't think I should say any more.

*Hall*: Come on, Bill…

*Poole*: I was attacked by Maggie and the Rock God.

*Hall*: Maggie attacked you too?

*Poole*: She attacked first. The Rock God was still on the ground. Maggie hit me in the chest and I fell backwards. I tripped over the Rock God.

*Hall*: Did Maggie have a weapon?

*Poole*: No. She used her fists. Her stumps. She didn't have hands.

*Hall*: She was able to knock you to the ground with just the stumps of her arms?

*Poole*: She startled me! And I tripped…

*Hall*: Yes. Over the Rock God. That's when he attacked you?

*Poole*: Yes. I raised my palm laser but before I could fire, he grabbed me, and…

*Hall*: What happened next?

*Poole*: He tore my arm off and threw it away. Then he picked me up by the ankle like I was a rag-doll. They laughed about me being disarmed. I thought he was going to tear me apart, but then the Rock God put me down and they both walked to the back of the warehouse. I couldn't see them.

*Hall*: Why do you think they let you live?

*Poole*: The Rock God wanted to kill me. Maggie stopped him.

*Hall*: Why?

*Poole*: Because…she's all merciful and just?

*Hall*: Are you a Maggot, Lieutenant Poole?

*Poole*: I wasn't before today.

*Hall*: I'm sorry about your arm, Bill. Truly. I'm confident our guys will hook you up with a worthy replacement. You need to take your time and heal. You're off duty now, soldier. Rest up and take care of yourself. Think about your family, Bill.

*Poole*: I don't have a family.

*Hall*: What about your parents?

*Poole*: They're assholes.

*Hall*: Bill, I want you to understand that the official report on this incident will be that you were attacked by one—possibly two—terrorists. Rebel soldiers in tactical body armor. The attackers blew themselves up along with the warehouse, along with Maggie.

*Poole*: What do you want me to say to that, Alex? I guess you're an asshole too.

*Hall*: Everything you've told me here tonight will be kept in confidence. You'll need to recount these events numerous times over the coming days and weeks, I'm sure. Say whatever you'd like. But I want you to know in advance what the military report will say.

*Poole*: If I tell the truth I'll sound insane.

*Hall*: It's your truth, Bill. Believe in it. That's what makes our nation great.

*Poole*: Burying the truth in layers of bullshit?

*Hall*: Everyone is free to believe what they'd like.

*Poole*: I gave my arm defending this country. I won't be silenced, Alex.

*Hall*: That kind of fire and conviction will take you a long way, Bill! Use it! But, as a government agency, we need to back away from your truth and embrace a truth with a broader, more palatable public appeal.

*Poole*: People loved Mother Maggie. I don't know why you locked her up in that warehouse in the first place.

*Hall*: Not our place to question decisions, Bill, just clean up the mess when it's over.

*Poole*: *You* made this mess! Maggie and the Rock God were *not* destroyed in the warehouse explosion. They left before the building exploded.

*Hall*: How do you know?

*Poole*: They came back. From the rear of the warehouse. I couldn't get a shot off…I was too weak.

*Hall*: They didn't return to attack you?

Poole: No. They came back for the dog. The dog's ashes. The Rock God scooped a handful of charred dust into a plastic bag and they left.

*Hall*: The dog…a fucking stone dog. Really, Bill?

*Poole*: Really, Alex.

*Hall*: Was its name Rocky or Pebbles?

*Poole*: Fuck off.

*Hall*: Seriously, it was a real dog in combat armor? Like the Virtus-4K9?

*Poole*: No. The dog was made of stone. Like the man. Like Maggie.

*Hall*: I don't think the Virtus has stone camo, but they may have modified a Talos.

*Poole*: It wasn't a modified Talos, Alex! They were made of stone! Speaking of which, my Talos exoskeleton was supposed to protect against grave bodily injury. What the fuck happened?

*Hall*: You bring up a good point. I think you've got a slam-dunk lawsuit against Talos, Bill.

*Poole*: You disgust me.

*Hall*: I'm sorry you feel that way. I'm just doing my job, Bill. I wish you luck and a speedy recovery, Lieutenant. Oh, I'm going to leave the stone dog out of my report…just so you know.

*Poole*: Go fuck yourself.

*Hall*: Thank you, Bill. Get well soon.

*Blocking notes for the 2265 Galaxy Theater production of* 60MM, *March 10-31, 2265.*

MUSIC: 'OVERTURE' ENDS. 'MAIN THEME' BEGINS.

REAR LIGHTS/RED GELS rise slowly on two figures, statues. The statue STAGE LEFT is a large male, covered in vines as if tied down. This is THE ROCK GOD. The statue STAGE RIGHT is female, standing on a pedestal, clutching a swaddled baby to her chest. This is MAGGIE.

MUSIC: 'MAIN THEME' GIVES WAY TO 'DARK THEME.'

TWO FIGURES, dressed in yellow jumpers and red hats, cross the stage, crouched low, holding flashlights. They shine their flashlight beams on MAGGIE's face, then lower the beams to the baby on MAGGIE's chest. The TWO FIGURES move their arms through the flashlight beams, casting long, chopping shadows on MAGGIE. [*Arm motions accented with horn blasts.*] The flashlight beams swirl and when they settle on MAGGIE again, her baby is gone and her hands are missing. Flashlights click off abruptly and TWO FIGURES exit STAGE RIGHT.

MAGGIE is flooded with bright white light. TWO SOLDIERS enter carrying sections of cage walls. The soldiers build a prison cell around MAGGIE, step back to inspect their work, are satisfied by what they see, and exit STAGE RIGHT. Lights dim so that we see only the two statues. Both are imprisoned—one with steel bars, the other with vines.

MUSIC: 'DARK THEME' GIVES WAY TO 'HOPE THEME.'

GHEE enters STAGE RIGHT, glancing over her shoulder at the TWO SOLDIERS that passed her. GHEE also wears a yellow jumper and a red hat. She looks at the damage MAGGIE has sustained, looks OFFSTAGE RIGHT, and then back at MAGGIE. GHEE hangs her head.

BROTHER ROBERT, CALIPH MUSTAFA, and RABBI SOLOMON enter from CENTERSTAGE REAR, emerging from the shadows between the two statues. They follow a dog, though no dog is visible. The invisible dog leads them to GHEE. All four join hands and hang their heads before MAGGIE.

The invisible dogs jumps on their legs until all four follow the invisible dog across the stage to the stand before the ROCK GOD.

MUSIC: 'DARK THEME' GIVES WAY TO 'STONE THEME (REPRISE).'

BROTHER ROBERT, CALIPH MUSTAFA, and RABBI SOLOMON drop to their knees in reverence. GHEE steps forward and puts her hand on the ROCK GOD's chest, the same spot where MAGGIE lost her baby. The ROCK GOD jolts to life and rises, breaking the vines that bind him to the earth. [*Arm motions accented with horn blasts.*] He stands two feet taller than GHEE, BROTHER ROBERT, CALIPH MUSTAFA, and RABBI SOLOMON, and twice as wide. The ROCK GOD takes GHEE's hand and they cross DOWNSTAGE, followed by BROTHER ROBERT, CALIPH

MUSTAFA, and RABBI SOLOMON. They slowly begin to march across the stage toward MAGGIE.

MUSIC: 'STONE THEME (REPRISE)' GIVES WAY TO '60MM THEME.'

They only make it a few steps before the TWO SOLDIERS return from STAGE LEFT, each holding a car tire. The ROCK GOD pushes them aside. The TWO SOLDIERS exit STAGE LEFT. They walk a few more feet. HOODED FIGURES (two/three) locked arm-in-arm, enter STAGE LEFT holding signs ("We heart GHEE! We heart ROCK GOD!") and join the march, positioning themselves safely behind BROTHER ROBERT, CALIPH MUSTAFA, and RABBI SOLOMON.

The TWO SOLDIERS return from STAGE LEFT. This time they throw sparkling sleeping powder on GHEE, the ROCK GOD, BROTHER ROBERT, CALIPH MUSTAFA, RABBI SOLOMON, and the HOODED FIGURES. Everyone falls to the stage except for the ROCK GOD, the invisible dog, and the TWO SOLDIERS. The ROCK GOD picks up GHEE and pushes the TWO SOLDIERS aside. TWO SOLDIERS exit STAGE LEFT. ROCK GOD continues across the stage with GHEE in his arms. The invisible dog follows.

A few steps later, three gunshots ring out. The ROCK GOD bends over and protects GHEE with his body. The bullets do not stop him. The ROCK GOD and GHEE travel a few more steps and a net falls from above. The ROCK GOD pulls the net off, tosses it aside, and keeps walking.

The TWO SOLDIERS return, STAGE RIGHT, standing before MAGGIE. The HOODED FIGURES—their numbers multiplied (*with mirrors, projections or cutouts*)—stand before the TWO SOLDIERS, arms interlocked.

The ROCK GOD puts GHEE down. The invisible dog scampers at their feet. They walk hand-in-hand toward MAGGIE. The HOODED FIGURES part before them.

MUSIC: '60MM THEME' RETURNS TO 'DARK THEME.'

The TWO SOLDIERS stand behind the bars, inside the cage with MAGGIE.

The ROCK GOD raises his arms, hands balled into fists, as if to smash the walls of the cage. GHEE puts her hand on his chest and stops him. The ROCK GOD lowers his arms and GHEE climbs into them. The ROCK GOD lifts her up, until GHEE stands taller than the cage, taller than anyone else on stage except for MAGGIE on her pedestal. GHEE smiles and takes a triumphant step over the wall of the cage.

ABRUPT DARKNESS. MUSIC CUTS. GUNSHOT.

FRONT LIGHTS/RED GELS rise slowly on GHEE's body. We see her legs and the bottom of her shoes, but her head is UPSTAGE, hidden in darkness. Her red hat lies overturned at her feet. The stage is empty except for GHEE. The pedestal where MAGGIE stood is empty.

MUSIC: 'GHEE THEME.'

SOFT SPOT follows TWO FIGURES dressed in yellow/red hats as they ENTER STAGE RIGHT. The TWO FIGURES cross to GHEE's body and stand over it, shoulders slumped with grief. They look at each other and look away, ashamed. They stand back-to-back for a moment before slowly walking away from each other, one EXITING STAGE LEFT, the other, STAGE RIGHT.

SOFT SPOT follows BROTHER ROBERT, CALIPH MUSTAPHA, and RABBI SOLOMON as they ENTER STAGE RIGHT. They hold hands over GHEE's body and pray in unison. Prayers complete, the trio moves DOWNSTAGE LEFT, following the path they took during the march only in reverse. They stop DOWNSTAGE LEFT and stand ten feet apart, arms outstretched, prepared to preach.

SOFT SPOT follows TWO SOLDIERS as they ENTER STAGE RIGHT. They stand over GHEE, their body language similar to the TWO FIGURES in yellow/red, shamed, accusatory. THE TWO SOLDIERS stand back-to-back, but instead of walking away in opposite directions they turn and face each other. Working robotically, one SOLDIER grabs GHEE's feet, the other her arms, and they drag her body off into the shadows, EXITING UPSTAGE CENTER.

Only GHEE's red hat remains.

MUSIC: 'GHEE THEME' GIVES WAY TO 'DARK THEME (REPRISE).'

FRONT & REAR STAGELIGHTS RISE to mimic DAY. The HOODED FIGURES enter, one STAGE RIGHT, the other STAGE LEFT. The HOODED FIGURE from STAGE LEFT must weave through BROTHER ROBERT, CALIPH MUSTAFA, and RABBI SOLOMON. The holy men reach out, but the HOODED FIGURE avoids their touch.

The HOODED FIGURES cross the stage quickly, heads down, ignoring each other. They cross on the spot where GHEE's body had been, but they do not stop, do not slow, do not acknowledge one another. One of the HOODED FIGURES absently kicks GHEE's red hat and it sails offstage (or into audience).

The HOODED FIGURE exiting STAGE LEFT weaves through BROTHER ROBERT, CALIPH MUSTAFA, and RABBI SOLOMON. The holy men reach out, but the HOODED FIGURE avoids their touch.

The HOODED FIGURES gone, BROTHER ROBERT, CALIPH MUSTAFA, and RABBI SOLOMON look at each other, hang their heads, and EXIT STAGE LEFT.

MUSIC: 'DARK THEME' GIVES WAY TO 'MAIN THEME.'

FRONT & REAR LIGHTS dim. Rippling BLUE GELS make the lower half of the stage appear underwater. The top half of the stage looks like blue sky, complete with puffy white clouds. The pedestal where MAGGIE once stood has been altered to appear like a stone rising above the surface of the water. A scrawny tree grows atop the stone.

The ROCK GOD and MAGGIE stand "underwater" at the base of the stone. The ROCK GOD helps MAGGIE climb to the top. The ROCK GOD climbs up and sits beside her. They look out over the surface of the water. MAGGIE lays her head on the ROCK GOD's shoulder. He rests his cheek against the top of her head.

Lights dim so ROCK GOD and MAGGIE are merely shapes, shadows against the blue backdrop of night. Together, they climb down off the stone and back into the dark sea.

For a full minute, we see the shapes of MAGGIE and the ROCK GOD moving under the sea, appearing, disappearing, re-appearing. Their shadows eventually get lost among the other undersea rocks.

FADE TO BLACK

# 7

## *Mudspeak III*

Ghee's body slipped from my grasp and tumbled forward over the fence. She wasn't Ghee anymore, just a headless body, dead meat. Ghee lived in the sky now. And in my veins. I roared with rage and sorrow.

The fence collapsed inward as the crowd surged, carrying me with it. I didn't think people still had the power to move me, but I was overwhelmed, my feet lifted off the ground as the human wave carried all two tons of me into the warehouse parking lot.

A couple of people reached the tank on the far left and climbed atop. But the tank jerked backwards thirty feet, tossing the climbers to the pavement. The black-bubble machine-gun turret began to rotate.

*No way will they open fire on these people. They're just civilians.*

Machine-gun fire exploded from the tank turret, cutting people down in waves. A few bullets bounced off my chest, but most sailed into the crowd and found soft targets. People crumpled and fell like mowed weeds. Within seconds I stood in a parking lot full of dead bodies. Good God, when will people stop coming up with faster and easier ways to kill each other?

Two strides and I was climbing the tank, metal screeching beneath my feet. I punched through the machine-gun turret, black glass shattering to reveal a surprised face that turned to red paste beneath my fist. The entry hatch peeled away like the top of a can of cat food. Two more surprised faces looked up. I reached in and grabbed one soldier by the head, crushing it—helmet and all—in my palm. The other soldier hid somewhere low and out of reach.

Motors whirled behind me. The other tank swiveled its cannon, the muzzle a black hole the size of my fist. I jumped to the pavement and grabbed the barrel of the tank beneath me. I tried to swing it like a baseball bat but the best I could do was drag the vehicle across the parking lot in a wide, sparking arc. It smashed into the other tank, the impact causing both vehicles to tip.

Miss Polly and I marched across the parking lot. The soldiers with the glowing shields fled to parts unknown. A man carrying a pump-action shotgun and wearing a faded Def Leppard t-shirt fell into step beside us. He wore an upside-down metal cooking pot on his head, the insulated handle sticking out behind him like the bill on a backwards baseball cap. Had he brought the shotgun to the march? Did he live nearby and came running once the battle started?

"We're with you, brother! We're with you!" the man said to me, a look of pure bliss on his face. Polly growled but I didn't need her to tell me the guy was bad news. I put an open palm in the guy's face, keeping him at arm's length. He looked dejected, but stopped following us. He wasn't alone, however. Several other survivors crossed the parking lot, skirting around the wrecked tanks and fallen bodies. Damn, I didn't want their help, didn't want to be responsible for more deaths.

The bay door on the side of the warehouse faced the

parking lot. Polly and I walked up to it. I knocked politely. No answer. I grabbed the metal frame and tore the door off its hinges, tossing it over my shoulder. It landed with a loud clatter that I hoped would deter any followers.

Polly and I stepped inside.

The first thing I saw were three guys with stone bodies like mine standing right inside the doorway.

*Was this a trick done with mirrors?*

A closer look revealed seams in the armpits, neck, and groin. The eyes were black-mirrored cue balls. This was an animatronic version of me, something you'd see at an old Disney theme park. What did I expect? I acted like a monster and they treated me like one. Maggie acted like a saint and became one. You are what you do.

One of the stone soldiers rushed me. I raised my fists but Miss Polly's counterattack was quicker. With a hellish howl, she bit into the soldier's crotch and locked her jaws with a sound like crushed glass. The stone soldier panicked and beat at the dog. A blast of orange from the soldier's hand turned Miss Polly into a cloud of dust. But he had inadvertently blown a hole in his armor. Blood poured from between his legs. He fell at my feet, so I kicked him in the head. Half the stone skull and one big, black eyeball flew away. These weren't robots, just men in oversized suits. The guy inside this one looked barely out of his teens—not much older than Ghee. Another young life lost to a senseless cause…and with the added indignity of dying inside a silly costume.

The other soldiers charged me. More foolish men—foolish children—who wanted to die heroes. Heroes! Thirty minutes ago, I was called a hero—a *savior*! Now, most of my followers lie dead in the parking lot. You're only a hero if you die for the winning side, otherwise you're a forgotten schmuck, a statistic in the long equation of failure.

I wrapped my hands around one soldier's neck, intent on

ripping his head off. *This one's for Polly, asshole!* But the other soldier hit me in the hip with an exploding punch. Half of me went numb. I fell to the floor with a grunt that sounded like boulders tumbling downhill.

The soldiers stood over me. Damn, I'd seriously underestimated their firepower. I'd rushed in like a foolish cowboy. So much for my big rescue mission. Sorry, Maggie. Sorry, Ghee. All I did was get you, Miss Polly, and hundreds of innocent people killed. Now I was a goner too.

One of the stone soldiers balled up his fist. Was there a sonic blaster in there? Whatever it was, he packed a lethal punch. He drew his arm back to deliver the deathblow.

I needed a miracle.

I got one.

"Stop!"

The stone soldiers obeyed.

Maggie emerged from a dark corner of the warehouse, glowing radiant white and exquisitely beautiful. She walked with grace and poise, practically gliding across the warehouse floor. Her outstretched arms ended at the wrist, a scratched-out hollow on her chest where she used to cradle a child. My child. *God, Maggie looked so much like Sarah!*

"Drop to your knees before the Queen Mother!" Maggie said. Who knew she could speak?

One of the soldiers dropped to his knees, the other stayed on his feet.

"Kill him!" Maggie shouted.

The kneeling soldier sprang up and swung his fist but the standing soldier was ready, delivering an explosive punch that drove the other man to his knees, a cloud of red mist and pulverized skull where his head used to be.

Maggie lunged at the remaining stone soldier, pushing him back with the stumps of her wrists. She screamed and the metal walls of the warehouse reverberated with her rage.

The soldier staggered back and I grabbed his leg, wrapped myself around him until he fell to the ground. I got to my knees. The soldier threw a weak punch while lying on his back. I grabbed his arm and tore it off his body, tossed the dead limb across the warehouse. A spurt of blood gushed from the wound, but it quickly stopped, evidently sealed by the armor suit. The soldier screamed and gurgled inside his helmet. He tried rolling away, but I grabbed his left ankle. Tearing him limb from limb sounded like a wonderful idea in light of what happened to Miss Polly…and Ghee. I'd let them down. But I'd make this puny soldier pay. I lifted him off the ground and grabbed his other leg, ready to play wishbone. (Whoever gets the half with his head wins!)

"Stop!"

The shock and disgust in Maggie's voice shamed me, instantly drained my bloodlust. I hung my head, but kept my grip on the soldier's ankle.

"Put him down! He's…disarmed."

Maggie started to giggle. She tried covering her mouth with her hands but had to settle for resting her stumps against her chin. I laughed too, the strange boulder-clack sound echoing like an earthquake. It felt good to laugh. It was just about the best feeling ever.

I laid the one-armed soldier back on the ground. He rolled on his side and tried crawling away, but didn't get far before he collapsed in a sobbing, moaning heap. Disarmed, indeed.

Maggie smiled, spreading her arms wide. I hugged her and my knees buckled. Even though I stood a foot taller and twice as wide, Maggie was the true powerhouse. A great, healing energy radiated from her, similar to Ghee's touch, but more concentrated, more powerful. This was stone on stone. Maggie understood the depths of my soul, the fabric of my existence—*our* existence—like no one else could, not Sarah, not Ghee.

Was Maggie my true stone bride? Had George made her not for himself, but for me? It didn't seem possible. My father-in-law hated me. But holding Maggie in my arms made me realize how terribly, terribly lonely I'd been, sitting in the woods for centuries, waiting for…what? Rock doesn't die, just weathers away. Rock transforms. If Maggie and I couldn't grow old together, maybe we could transform together.

If she'd have me.

Without thinking, I touched the terrible scar on Maggie's chest with my blocky fingers. What horrible monsters had done this? What chance did my child ever have to live? My kid spent its entire life swaddled up in grandma's arms. Maybe that's not such a bad existence after all. It sure beat mine.

"We should go," I said. Military reinforcements would be here soon. Maggie shook her head.

"Here first," she said.

She led me to the back of the warehouse. Sitting in the shadows were boxes and crates marked "Franz Rock Excav" in neat stencil letters. Maggie pointed to a crate with her missing fingers and I removed the lid. A dirt-covered urn lay atop brown packing straw. I tried lifting the urn out, but it shattered beneath my fingers. A plastic bag fell out, the writing on the label faded, but the orange biohazard circle still faintly visible.

"George," Maggie said.

Ah…the last time I'd seen my father-in-law, Sarah had stopped me from beating him to death. We were in his work studio, the Castle, out behind the Ottomeyer house, and George had caught Sarah and I making love. He attacked me and then the police arrived and I ran into the woods…the woods…where I stayed. Now here he was, not so tough after all, nothing but gray powder inside a one-gallon storage bag, dust to dust like the rest of us. Still, this man gave me a second chance, reborn as stone. Miss Polly too…and Maggie. Maggie was George's finest work, no question about it. Maggie was a masterpiece.

Where did George get the power to animate mud and clay like a god? It happened after an accident at a construction site, some old church on Washington Avenue in Paterson. George swore angels spoke to him while he was trapped beneath a pile of rubble. What had the angels told him? The angels' secrets died with George. He was a creator, but he was not a god. In the end, he was only a man, nothing but a bag of dust. Add water, make mud.

Helicopters rattled the warehouse roof. We needed to go. But Maggie touched my elbow and drew me over to another crate, this one already opened. There was a clear plastic bag inside. I picked it up and studied the contents. Bits of stone and loose dust mostly, but the profiles of certain fragments suggested something more. I turned the bag over and saw half a tiny face, delicate fingers curled beside a cherub cheek, eye closed, asleep and dreaming.

Maggie's child, the one vandals had chipped away. Was this the baby Sarah and I never got to have? Was this sad bag of sorrow and loss all that remained of my child? I looked at Maggie. She nodded knowingly and pulled me into her arms. I laid my head on her shoulder and sobbed like a rockslide.

The front of the warehouse shook as the helicopters landed.

"We have to go," Maggie said.

I looked toward the front of the warehouse.

"Miss Polly," I said.

Maggie followed my gaze. Voices came from the darkness. Troops were inside.

"Hurry," Maggie said.

We ran toward the front of the warehouse. Surprisingly, the

one-armed soldier was there, curled into a ball near his dead comrade. The wounded soldier appeared unconscious; at least, I thought so until he rolled over and pointed a shaky arm at me.

"We're not going to hurt you," I said, but it came out sounding scary.

"We're not going to hurt you," Maggie repeated, her voice far more pleasant. "Don't *make* us hurt you."

The soldier lowered his arm and curled back into a ball.

"Fire!"

Muzzle flashes illuminated the far side of the warehouse with a strobe-like effect. Bullets pinged off my chest. Maggie staggered but got her footing and stood firm against the assault. A few strays clipped the one-armed soldier on the ground and he curled up tighter.

"Hurry!" Maggie said.

A handful of burnt sand was all that remained of poor Miss Polly.

"Put her in George's bag," Maggie said. I gave her half-a-look over my shoulder. "He loved that dog. He won't mind."

I scooped as much of Miss Polly into the bag of George's ashes as I could, but struggled getting the bag closed with my clumsy fingers. I looked to Maggie for help and she raised her stumps in reply. Fine, I'd hold the bag closed. We weren't going far.

Another wave of bullets bounced off our backs as we ran into the depths of the warehouse. Why did they keep wasting ammunition?

The door at the back of the warehouse was locked, but Maggie opened it with a swift kick. We stepped out into twilight.

We walked the waterfront until the docks and bulkheads gave way to a small weedy beach. Sirens pierced the falling night and a Coast Guard cutter swung a lazy spotlight over the shore. Maggie and I stayed out of sight. The warehouse exploded a few minutes after we left. Maggie wanted to stay and watch it burn, but I urged her to keep going. We had to get to the water.

I tore away a security fence and Maggie and I walked into Newark Bay. Maggie spread her arms wide, allowing the ashes of George, Miss Polly, and the unborn baby to scatter. The bigger pieces sank immediately, but the ashes formed a murky ring around Maggie and I, clinging to our bodies. I wished I could have gone back for Ghee. She was family too. I tried to tell Maggie but stopped when I saw blood streaming down her cheeks. I pulled her close. Was she hurt? She shook her head. No, they were only tears.

We sank beneath the bay, brackish water washing Maggie's bloody tears away, cleaning the ashes from our bodies. The remains of George Ottomeyer, his faithful beagle, and his unborn grandchild rode currents both natural and unnatural to the bottom of Newark Bay.

# 8

## *Second Final Report IV*

*NewsStream headline, May 7, 2222.*

Violent clashes between the Maggot Revolutionary Force and National Guard troops at protests in Columbus, Ohio and Albany, New York left two people dead and fourteen injured today… [*Read more*]

*NewsStream headline, May 15, 2222.*

Protests in New York City and Baltimore turned violent today, as local police and national peacekeeping forces fired on Maggot organizers… [*Read more*]

*NewsStream headline, May 20, 2222.*

Four dead and 16 injured as Maggot protesters storm Air Force military base in Chattanooga, TN… [*Read more*]

*President Ipson, public address, June 22, 2222.*

It is with a heavy heart that I must enact Marshall Law for all states across our nation. The violent actions of a handful of terrorist groups and Maggot extremists have left us no choice but to enforce nightly curfews and limit the size of public gatherings in order to ensure the safety of *all* our citizens. Effective immediately I'm asking all citizens to shelter in place…

*Vice-Presidential Debates: VP Taru Burnett (Freedom Party) vs. Roger Vahvonen (Patriot Party), July 16, 2222.*

BURNETT: You can't blame President Ipson. She did what she had to do in the interest of public safety. The Maggots left her no choice! Frankly, I think the Maggots *want* Marshall Law…the more unrest they cause, the happier they are.

VAHVONEN: It's unfair to call all Maggots violent dissidents. The Maggots are a divided group, but on the whole, they are peaceful. You can't define an entire group based on the extreme actions of the Maggot Revolutionary Force.

BURNETT: Understood, Roger, but these are organized terrorist attacks against our country being carried out in the name of Mother Maggie! You have to acknowledge that!

VAHVONEN: Frankly, Taru, much of the current civil unrest stems from the public execution of Ghee Dorfhouse! The government has yet to answer for the murder of that girl!

BURNETT: And the MRF has yet to take responsibility for killing three American soldiers at Newark Bay, as well as destroying two tanks, a warehouse, and Mother Maggie herself! Maggots should be angry at themselves for allowing their violent tendencies to destroy that which they hold so dear.

VAHVONEN: Most members of the Maggot Revolutionary Force are driven by the fight for chemical-free air and water rather than by spiritual beliefs. Again, you can't lump all Maggots in with—

BURNETT: No one believes this uprising is about Sukadom-Benzyril ring poisoning. That was an issue a century ago! Changes have been made! Nobody's hooked on that stuff anymore. This is about vengeance for the death of Ghee Dorfhouse and the destruction of the Maggie statue, both incidents born of Maggot aggression. You have no one to blame but yourselves!

VAHVONEN: Maggots didn't confiscate Mother Maggie…

BURNETT: Jasmine and Lucas Dorfhouse, Ghee's parents —both practicing Maggots—were found guilty of defacing the Maggie statue last year. Fear of additional acts of vandalism forced President Ipson to relocate the statue to a secure facility—

VAHVONEN: Obviously, *not* a very secure facility. Does President Ipson have an answer for *why* there was so little security protecting the Maggie sculpture and keeping the peace in Newark?

BURNETT: We couldn't have predicted the vast number of Maggot protesters converging on Newark Bay, nor that they'd arrive with a fully weaponized robotic soldier.

VAHVONEN: They walked for a day-and-a-half, live-streamed for the world to see! How could *your* administration *not* come up with a more peaceful conclusion to the Sixty Mile March?

BURNETT: We were certainly unprepared for the level of Maggot aggression we encountered. It caught us all by surprise.

VAHVONEN: And your solution was to murder Ghee Dorfhouse?

BURNETT: Of course not! Evidence indicates Ghee Dorfhouse was killed by an accidental gunshot. Until the investigation into Ghee Dorfhouse's death is complete, we won't know for sure who fired that bullet. Maggots came armed to the so-called "peaceful protest" in Newark, as we all know.

VAHVONEN: So did your administration, Ms. Vice President. But it only took one taxpayer-funded bullet to kill

Ghee Dorfhouse.

BURNETT: Allow the Newark Bay Commission to finish its report, Roger. It's bipartisan and some of the best minds in the country are working on this investigation.

VAHVONEN: We all saw the muzzle flash come from the tank turret, Taru.

BURNETT: Perhaps the investigation will show Ghee Dorfhouse wasn't trying to save the Maggie statue, but destroy it, finish the work her parents started.

VAHVONEN: How dare you! Is that your idea of justice? Savagely murder—slaughter like a lamb—a teenage girl climbing a fence? Is that Ipson's America?

*Private debriefing, President Loren Ipson and Vice President Taru Burnett, July 17, 2222.*

IPSON: Whose side are you on, Taru?

BURNETT: I'm sorry. I fucked up.

IPSON: You fucked up. You fucked *me* up. Up the ass, Taru. How am I going to go out there next week and debate Layton when you laid down like a fucking pussy before Roger Vahvonen? My numbers have dropped three points since last night's debate. You're a fucking albatross.

BURNETT: I apologize. I did the best I could. Being Vice President of the "Marshall Law Administration" isn't easy.

IPSON: It's not half as hard as being the President of one. You're making it even harder, Taru. You're a shit VP. I should've picked Phyllisa Dokenski for the job four years ago.

BURNETT: I wish you had. It's a shit job. Yours is even worse. The White House turns good people bad. Maybe it always has.

IPSON: Most are bad before they get here. You were.

BURNETT: You chose me four years ago because I promised you the gays and the senior citizens, and I delivered those votes. I didn't expect you to turn the country into a fascist police state that locks away holy relics and murders little girls on live-stream.

IPSON: Fuck off, you withered dyke!

BURNETT: Thank you. Good luck in next week's debate, Loren. Seriously. Go out there and tear Layton apart. I don't want to get a real job next year.

IPSON: Me neither. But you took a shit on stage last night and now I have to clean it up.

BURNETT: Shit was already there, I just slipped in it. You'll do better. Wear your boots.

IPSON: Fuck.

*Excerpt, First Presidential Debate, President Loren Ipson (Freedom Party) vs. Grant Layton (Patriot Party), York, PA, August 13, 2222.*

IPSON: America is a nation of strong individuals. I know the American people. I've spoken with them. I've *listened* to them for the last four years. I've learned their opinions and the strength of their convictions. I am also a person of strong convictions and I am convinced we can get through this troubled time with strong, steady, consistent leadership.

LAYTON: I agree with you there, Loren. We *do* need strong leadership during troubled times. But you're not that leader. Your administration has led this country to the brink of civil war. We live in the most dangerous time in American history because of your actions and decisions.

IPSON: Americans have come through tougher times than these, emerging stronger and unified. Change is never easy, but a strong government and a strong executive office—an *experienced* executive office—is needed to steer the ship to calmer waters. What the country *doesn't* need right now is additional upheaval caused by a change in administration.

LAYTON: A change in administration is exactly what this

country needs—

[A MASSIVE POWER FAILURE IN CENTRAL AND WESTERN PENNSYLVANIA CANCELS THE REMAINDER OF THE DEBATE.]

*From Action NewsStream, August 14, 2222.*

Authorities blame last night's power failure during the Presidential Debate in York, Pennsylvania on a faulty offshore power cable. Despite rumors the Northeast power grid was sabotaged by the Maggot Revolutionary Force, the MRF has not claimed responsibility. Clashes between MRF fighters and authorities last night in Detroit and Sturgis, Michigan…

*Private line transcript, candidate GRANT LAYTON and campaign advisor MARTIN MORRIS. August 14, 2222.*

LAYTON: Christ, Martin, you're *sure* the MRF had nothing to do with this?

MORRIS: Nope. It's a happy accident, Grant. The power failure made Ipson look weak. Just roll with it. Maybe we'll catch a miracle and it will happen again next week.

LAYTON: Don't even joke, Martin.

*From Chemolco College Student Politics Streamcast, hosted by CARA LEWIS and IZZY BLOCH, Second Presidential Debate, President Loren Ipson (Freedom Party) vs. Grant Layton (Patriot Party), Derby, New Hampshire, August 21, 2222.*

LEWIS: I can't believe this has happened again, Izzy. One power failure during the debates is an accident, but two…

BLOCH: It's terrorism. Yes. It's scary.

LEWIS: I think the most unsettling part is that no one is taking responsibility for this. The MRF is the most obvious candidate, but there are other revolutionary groups out there. And you have to wonder…is this some kind of campaign tactic by Layton's camp?

BLOCH: I mean...oh my God. Do you think? How could scaring the crap out of everybody help you win the Presidency?

LEWIS: Plenty of candidates have campaigned on fear in the past, Iz. It can be an effective strategy.

BLOCH: Yeah, but killing the power grid to half of New Hampshire and Vermont? They still haven't restored power to Pennsylvania yet! Look! Look at this! They're reporting Maine's gone dark now!

LEWIS: Shit...excuse my language. But this is unreal... what is the MRF doing?

BLOCH: We don't even *know* if it's the MRF! Whoever's doing this...it's a vulgar display of power.

LEWIS: It is. I mean, this is all-out revolutionary war, right?

BLOCH: Oh, Cara! I'm frightened!

LEWIS: Deep breaths, Izzy. We'll be okay. You know I was at the Battle of Newark in May. I saw Ghee Dorfhouse murdered. I was there when the fences fell. It was a terrifying day. I'm not going to lie. I was there to protest, not to fight, and when the violence started, I ran. That was scary. But this...this is a different kind of scary. That was a mob scene. These are cold, calculated attacks against our nation. Organized attacks. How deep does this go, Iz? How big must the MRF be to pull this off? There must be insiders in the infrastructure, at the very least. But who could fund a group that large and organized? It must be a foreign government, right?

BLOCH: Christ, Cara! Stop it! You really think this is civil war?

LEWIS: I don't know, but it sure seems like someone is attempting to sabotage the November Presidential elections.

BLOCH: Ah! Ah! Power's out in Massachusetts now! Connecticut! It's coming down the seaboard! I'm scared,

Cara! Hold me!

LEWIS: Get a grip on yourself, Izzy. We're okay here in Jersey. It won't get this fa—

[BROADCAST TERMINATED DUE TO POWER FAILURE.]

*From Euro-News with TOM BLUE and MARY SUE (holo-hosts parented by EUNewsMedia), August 22, 2222.*

MARY SUE: Massive power grid and communications failures throughout the American Northeast, as far south as Maryland, have crippled the United States, the second and most devastating attack in the past week. Members of the Maggot Revolutionary Force seized control of government facilities in New York, Boston, Philadelphia, Hartford, and countless smaller cities and communities throughout the United States. US military forces are battling revolutionaries on a number of fronts, but, as you can imagine, Tom, they're doing all this without adequate power and communication.

TOM BLUE: They're fighting in the dark. You have to wonder, Mary, if we're witnessing the start of an all-out revolution against President Ipson's administration.

MARY SUE: Hard to imagine how this will impact the US Presidential election this November. It's scary to think a terrorist or revolutionary group—depending on how you look at it—could pull off such a sophisticated attack.

TOM BLUE: It really is frightening, Mary. It's going to be interesting to see how these latest events in America impact the Maggot community here in the UK and throughout the world. As you know, Mary, global tensions are high following the apparent destruction of the Mother Maggie statue and the murder of Ghee Dorfhouse in May.

MARY SUE: Absolutely, Tom. It's been a very difficult, very troubled year for America and our hearts go out to everyone in the United States affected by this tragic turn of events.

*From President Ipson, public address, August 22, 2222.*

Let me make this perfectly clear to everyone in the United States who can hear my voice. There *is* no American revolution. The White House is safe. The banks are safe. Businesses are safe. People are safe. *You* are safe.

A little over forty-eight hours ago, several undersea cables off the northeast coast of the United States were damaged, mostly likely due to an undersea quake or some other natural phenomenon. We have a top team of military scientists looking into the exact cause, but I can tell you with utmost certainty that it *was not* an act of terrorism committed by the Maggot Revolutionary Force or any other terrorist group.

A handful of unruly malcontents took advantage of the blackouts to break some windows and enter a few vacant government buildings, but these acts of vandalism were short-lived and easily dispelled by local police. No US troops were injured in the reclamation of these government facilities. A handful of insurgents were killed, but the vast majority surrendered and were taken into custody without a shot fired. I repeat, this is *not* a revolution. It's nothing more than a blackout and the looting of a few empty government offices. The power grid will be completely restored in a matter of hours and we can all get back to life, liberty, and the pursuit of happiness. God Bless America!

*Private debriefing transcript, President Loren Ipson and Vice President Taru Burnett, August 22, 2222.*

IPSON: I'm fucked, Taru. Sorry I'm dragging you down with me.

BURNETT: Don't be so sure. The MRF scares the shit out of everybody. Will people vote for Layton if he's backed by madmen with the ability to crash the power grid?

IPSON: The MRF didn't do it.

BURNETT: Who did?

IPSON: Military thinks it's the walking stones.

BURNETT: No shit? They made it out of Newark Bay?

IPSON: According to Alexandra Hall's report. Shhh. It's classified.

...[INFORMATION REDACTED]...

BURNETT: Alright. Okay. Either way, voters think the MRF is responsible for sabotaging the power cables. That will scare them.

IPSON: Will it scare them enough to keep them from voting for Grant Layton?

*VR Meeting transcript, candidate GRANT LAYTON, running mate ROGER VAHVONEN, and campaign advisor MARTIN MORRIS, August 30, 2222.*

LAYTON: I'm fucked, Roger. Sorry to drag you down with me.

VAHVONEN: Don't be so sure, Grant. Ipson looks weak, like she doesn't have control of the country. People are scared.

LAYTON: Fuck, I'm scared too! Where did the MRF get the power to shut down the grid?

MORRIS: They say it's Maggie and the Rock God.

LAYTON / VAHVONEN: What?

MORRIS: Well, that's what the Maggots believe, of course. But there's a government report filed recently that cites the walking stones, too.

LAYTON: The walking stones? Come on, Martin. A guy in body armor fought at Newark Bay. Enough with the fairy tales.

MORRIS: Whether it's true or not is irrelevant. It's what your *constituents* believe, so you'd better get on board too.

LAYTON: I can't control the Maggot Revolutionary Force! I didn't ask them to attack the goddamn power grid. What will they do next?

MORRIS: They're not going to do anything, because they *can't* do anything. The MRF is barely more than a couple dozen guys with hunting rifles and metal pots for helmets. Seriously, there's no way they pulled off the grid attack.

VAHVONEN: Then who did?

MORRIS: It doesn't matter. What matters is that we use it to our advantage. All you two say is, "No comment." If somebody asks you directly if you're behind the MRF, the Rock God, or sabotaged undersea cables, you smile and move on to the next question. Understood? If you're pressed, say you trust the results of the FBI investigation.

LAYTON: But I don't.

MORRIS: Well, you can't say that until you're president. While you're a candidate, you respect the cogs in the wheel. Once you're in charge, you can screw with the cogs all you want.

LAYTON: Shit, Martin. I'm never going to be President. Not now.

MORRIS: Don't be so sure, Grant. There's still two months until election day. Anything can happen.

*From KnowNet,* "Transatlantic Cable Failure of 2222," *last updated: March 2, 2299.*

The failure of several undersea cables on August 13 and 21, 2222 resulted in loss of power for much of the eastern United States. Leaders of the Maggot Revolutionary Force used the power failure to their advantage, taking control of several key government buildings during the blackout.

*Overview*

At 7:51 am on August 13, 2222, the first TransAtlantic cable, CapeOne, was severed off the coast of Massachusetts, presumably by an illegal fishing trawler. The failure of CapeOne cut electrical power and communications to much of Central Pennsylvania and the Ohio Valley, resulting in the interruption and cancellation of the first Presidential Debate between President Loren Ipson and Patriot Party candidate Grant Layton, launching the idea that the cable failure was an act of sabotage perpetrated by the Maggot Revolutionary Force.

This theory gained traction eight days later when a second and more serious cable failure cut power to much of the Eastern seaboard. This second blackout occurred in the middle of the second Presidential debate between Ipson and Layton, leading many to assume it was a targeted attack.

At 8:45 pm, August 21, 2222, Helax767, a power and communications cable off the coast of New Brunswick, went offline. The destruction of the SyntechCorp, ATTInfoLink, and CommStat undersea cables, occurred at 9:47 pm, 9:55 pm, and 10:01pm, respectively. This trio of cables lay clustered 57.4 nautical miles off the coast of Northern Canada, 2.8 nautical miles north of the Helax767 cable. The destruction of these cables caused a complete shutdown of wireless communications throughout New England, New York, and the eastern seaboard as far south as Maryland. Military communications were also severely compromised, as emergency relays were channeled through networks in Savannah, GA and San Diego, CA.

At 10:22 pm, a nationwide state of emergency was declared by President Ipson, though it is estimated that less than 40% of Americans received the initial message due to power outages. The Canadian Coast Guard vessel, *Greekout*, reported suspected sabotage to Helax767 ("the end of the cable is all frayed...like it's been chewed through," reported *Greekout* Captain JB Walker), and the United States Navy and Maine Coast Guard immediately dispatched vessels to the site of the damaged SyntechCorp, ATTInfoLink, and CommStat undersea cables. Navy Cruiser, *USS Rampalla*, at the time the fastest combat ship in active service, arrived first on the scene, armed with depth charges and B45 guided torpedoes. Although sonar and radar revealed no attacking vessel, either on the ocean surface or submerged, several unauthorized depth charges were deployed by the military. An automated bathyscaphe located the SyntechCorp, ATTInfoLink, and CommStat cables on the sea floor at a depth of 324 meters, and confirmed they were also damaged in a similar fashion to the CapeOne and Helax767 cables ("like God himself twisted them around his finger and snapped them like strands of spaghetti," according to ret.-US Admiral Amos Westee).

Over the course of the next 39 hours, a total of 22 undersea cables were rendered inoperable, including the BrightLight fiber optic trunk, the Kitchman TransAtlantic FiberTrain, and several regional communication cables.

The undersea cable failure culminated in the loss of the LaForme Undersea Transformer, 75 miles off the coast of Newfoundland. The failure of the LaForme Transformer resulted in total loss of electrical power and wireless communications for the entire Northeast of the United States, as far west as Toledo, OH, and as far south as Charlotte, NC. Canada also "went dark" as far west as Manitoba and as far north as the Arctic Circle.

Public unrest—already high following the Battle of Newark Bay—reached a fevered pitch in the initial hours following the power and communications failures. Many believed the Ipson regime was no longer able to protect American citizens. [*citation needed*]

Due to the chaotic nature of the situation, proper protocols were not followed, allowing the government's military and administrative communications lines to remain unsecured for a period of nearly 70 hours (see "Three Days Of Blabber"). As a result of information gained during this period, combined with additional communication and power failures, MRF troops led by Dorothy Landis, Paul Arborgast, and Irma

Mollins were able to seize control of key government facilities along the East Coast, including the Albany Statehouse, Keystone Federal Building in Pittsburgh, PA, and the Treasury Reserve in Louisville, Kentucky. A military standoff in Pennsylvania (see "Scranton Showdown / Scranton Armistice") ended peacefully and democratically.

*Cause of Cable Damage*

US military scientists concluded in a January 2223 report that a low-tension seaquake caused the cables to twist and break. A number of undersea cable installation improvements were made in the wake of the military report, including flexi-cable, stainless steel casings, and deeper cable burying requirements.

*Aftermath*

The TransAtlantic Cable incident is one of several factors sited—along with the Battle of Newark Bay and The Iceland Incident—that led to the defeat of incumbent President Loren Ipson by Maggot-based Patriot Party candidate Grant Layton in November 2222.

(See "The Week America Changed," docucast)

(See "The FreeAir Revolution," "The Stone Revolt," "Wake Up & Breathe!")

(See "Battle of Newark Bay," "Sixty Mile March," "Public/ Military Conflict, Newark 2222")

(See "Inciting Incident: Second American Revolution)

(See "The Iceland Incident / (Unidentified Offshore Military Engagement, Iceland 2222")

*Excerpts from the Docucast,* "Revolution In The Dark: Survivors Recall the Blackout of 2222," *PinchesPictures, 2259.*

*Arthur, 55, Springfield, MA*

Survivors thrive. That's the way it is. We survived those fucked-up few months in 2222 and we thrived. We replaced our elected officials, practically the entire government. Fuck 'em. Crooks.

You don't know. We thought it was the end of the world. There was so much tension—all that fighting in New Jersey—and then the grid went down. I thought that was the end. We all did. I mean the grid was powered back up in a few days, but it was a scary time. Nothing was ever the same again after that, not really.

I'd never lived through something like that. I mean, who could have predicted America would still have blackouts and civil unrest in 2222?

*Patty, 64, Cold Spring, NY*

You turn out the lights and people freak out. Maybe we're all still afraid of the dark on some level. Things you can't see will kill you. But the Blackout of '22 didn't bother me none. We're up on the farm, where we lose power for a spell each winter, even in the spring when the rains are heavy. We always got preserves down in the cellar, so I wasn't worried about us starving none. I mean this is how people are supposed to live, hunkered down, minding their own B.I. Business. Problems happen when everybody's crowded in, gettin' up in each other's shit. You mind your B.I. Business, you don't have problems. No, I ain't afraid of the dark... darkness is natural. You can't have day without it. But I don't like how people behave in the dark. No, sir. They get scared and mean and things go to shit right quick. Everybody blamed President Ipson for the loss of control. I did too, even though I voted for her in 2218. Looking back on it, though, I'm not sure any President could have done better. It was a fucked-up time and people were fucked up. Still, if the military hadn't shot that girl in Newark—Grief? Greed? What was her name?—I suspect the whole mess could have been avoided.

*Randy, 77, Crooksville, PA*

I hate when people call it a blackout or a power failure. It's demeaning. What happened in the summer of 2222 was a revolution, every bit as powerful and important as the one American colonists fought against England in the 18th century. We freed ourselves from oppressive leaders who poisoned our air and water supply! We turned the tide of public consciousness. We voted those bums out of office. A blackout is an accident. What happened in 2222 was no accident. We shut the power down, then took the power back!

*Troy, 70, Bangor, ME*

The Maggot revolution is bullshit. A few isolated groups of assholes vandalized a couple of government buildings. That's hardly a military coup. If you examine the spike in crime that took place during the 2222 Grid Failure, you'll see the Maggot nonsense was barely a blip. There was a 22-percent jump across the board in violent crimes during the blackout. Murder, rape, assault—that says more about the state our society was in at the time than it does about the Maggot influence. I mean, if people were truly following the teachings of Mother Maggie, why were they treating each other so terribly? What did the Maggots even stand for? I think that's why people abandoned that movement in droves after 2222. It was a wake-up call. At a time when everybody should have stuck together, we fell to pieces as a nation. It was shameful. Shameful.

*Adam, 58, Barnsworth, NJ*

Maggots win because Mother Maggie and the Man of Stone are *real,* not some imaginary spirits in the sky. *They walk the earth!* The Rock God snapped those undersea cables like strands of thread! Then he and Maggie walked over to Iceland where they were attacked by the British Navy and a cadre of Illuminati ninjas.

*Elizabeth, 66, Chester, PA*

Illuminati ninjas? Really? This is why the Maggots lost momentum—because of fools like Adam. Let me guess—after

Iceland, Maggie and Mr. Mud went to stay at the Martian Bed and Breakfast at the North Pole, right? Did they meet Santa Claus there? *Idiot*!

*Chemolco College Student Politics Streamcast, hosted by CARA LEWIS and IZZY BLOCH, from the basement of Cara Lewis's parents' house, Princeton, New Jersey, August 22, 2222.*

LEWIS: Okay. You with me, Izzy.

BLOCH: I am, Cara.

LEWIS: We're broadcasting live from the basement of my parents' house near Princeton, New Jersey. The power is out. It's been out for…what time is it, Izzy?

BLOCH: It's just after two in the afternoon. The power went out *again* during the Presidential debates last night, so it's been out for about sixteen hours now.

LEWIS: Sixteen hours. My parents have a solar generator, but it ran all night so I'm not sure how much longer it's got.

BLOCH: I think we should power down after sundown anyway. No lights. Don't attract attention.

LEWIS: That's…a good idea. Communications have been really sketchy since the blackout, but my parents heard on the wireless this morning that Maggots took over the state house in Albany and were preparing to do the same in Trenton. We listened to the news on the bus back to campus last night, but they didn't report anything other than there'd been other major power failures. They didn't even say it was a terrorist attack, even though everybody knew what was happening. Two blackouts, a week apart, both shutting down presidential debates? That's no coincidence—that is an orchestrated attack. The only question is, did the MRF have help? If so, who? How deep does this go?

BLOCH: Gosh, Cee-Cee, do you think my parents are okay?

LEWIS: What? Why…your parents are out in

Pennsylvania, aren't they?

BLOCH: Wilkes-Barre, yeah.

LEWIS: You talked to them?

BLOCH: The call didn't go through, but I sent a message.

LEWIS: Did they reply?

BLOCH: Yes. They said they're okay.

LEWIS: Then why do you think they're in danger?

BLOCH: Well, the power's out and...I don't know... everything's just so scary! What if the Maggots start burning houses in the suburbs! My parents can't defend themselves! They're almost sixty years old!

LEWIS: Okay, Iz...take a breath...

BLOCH: Don't try to calm me down, Cee-cee! This is scary! Admit it! Admit it's scary!

LEWIS: Yes, Izzy. It is kind of scary. We've never seen anything like this, and the unknown is always kind of scary. Unpredictable. But we'll get through this, Iz. Just breathe, okay? We're somewhere safe where we can shelter in place until all this gets sorted out.

BLOCH: That's easy for you to say! Your parents are right upstairs! You don't have to worry about them getting murdered or burned to death by some Maggot...*assholes*!

LEWIS: Izzy, there are no reports of the MRF attacking the homes of private citizens. That didn't happen during the last blackout and it won't happen this time either. The MRF is fighting our corporate-controlled government on behalf of the people...

BLOCH: *What* people, Cara? I didn't ask for this! Nobody did. Your fucking Maggots cut the lights, seized control and forced this shit on everybody. They're violent maniacs! And they inspire other violent maniacs. You don't know how far this will go! You don't know where it will end!

LEWIS: Last time they had the grid restored in forty-eight hours. I'm sure this will be about the same, maybe even sooner…

BLOCH: What if it's not, Cara? What if instead of just the Northeast, they black out the whole country? What if they start blowing up buildings or using biological weapons… what then? What are we going to do then?

LEWIS: Izzy. Breathe. The past couple of days have been very stressful. Let's be honest, Iz, this whole year has sucked, especially these last few months. I know you're worried about your parents. We'll take my parents' transport out to Wilkes-Barre tomorrow morning, whether the power's back on or not.

BLOCH: (*crying*) I wish you'd never gotten me involved with Ghee *Dork*house and the goddamn Maggots!

LEWIS: Izzy…Iz. I-I…listen, you're right. The Maggot Revolutionary Force is awful for doing this. Nobody wants violence and fear. It's not the way things are done in this country. It's not fair. The MRF should be ashamed of itself. They do not speak for the Maggot Movement. Mother Maggie teaches us to love one another, to be kind and care for each other. And Ghee…Ghee… I'm not even sure Ghee Dorfhouse *was* a Maggot. She was just a girl who tried to make a difference, to right a wrong, and the movement just swept her up…

BLOCH: Maggots suck!

LEWIS: No! The MRF sucks, but the teachings of Mother Maggie are pure of heart and clear of mind.

BLOCH: Enough with that bullshit! I don't want to hear it, Cara! Ever again! Do you understand me?

LEWIS: I do. I do. I love you, Izzy. We'll get through this together, okay? No worries. It's scary but we'll be okay. Let's wrap up this gram, okay?

BLOCH: Nobody's watching, Cara. Nobody's listening. Nobody cares.

LEWIS: I still care, Izzy. I care about you. I care about my family and friends. I care about this country. And I care about this gram. I believe people *are* listening. We're doing our part, Izzy, however small, to make this country—this *world*—a better place.

BLOCH: Not me. Not anymore. *You* change the world, Cara Lewis. It's…too much for me. Too intense. I don't care like you do. I'm out.

*Excerpt from* THREE DAYS IN THE DARK, *written and directed by Darcy Valero, Meridian Theatre Company, February 4-September 30, 2230.*

ACT II, Scene iii

*GRANDMA, FLO, and MARY sit in silence around the kitchen table, staring at a candle. There are more candles on the countertop. There's a shotgun lying beside the candle.*

*Banging on the kitchen door. FLO and MARY jump to their feet. GRANDMA remains seated.*

GRANDMA: See who it is.

*FLO picks up the shotgun and places the stock against her shoulder, points the barrel toward the door. MARY climbs up on the kitchen countertop, lifts a corner of the curtain and peers out the window.*

MARY: It's Joe and John!

*FLO nods and lowers the barrel, but keeps the stock against her shoulder.*

FLO: Let 'em in. But make it quick.

*MARY climbs off the countertop and crosses to the kitchen door. She unlatches several locks and opens the door. Neighbor JOE and his son JOHN step inside. JOE's holding a hunting rifle. MARY quickly closes the door and locks it behind them. FLO puts the shotgun down on the kitchen table and motions for JOE and JOHN to sit. JOE takes a seat beside GRANDMA, but JOHN remains standing beside MARY. FLO approaches the kitchen table but doesn't sit.*

FLO: What's the word?

*JOE opens his mouth to speak but JOHN cuts him off.*

JOHN: Town hall's on fire. Police station too.

GRANDMA: They putting it out?

JOE: We heard sirens but didn't see any fire trucks.

FLO: How long did you stay?

JOE: About ten minutes.

*FLO looks at GRANDMA*

FLO: They're gonna let it burn.

GRANDMA (*shaking her head*): Firemen are busy tonight. They'll get to it.

FLO: It's all coming down, Ma. From the White House to borough hall. This is the big one.

GRANDMA: Hush, silly girl! Power goes out and people panic. We wait this out. The lights'll come back on. Everything'll be normal again, except for people feeling bad they acted like fools in the dark.

JOE: I heard Maggots took the state house in Albany.

JOHN: And the Governor's Mansion in Michigan.

FLO: Where did you hear that? Who told you?

JOE: Johnny's got a solar reader.

GRANDMA: The KnowNet is still up?

JOHN: Yes.

GRANDMA (*to FLO*): See? Nothing's going down as long as the Net is still up.

FLO: KnowNet can't help if you can't access it! Power's been out for two days. No transporters, no information, no deliveries…nothing! The army hasn't shown up. No national guard. We haven't even seen a cop since the grid died. Now the police station is on fire! It's finally going to shit, Ma.

JOE (*looking up*): Do you think the air will spoil? If the filters aren't working?

GRANDMA (*exhales dismissively*): Air don't spoil! It's air!

JOHN: The purifiers probably have solar back-up.

JOE: I told you! You can't tap those solar cells without a converter and you need electricity for that!

JOHN: Maybe they got gas or a T-cell starter.

GRANDMA: I'm telling you it don't matter. Air is breathable! It always has been. Damn Pharm industry convinced everybody it isn't.

FLO: Christ, Ma! That was a hundred years ago! Everything's changed now.

GRANDMA: Nothing ever changes. Not really.

FLO: It's changing now. Our government. The world. People are sick of the lies and they're taking the power back. This isn't just a power failure. It's a power exchange.

MARY: It's scary.

GRANDMA: Don't be frightened, girl. We'll get through this.

FLO (*to JOE*): Are they looting out there?

JOE (*nods*): Foodworld's ransacked. All the windows are broken. Saw a group of twelve or so guys walking south on Main. Johnny and I didn't want to get closer.

MARY: Will they attack our house?

GRANDMA: Don't worry. We're safe here, child.

FLO (*nodding at the shotgun*): Armed and dangerous.

MARY: Are we going to have to shoot someone?

FLO: Hopefully not. Probably not.

GRANDMA: *Certainly not!* Put those guns away! All you're going to do is hurt yourselves. Nobody's getting shot in this house.

FLO: Better safe than sorry.

GRANDMA: Guns don't make people safer. Guns get people killed.

FLO: I'm not putting the gun away.

MARY: Don't. I feel safer with it here.

GRANDMA: Even though it's the most dangerous thing in this room?

FLO: The most dangerous thing in this room is your narrow mind!

GRANDMA: Or your high-minded ideals?

MARY: Just leave the gun on the table. Please.

*MARY folds herself into JOHN's arms.*

MARY: Christ, Johnny, I've never been so scared.

GRANDMA: There's no call for fear or foul language, child. Be strong, girl!

MARY: We have no power! No lights! People are fighting…

GRANDMA: People are forever fighting about some thing or another. We're safe. We got a roof. We got a warm fire. We got food. We'll survive this. Florence, step up. Be strong for your girl!

FLO: I am! I'm showing her how to stand up for what's right!

*While FLO and GRANDMA argue, MARY pulls JOHNNY into the kitchen pantry.*

MARY: We have to get out of here, Johnny. Now. Tonight. Start over someplace new, where we can live by our own rules, not the rules of our parents and grandparents!

JOHNNY: I…I don't want to leave my father.

MARY: Those old farts in the other room are going to get us killed! My mother…my grandmother…they're both wrong, but they can't see it. They're so blind. Politics has made them blind…and deaf. Neither will listen to anyone else.

JOHNNY: But my father…

MARY: Your father is no better, John! He wants to avoid conflict. He wants to hide. But you can't bury your head and let somebody else figure it out. The fighting is already here, right outside our door!

*Gunshots explode in the kitchen. A woman screams. MARY and JOHNNY race back into the kitchen. MARY screams.*

FADE TO BLACK

*Lyrics,* Ballad of the One-Armed Soldier *by punktronic musical act, Mobile Stone Entities, 2235.*

Ouch! Ouch! Ouch! That hurts!
Stop! Stop! Stop! That's my arm!
Hey! No! Wait! Give it back!
Fuck! Shit! Damn! You tore my arm off!
Threw it away, like garbage.
Fuck! Shit! Damn! You tore my arm off!
Fine. I got a shiny new one.
Made of heavy metal!
Made of heavy metal!
U-S-A! U-S-A! U-S-A!

*BiblioFriend Search: Books by Captain William Poole. SERP / summaries / excerpts / sample chapters.*

*Excerpt,* Monsters Tore My Arm Off: A First-Hand Account Inside The Battle Of Newark Bay, *non-fiction, January 2224.*

Talos suits are equipped with palms charges, but the Rock God moved too fast for me to get a clear shot. Before I knew it, Maggie attacked from behind. She bludgeoned me with her stone arms and I was dazed, defenseless. The Rock God grabbed me and pulled me down to the concrete floor. I raised my hand to fire on him, but he was quicker, grabbing my arm and twisting.

It happened so fast, I felt no pain. One moment my arm was there and the next it was gone, tossed across the warehouse like a piece of scrap. All I felt was a sudden tug, a jerk, and my arm was gone. Talos suits are built to withstand 10K PSI, yet the Rock God tore through it like paper.

The Talos suit cauterized my wound and injected me with antibiotics, but it didn't stop me from going into shock. I rolled onto my side and tried to crawl away, but the Rock God stopped me. He grabbed me by the ankle and lifted me up, all the way up, until I hung upside down with my head a foot off the ground. I kicked and twisted, trying to free myself, but the monster's grasp was like iron. Dear Lord, he was going to pull me apart like a wishbone! I was powerless to stop him. I needed a miracle.

I got one.

"Stop!" Maggie spoke and the Rock God obeyed.

Maggie.

Spoke.

*Excerpt,* Healing From A Monster Attack: My New Life, My New Arm, *non-fiction, March 2226.*

The agent who debriefed me after the attack had the audacity to tell me, "The military will get you a new arm that's better than the old one." The comment offended me at the time, as well it should. But that agent was right. The bio-synthetic limb developed for me by the Army Corp Of Engineers is a marvel of technology. The nano receptors integrate so seamlessly with my nerve endings that I can feel all degrees of heat and cold. I can even feel something as light as the touch of a butterfly landing on my arm. My new right hand has the dexterity to sort grains of sand and the power to crush stone.

# 9

## *Mudspeak IV*

The walk took forever. At least it seemed to. I mean, forever is a long time, even if you're a stone. There are no clocks at the bottom of the sea, no sun, no seasons. Time moves differently down there. I like it. We both did. Deep-water time is first cousin to geologic time, slow and steady, the time of erosion and plate tectonics. It felt familiar to us both, connected with our deepest granules, our innermost grains. At least it did for me. I think Maggie felt it too.

I couldn't see, not really, but I could sense the topography of the ocean floor in detail. The sand beneath my feet was a part of me, a part of everything around us, and it told me (almost) everything I needed to know.

Black, oily glue coated the bottom of Newark Bay. It grabbed our ankles and wouldn't let go. I'm not being flowery here; the seabed grew gummy appendages with every step, long black fingers like seaweed or bolero whips, snaring us, snagging us, climbing our calves until we tore ourselves free. Everything at the bottom of Newark Bay was stuck in that muck; fish bones, human bones, three rusted commercial cargo planes, dozens of decaying automobiles, thousands of old tires. If we stayed in one spot for longer than a minute, the black goo threatened to make us part of the landscape forever. We kept moving, but it took days to escape the bay.

We stayed about fifty miles off shore, walking through water between fifty and a hundred and fifty feet deep. The corals envied our mobility. Barnacles, snails, and anemones hitched rides on our backs. When the hitchhikers grew cumbersome, Maggie and I scraped each other clean and walked on.

We stayed on the continental shelf, heading north, skirting the tip of Long Island, cutting between Martha's Vineyard and the Massachusetts coast. Twice we got caught up in fishing nets. I freed Maggie from a net full of tuna, tearing the intersecting ropes until both my mother-in-law and several hundred bluefins tumbled out. Maggie later returned the favor, freeing me from a nylon grouper trap, no easy feat for a woman with no hands. What would happen if we were both swept up with the catch? Our combined weight would probably capsize any but the hardiest of boats, but I'd love to see the look on the fishermen's faces.

Gold coins glittered on the seabed off the coast of Nantucket, part of the debris field from an ancient wooden ship that lay crumbling, half-buried in sand. Maggie and I counted nearly two dozen coins. Shortly after that, Maggie stepped in an eel hole and cartwheeled down a long, sandy slope. When she landed (ungracefully on her face), the seabed quaked all around, sand rising up like mist. I grabbed her arm and helped her to her feet, as the water around us filled with soft bodies and black-purple limbs. Octopi swarmed around us, trash bags with tentacles and beaks, spraying us with black ink. The attack tickled. Sorry, little guys. The octopi moved off in a swarm like a flock of birds, many steered by one mind.

Maggie felt bad. An octopus sits on its eggs for four years before they hatch, and she had crushed so many when she landed. But accidents happen…like the cable I tripped over.

It snagged my ankle and I pulled six feet of it out of the sand and muck. The cable looked like a tree limb, but there were no trees at the bottom of the sea. I grabbed it, gave it a tug, followed it for while. It ran all the way back to shore, in one direction and off into the deep water in the other.

The cable was an ugly, unnatural thing. It didn't belong here at the bottom of the sea, trying to hide, half-buried in the sand, more man-made garbage. Our walk across the ocean floor meant constantly navigating giant mountains of trash, an underwater obstacle course of rusted cans and dirty diapers. Massive balls of soft plastic rolled and swirled along the bottom like tumbleweeds. Maggie and I walked for miles through a cloud of empty water bottles that floated around us like thick fog, wading through discarded coffee cups up to our knees. The ocean was a shit pit. Literally. Humanity made it their toilet bowl and trash bin.

The undersea cable in my hands embodied everything that sucked about the bottom of the ocean, namely, human pollution. Here was one of mankind's veins, a big, ol' artery pulsating knowledge and information beneath my fingertips. If I pinched it hard enough, crimped it like a garden hose, could I cut off the flow of information inside? Maggie and I decided not to take any chances. We played tug-o-war until the cable broke.

We found another cable several days later and snapped that one too. We broke cable after cable as we walked along the east coast. Some were as thick as my arm and covered with slippery green algae. Others were thin, white, and could have been laid yesterday. Did these wires cross the ocean floor all the way to Europe? Africa? Maggie and I didn't know, nor discriminate. We destroyed every cable we found.

I'm not sure what we hoped to accomplish, but breaking the cables felt right. Maggie seemed to enjoy the vandalism as much as I did. Maybe we broke the internet. I hoped so. From what I'd seen, the information superhighway was another polluted road to nowhere.

I counted twenty snapped lines by the time we reached the tip of Nova Scotia, where we found a big metal box the size of a pickup truck bolted to the ocean floor. A thick, knotted rope of cables wormed into one side of the box and out the other. Maggie and I kicked and punched the contraption until it burst into a shower of sparks. I'd never seen flames burn underwater before, blooming orange balls that lit up the sea. It was wild.

The explosion that followed was wilder still, blowing us off the edge of the world.

I figured we were close to the continental shelf—the ocean currents had grown progressively darker and colder for miles—but I didn't realize *how* close.

Maggie stumbled back, pinwheeling her arms. I reached for her, but she was already falling backwards off a cliff. She was gone into the dark depths before I even got to the ledge—then the ledge itself gave way beneath my feet (likely *because* of my feet and the tonnage atop them), and suddenly I was falling too, part of an underwater landslide.

I was free, free-falling, for well over a mile, probably two. It felt like a hundred. Falling underwater is different, but not much when you weigh a ton. I tumbled like a snowball, gathering a cocoon of sand and muck around me. By the time I stopped rolling downhill—which felt like it took a week—I was the core of a ball as big as a house, buried under a thousand feet of sand.

Digging out. Clawing out of your own grave. It keeps you very single-minded and focused. Dig, dig, dig, as if your life depends on it…because it does. Don't get me wrong, I wasn't in danger of suffocating or getting crushed, but it's claustrophobic beneath tons of wet sand. Part of me was content to stay buried at the bottom of the ocean. What did it matter to a rock? But my remaining humanity screamed for freedom. Dig, you stone ape! Dig, dig, dig! Swim, climb, kick, and squirm through mud as thick as yourself. If I needed to breathe I would have been a goner. I emerged from the sand nearly a mile from where I'd fallen. Maggie wrapped her forearms around my hand and pulled me from the landslide. Maggie was strong, much stronger than she appeared.

We landed in another world. The water was different, the pressure, the light. This was true darkness, a land that never knew sun, had no use for a burning ball of fire in the sky, nor the sky itself. The bottom of the sea, the true bottom, defied the sun.

The abysmal plains were aptly named. The only moniker more appropriate would have been "Hard As Fuck To Walk Through Plains." The sea bed was low and flat for miles and we sunk into powdery silt up to our necks, like quicksand, swimming through miles of dense dirt before we got solid footing. We walked on, sand up to our chests, then our waists, our knees, our ankles, until the earth released us at last.

Sea life was more sparse down here than up on the shelf. Or maybe it seemed that way because everything was so spread out. Fish, like humans, flocked to the coasts. The dark deep was the heartland of the ocean...or the sticks, depending on how you looked at it. Either way, it was rural, the landscape rugged and bare.

Life at the bottom is about trying not to get eaten. Maggie and I did our best, but we were an anomaly here, pedestrian intruders in an undersea domain. Our intentions were constantly being tested; were we predator or food? Countless crabs pinched our ankles, climbed our calves. Crabs are assholes.

A school of grouper swarmed us off the coast of Newfoundland, knocked us flat, buried us in the sandy seabed. Maggie got to her feet first, but as soon as she stood upright, a shark the size of a bus barreled into her and clamped its jaws around her midsection. It happened in a flash; all I could do was watch the fish swim away, shaking Maggie in its jaws like a puppy with a slipper. After five hundred yards or so, the shark spit Maggie out, along with a cloud of broken teeth. Maggie and I shared a good laugh when I caught up with her. Fucking sharks, always bolting out of the dark, mouths open wide, bite first, ask questions later. Actually, the bite *is* the question—are you edible? Fortunately for Maggie and I, the answer was no.

Things grow big at the bottom. Deep sea gigantism is real. Jelly fish with legs a hundred feet long. Spindly sea spiders the size of small cars prowling the ocean floor like wraiths. An oarfish swam past like a Chinese dragon and kept going, its body impossibly long, while isopods carpeted the seabed like prehistoric terrors. Squid with heads like massive strawberries, or hot air balloons, drifted alongside spaghetti-like plankton chains. Fish that glowed from within. The hypnotic, feather-like arms of sponges, the interpretive dance of weightless jellies performed only for Maggie and me. We walked through a field of microscopic creatures illuminated like tiny Christmas bulbs, allowing me to see, really see, Maggie's smile for the first time. So beautiful, so like Sarah's smile. Maggie and I tried to hitch a ride on the back of a massive stingray, but it shook us loose after a hundred yards.

A two-piece shipwreck in the North Atlantic may have been the Titanic, but Maggie and I didn't venture over for a closer look. We walked through the debris field of a wrecked cargo ship, metal shipping containers broken open, spilling

Adidas sneakers all over the sea floor. Algae covered the laces, and crabs made homes in the interiors. We passed a rusty mountain made of hundreds of cars and trucks; Nissans, Toyotas and Hyundais by the dozens, windows smashed, frames buckled by the pressure and rotted by saltwater, reborn as an ecosystem for coral and crabs. Sharks may be the apex predators of the ocean, but crabs ruled the seabed. Nasty assholes.

The water grew slick and heavy. A few miles later we found a broken pipe, nearly a foot wide, sticking out of the ocean floor, spewing a plume of oil. Maggie and I tried to plug the leaking pipe with rocks and sand. It helped, but oil continued to seep out. We eventually moved on. You can't fix everything, but you do what you can.

The plains eventually gave way to the fracture zone, where lines of seamounts rose in the east. The seamounts ran parallel on either side of us, meeting at the horizon. These low, rugged mountain ranges were the stretch marks of the Earth, the pregnancy scars of new land born at the Mid-Atlantic Ridge. Tremors and quakes radiated from the ridge in waves, drawing Maggie and I on.

Maggie and I climbed along a ridge that throbbed like a vein. Sometimes it did more than throb, rumbling so violently, Maggie and I toppled to the sea floor and had to climb back up once the shaking stopped.

We made better time walking the ridge, but sections were pitted and split. Maggie fell into a transform fault that took her days to climb out of. She didn't need my help, so I waited patiently while she climbed back up, listening to her cuss a blue streak. Maggie was a good cusser.

I spotted a plane crash just off the ridge, an old Boeing 727, rusted, coated with orange algae, and nearly hidden beneath green-brown seagrass. The left wing and tail stuck out of the sandy sea bed about a hundred yards south, but otherwise the plane was surprisingly intact. Maggie and I climbed down. I peered into one of the oval passenger windows and saw skeletons strapped into the seats. Maggie looked too and I saw her shiver. Dying in a plane crash, especially one that dragged you down to the bottom of the ocean, was a rough way to go.

The Mid-Atlantic Ridge loomed above us, black spires against the black sea. A few peaks glowed with orange fire. We could make it to that fire. We were close, nearly there.

A starfish, at least a foot taller than Maggie or I, emerged from the darkness ahead of us, sometimes walking on two legs, sometimes crawling on four, sometimes cartwheeling on all five. As the creature got closer, I saw eerily human faces on the underside of each of its five legs. The faces differed slightly, but bore familial resemblances; pug noses, thin lips, almond eyes. The starfish sang through a set of gills that expelled water in different frequencies. I assumed this was how the creature communicated, until it spoke in a language Maggie and I understood.

*Hail, visitors of stone. Please state your purpose for coming to the city of Ergan.*

*We came upon your city by accident,* I said. *We seek the Mid-Atlantic Ridge.*

*Why are you traveling to the seam of the Earth?*

*I don't see how that's any of your business,* I replied.

*Perhaps. But we cannot let you pass through Ergan.*

*Why not?*

The oldest face, on the bottom left limb, answered. *We have never had visitors in our city. We are not about to start now.*

*What are you hiding in there?* I asked.

*I don't see how that's any of* your *business,* the starfish replied. Maggie and I exchanged a look.

*Okay. I'm David and this lovely lady is Maggie,* I said. *We want to jump into an active volcano.*

*Why?*

I considered playing the "not your business" game, but thought better of it.

*Because that's where stones go to die.*

The starfish folded its limbs together so the tips almost touched. It looked like it was praying, but the faces whispered urgently among themselves in a language that sounded like bubbles popping. Eventually the starfish popped upright and all five faces began speaking at once, the two younger faces on its right side outshouting the older faces on the left. The middle-aged face on top silenced them all with a harsh command shouted in bubble language. The faces fell silent. After a pause, the oldest face spoke first, but each face said its piece.

*We can guide you to a suitable lava spout…*

*…but this is where stone is born…*

*…stone never dies…*

*…it is transformed…*

*…in subduction zones.*

Maggie and I looked at each other, then I looked away in embarrassment. I hadn't considered this. I was so fixated on the idea of the two of us swan-diving into a volcano, I never considered I might be wrong. I mean, it *could* work, but it wasn't *right*. I needed to do the right thing. I'd walked halfway across the ocean but there was still blood on my hands, even if I was the only one who could see it.

*Where is the nearest subduction zone?* Maggie asked. I knew, but didn't want to say it aloud.

*The Bering Trench is closest, but there are deeper spots if you follow the trench south.*

*South?*

*Well, you'll have to travel north first, of course, and cross over.*

*Cross over? The…north pole?*

*Yes.*

*The other side of the world,* I said, looking apologetically at Maggie. She shrugged nonchalantly, but couldn't hide the disappointment on her face. She'd followed me without question since the moment we stepped into Newark Bay; she trusted me and I'd led her astray. My grand plan was shit… all my plans were shit. Now I'd gone and splattered my shit all over Maggie the same way I had her daughter, Sarah. Why couldn't I stop hurting the women I loved?

*We can still jump into a volcano,* I suggested. I looked to the starfish for support.

*We can guide you to a suitable lava spout…* The bottom left face repeated.

*But you cannot pass through Ergan,* the middle face spoke.

*Are you going to stop me?* I said. I rolled my shoulders back and stood upright, but the starfish was still a foot taller. It snapped into tip-touching position again and the faces resumed whispering. A moment later it popped upright. The youngest face spoke first, but the message was delivered limb by limb, counter-clockwise around the starfish.

*We come in peace…*

*…but will proudly sacrifice ourselves…*

*…to protect Ergan…*

*…we are one of an infinite race…*

*…we spend our lives attached to rock.*

The starfish slowly spun around, showing off its countless rows of short, suckered feet and an orifice lined with blunt teeth in the center of its body. Maggie put a hand on my shoulder before I said something else stupid.

*We also come in peace and mean your city no harm,* she said. *We don't want to destroy anything, we only want to…complete our journey.*

I thought about the cables we'd vandalized. That destruction didn't count. I'm sure the starfish would agree.

*We can guide you to a path atop the ridge,* the middle face said.

Maggie nodded to me and then to the starfish. The starfish climbed down the side of the seamount. Maggie and I followed. The creature rolled across the sea floor on the points of its limbs, like a wagon wheel.

*Are all the creatures in Ergan like you?* Maggie asked.

*We celebrate individual diversity,* it said. *But we are all of a kind. One mind.*

*One mind,* I echoed. *There's not one diverse individual in your city who will allow us to pass through?*

*No.*

*You're certain?*

*Of course. We are one mind. It was decided as soon as we became aware of your arrival.*

*You saw us coming?*

*We heard you. Felt you. Neither of you are light on your feet.*

*True.*

*What do you do in your city?* Maggie asked.

The starfish regarded her suspiciously, especially its younger faces.

*What do* you *do in* your *cities?* it replied.

*We...make things. Conduct business. Build places for people to live,* Maggie said.

The starfish nodded its top face. The old face on its left leg appeared asleep, eyes closed, puckered lips parted and wet. I watched the sleeping geezer spin around and around until it made me dizzy.

*Our city is the same,* it said. *Plus, we wait for the water to recede and the ridge to rise.*

*You've got a long wait,* I said.

*We are patient,* the starfish replied. *A man of stone should understand.*

We walked in silence for a long time. Days? Months? The starfish led us northeast to the base of the next seamount. A narrow gully climbed up through the foothills. Volcanic peaks towered over us, radiating heat. The starfish made the climb look easy, suckered feet and supple limbs deftly scaling steep rock faces. Maggie and I had a harder time; Maggie's lack of hands really made it tough. We slipped or fell two steps for every three we climbed. But we carried on, higher and higher, the sea floor spread majestically to our left, an abysmal plain, but beautiful nonetheless. It's a kind of death down here in the cold, dark deep—a death brimming with life.

*What do you eat?* I asked.

*We self-consume,* the starfish said. It demonstrated by lifting its oldest foot and shoving it into the tooth-lined opening in the middle of its belly. The elder face awoke with a start, but didn't cry out. The mouth clamped down, biting into the face. The old face grimaced as if screaming, but didn't make a sound. The remaining four legs readjusted, allowing the starfish to keep rolling on without missing a beat. It took a while, but eventually the starfish devoured its entire leg. Gruesome as it was, Maggie and I couldn't look away.

*Does that hurt?* Maggie asked. She sounded as repulsed as I felt.

*We don't feel physical pain.*

*Does it hurt your feelings?* I asked.

*Asshole,* the youngest face replied. The next oldest face echoed the sentiment. *It doesn't feel* good. *There is a lot of pressure. But eating yields an equal measure of contentment. It all balances out.*

A new leg-arm grew from the chewed stump of the old. The limb was thin, worm-like, its face infantile. The other four limbs took up the slack until the new limb reached full length and was able to do its share of climbing and cartwheeling. The starfish was whole for a time, until it grew hungry and chewed off its oldest face again. Baby limbs grow up so fast.

*So, you eat yourself,* I said, after weeks of silence. The top of the ridge grew larger, but didn't seem to get closer.

*We self-consume and self-reproduce,* the starfish clarified. *All we need is a limb and a bit of our core to clone ourselves. We are completely self-sufficient. We choose to live in groups for protection and companionship.*

*Do you...have family?* Maggie asked.

*We* are *family,* the starfish replied.

*I've got all my sisters with me,* I said.

Neither Maggie nor the starfish responded. They wouldn't even look at me. We climbed in silence for several weeks, until finally emerging onto a flat path that ran atop the Mid-Atlantic Ridge.

*Go north,* the starfish said. Maggie and I did just that, but stopped when we realized the starfish wasn't following.

*You're not coming?* Maggie asked.

*We promised to guide you to the seam of the Earth…*

*…we have fulfilled our promise…*

*…the great trench lies ahead…*

*…travel well…*

*…go in peace.*

It felt wrong. I'd grown attached to our starfish companion and I think Maggie had too. I guess the feeling wasn't mutual. Maybe starfish don't have feelings.

*What are you hiding back in your city?* I asked again, figuring we were far enough away that I might get a straight answer.

*Our past,* the starfish said as it rolled away.

*Thank you!* Maggie called, but the starfish did not respond. In continued its retreat, and, when it grew too small for Maggie and I to see any longer, we turned and followed the seam of the Earth north. Iceland lay somewhere up ahead.

# 10

## *Second Final Report V*

*BiblioFriend Search: Books by Captain William Poole, SERP / summaries / excerpts / sample chapters.*

*Excerpt,* Terror Beneath The Sea *(writing as BP Haas), novel, June, 2227.*

Stoneman and Martha reached the edge of a cliff. Neither could see the bottom below, only empty blackness.

"It's the continental shelf," Stoneman said.

Martha pointed to a series of thick cables snaking over the edge of the cliff. The cables hugged the side of the seamount before disappearing into the darkness.

"Yes," Stoneman nodded. "We can climb down on those."

Stoneman went first, wrapping his arms and legs around the cable and sliding slowly down the side of the mountain. He waited for Martha, but once he saw her above him, he loosened his grasp and slid down faster. This was fun, like an amusement park thrill ride! Stoneman thought he heard Martha laughing wildly above him.

But, halfway down the mountainside, the earth suddenly heaved and bucked like an animal in a trap. The cable snapped like the wispiest gossamer string. Stoneman fell backward, away from the trembling mountain, the broken cable still clutched in his grasp. Somewhere above him Martha screamed, but he couldn't tell where. Then gravity took him end over end and he was spinning, spiraling out of control.

It was a long fall to the bottom of the sea.

*Excerpt,* The Terror Beneath The Sea Vs. The Five-Faced Starfish People *(writing as BP Haas), novel, June, 2229.*

"Don't come any closer!" Stoneman shouted, but there was no way for him to know if the gigantic starfish pinwheeling across the ocean floor understood him. Angry faces snarled from the end of each of the creature's five arms, and a toothy, mouth-like opening gaped in the center of its body.

Stoneman raised his massive fists and planted his feet. The starfish got bigger as it barreled closer. Stoneman noticed all-too-human details on the creature's five faces; wrinkles, pimples, a red mole with a long, black hair sprouting from the center, tucked deep into a chin cleft.

Martha touched Stoneman's shoulder with her wrist stump and the fight drained out of him. He turned to face his Queen.

"Let them come," Martha said. "Let them come. Let them come."

The starfish came. Stoneman lowered his arms, but wouldn't unclench his fists.

*From KnowNet,* "The Iceland Incident" *last updated, March 4, 2301.*

The Iceland Incident, also known as the Iceland-Faroe Passage Assault, was a military engagement with a pair of unidentified assailants on the coast and in the waters off Iceland between Oct 26-Nov9, 2222.

An independent task force comprised of Norwegian, American, and Scandinavian soldiers, backed by government agencies in the United States, Russia, and China, responded to reports of an unprovoked attack on two journalists by a pair of military robots in Hofn, Iceland on October 29, 2222. Initial reports were passed off as a Halloween Hoax or part of East Iceland's annual Days of Darkness Festival.

*Inciting Incident*

Journalists Raimo Viskari and Olivia Lyy claim they were assaulted with "boulders of ice and snow" while trying to film the unidentified assailants along Road One near Hornafjordur. The attack resulted in three broken ribs and a fractured breastplate for Viskari, and prompted a joint-nation military response.

It's widely believed the assailants were the same or similar robotic soldiers to those connected with the Sixty Mile March and subsequent Battle of Newark Bay on May 3, 2222. The soldiers—using modified Talos T244 combat armor—were likely controlled by internal operators, remote users, or both.

These "stone saviors"—named for the rock-like appearance of their camouflage—are most often associated with Maggot mysticism and the North American legend of the Mud Man (see "Man of Stone: New Jersey"). In the wake of the Iceland sighting, many believed the Maggot Revolutionary Force controlled these "secret weapons." As a result, Maggot-backed candidate Grant Layton was elected POTUS by an overwhelming margin on Nov. 2, 2222. The election of Layton, and the rise of Maggot power, historians argue, signaled America's reemergence as a global and political power.

*Assailant Engagement*

Icelandic police engaged with the mechanized robots in Hofn, but were unable to stop the assailants from returning to the waters off the coast of Hornafjordur. Following initial misidentification as a Halloween hoax, an independent military task force was summoned to track and engage the robots. Following a series of undersea depth charge attacks on Oct 30-Nov1, the robots resurfaced near Gerpir, the easternmost point of Iceland on Nov1. The international task force engaged the robots, but were unable to apprehend them in the rugged terrain of Neskaupstadur.

The unidentified assailants were sighted five days later (See "99 Hours: Movie") on Nov6 near the coast of the Fontur land spur. How they traveled to this location is unknown, though the prevailing theory is the assailants entered Lake Lagamjot and followed the Lagadjy river system to the sea near Husey. Others, like Cambridge Military Historian Charles Todd Hill Jr., argue the assailants traveled overland, following a route parallel to Road One as far as Grimsstadir, and crossing the Burfellsheidl on foot to Porsholm and the Langanes peninsula.

Regardless of how they arrived at Fontur, a military altercation began there at 12:33 am, Nov7, with the firing of two F-22 Stinger-V missiles into a fortified cave in the mountains overlooking Fontur. Over the next 55 minutes, 62 Stinger-V missiles, 104 M9 rockets, and 150,000 rounds of .50 caliber ammunition was discharged along the Icelandic coast, but the unidentified assailants continued to evade capture.

Task Force Commander J. Daniel Moore blamed the mission's failure on debilitating weather conditions (Hurricane Albert was forming nearby at the time of the assault), as well as lack of technical weapons support. International weapons bans limited the scope of the engagement to the onboard weapons of the Scandiavian M-455 cutter ship (*Berthrama*) and one Norwegian F-22 fighter jet. These vessels were equipped with heavy ordnance, but—lacking the full military support of any single governing nation—were not fitted with nuclear warheads or payloads larger than four megatons, in accordance with the Global Peace Pact's Declarations of War. (See "Weapons Limitations

Of The Iceland Conflict.")

By 1:22 am., the battle moved to the sea, with the *Berthrama* dropping 512 depth charges along the coast between Fontur and Raufarholn. (This included several controversial discharges within environmentally sensitive Pistifjordur Bay that resulted in an "ecological dead zone" both in the bay and in portions of the Arctic Sea, an environmental disaster that influenced passage of the Save Our Seas Act of 2231.)

Shortly before 2 am, the *Berthrama* issued a distress signal, citing severe damage to its forward hull and rotors and a subsequent explosion in the ship's munitions hold. Historians debate whether the *Berthrama* sank due to a counter-attack or because it ran aground. Accounts from the captain and surviving crew conflict and forensic evidence proved inconclusive. Regardless of the circumstances, the *Berthrama* sank quickly, slipping beneath the Arctic sea at 2:44 am. Four Norwegian soldiers died in the onboard explosion, with 15 injured.

Satellite tracking picked up the unidentified assailants traveling north beneath the Arctic Sea approximately twenty miles from the wreck of the *Berthrama*. Russian, Scandinavian, and Icelandic governments—following a public outcry over the perceived military and ecological disaster—refused to support pursuing the assailants north of the Arctic Circle, leaving the United States military as the sole responder.

Radar tracking was lost on Nov9 after the assailants dropped into the Arctic's Nansen Basin, whose depths were impenetrable with 2222 satellite radar.

*Aftermath*

The warship assigned to follow the unidentified assailants, the *USS Ortiz*, was stationed in Nova Scotia and did not arrive on site until Nov11. It is interesting to note, the *USS Ortiz* was not the closest vessel to the Iceland altercation. Both the *SS Kronk*, docked in Norway, and the M-Class Aquatank

*USS Mary Sue* docked in Northern Ireland, could have reached the site by Nov8, and continued pursuit. But United States Secretary of Defense Amy Patel defended the move, claiming the *USS Ortiz* was better equipped for arctic conditions, a decision which not only led to Patel's dismissal six weeks later, but spawned endless debate among both military historians and conspiracy theorists.

Faced with embarrassment and public unrest, the Icelandic government officially declared the incident—from the Oct30 attack on reporters Viskari and Lyy to the Nov7 sinking of the *Berthrama*—"a catastrophic amalgamation of geologic and weather events." In his book, *The Monsters That Were Never There* (MarrowBooks), Icelandic historian and polymath Nomar Atkinson suggests the assailants never existed, blaming natural phenomena as diverse as sunspots, magnetic polar distortion, freak weather, the aureal borealis, and elk migration to explain the "false appearance" of the robotic soldiers. Atkinson also blamed the resulting military disaster on human error fueled by Commander Moore's personal pride and quest for career advancement.

(See "United States Presidential Election, 2222," "American Revolution, 2222.")

(See "The FreeAir Revolution," "The Stone Revolt," "Wake Up & Breathe!")

(See "The Sixty Mile March," "Battle Of Newark Bay." )

*From* "Mother Maggie In Iceland," *docustream, directed by Seth Brania, November 2225.*

*Robert R:* She touched me! She touched my hand as she passed and I was filled with peace and light. A calm washed over me and I knew everything would be all right.

*Helen M:* We followed the two of them along Road One. They were walking along the beach, out in the surf, waving to people. We drove north past Sturtz, where the road swings out over the beach. There was a big crowd there...people waving signs...singing songs. We saw Mother Maggie and the Rock God approaching and a cheer went up. Everybody hung over the safety rail, reaching out, and Maggie touched as many people as she could. She touched my hand. It was beautiful. Life changing.

*Charles H:* We heard Maggie and the Rock God were at Diamond Beach so my sister, Marie, and I drove up. Marie painted a sign on a piece of poster board that said "Welcome Mother Maggie!" We didn't see them at Diamond Beach so we kept driving north. There was traffic on Road One and we only saw Mother Maggie in the distance. My sister waved her sign out the window, but we were pretty far away.

*Mimi S:* My friends and I had a snowball fight with the Rock God and sang 'Loftsongur' with Mother Maggie beneath the aurora borealis!

*PDU College Thesis submitted by XXXX [name redacted], Social Science 302 : Prof. Burke, May 2294.*

*Anatomy of a Meme: The Mud Monster Snowball Fight Through The Ages*

*Theme*: We've all seen the footage of two camouflaged soldiers in combat armor throwing a snowball at journalists in Iceland. While the legacy of the Iceland Incident has faded along with the chaotic political and social upheaval of the time, the image of a super-sized, super-human making and throwing a snowball at the camera has become ingrained in our global psyche.

Apart from its origins during the Iceland Incident, the "monster with a snowball" image has been used for diverse causes, from promoting political revolution to selling rice cakes. It has been used to terrorize as well as reassure. As a meme on social networks, the Mud Monster snowball photo has never fallen far from public consciousness in the 70-plus years since it was first taken. What is it about this iconic image that continues to fascinate us?

*Background*: The "Mud Monster With A Snowball" photo was captured by photojournalists Raimo Viskari and Olivia Lyy on the afternoon of Oct. 30, 2222, after reports of a possible terrorist attack on the coast of Iceland. Viskari—the cameraman who captured video of the incident and was later injured by the tossed snowball—was informed by local fishermen about a pair of "walking statues" seen near a Hofn pier. Viskari and Lyy descended a hillside near Diamond Beach, Iceland shortly after noon and encountered the two "stone soldiers" emerging from the sea. When the journalists approached the soldiers, they were met with aggressive gestures, culminating in the soldiers attacking the journalists with balls of ice. Viskari suffered a broken collarbone and fractured ribs, while Lyy tore an ACL, helping Viskari escape the attack. Lyy's photography and video equipment was also damaged in the attack, though Viskari and Lyy managed to recover their video storage cells before retreating.

A joint military task force was able to successfully repel the stone soldier terror attack, signaling a prolonged period of global unity and a sense—however false—of increased public safety.

Viskari and Lyy were labeled "war mongering paparazzi" in the wake of the Iceland Incident, but today are considered brave journalists who prevailed in the face of danger. (Evidence of which exists right here on campus; the esteemed Viskari and Lyy Media and Fitness Center bears their name.)

*The Photo:* Taken during peak sunlight hours, Viskari's haunting photograph captures not only the incredulousness of the situation, but the stark beauty of Iceland. The use of a long lens pulls everything into sharp focus: the majesty of the ice floes in the dark sea in the photo's background juxtaposed against the unexpected greens of the tree branches and grass in the foreground. It's easy to see why the soldiers themselves were referred to as "monsters." Their armor (most likely a variation of the now-ubiquitous Talos T244 combat armor) gives the appearance of hardened mud or stone, and is designed to mimic landscape features. Additionally, the soldiers in Viskari's photo are covered with snow fallen from overhead tree branches, giving them a menacing "abominable snowman" appearance. Viskari's complete series of 247 photographs (in addition to Lyy's nearly three-minute video) capture the entire "snowball fight" from start to finish.

But it's Shot #203 that won Viskari the Pulitzer Prize in Journalism and became the iconic image we know today. The photo captures the larger of the two soldiers—an apparent male—approximately .67 seconds after releasing the snowball, which is visible as a blue-black blur in the lower right foreground of the photo. The figure is balanced on its right foot, left kicked out behind, right arm across its upper body; the classic finishing position of a baseball pitcher. The figure's face is tilted toward the camera, following the trajectory of the snowball, and he appears smiling, though experts agree his smile is an effect of lens distortion. Talos combat armor does not allow for traditional facial expressions.

The second soldier stands approximately eight feet behind the "pitcher" and three feet to his right. This soldier is smaller in stature and appears female. Her arms are raised, as if to cover her mouth or lower face, an expression of shock or amazement, but her hands are missing, truncated at the wrist. It's theorized the missing hands are modified weapon ports. Like the male soldier, the smaller female also appears bemused in the photo, possibly laughing, or on the verge of doing so. As PDU Prof. Ed DeLorenta notes, "The posture of the two soldiers resembles 1950s-era Norman Rockwell

Americana rather than a 23rd century terrorist attack. They look like high school sweethearts at a county fair; he's trying to impress his date by knocking the stack of empty milk cans over with his fastball...and, based on her expression, he's succeeding!"

Indeed, the subject matter, composition, and framing of Viskari's photo is extraordinary and helps explain why this image endures long after its function as a news photo ended.

*Initial Impact*: The image was originally published online at 10:45 pm EST, Oct. 30, 2222 by the Washington Kindle, and in print by the Times Tealeaf, at 5:45 the next morning. The photo's headline, "America's Pastime," was not written by Viskari, but by an uncredited member of the Kindle editorial staff. The headline stirred controversy by referencing both the troubles of Major League Baseball (which was in the midst of a players' strike that canceled the 2222 World Series), as well as criticizing American enforcement of Iceland's borders. The soldiers in Viskari's photo wear similar combat armor to US troops during The Battle Of Newark Bay six months prior, and public mistrust of the military and the administration of President Ipson was high.

Some political historians claim the release of the "Monster Snowball Fight" photo a mere 74 hours before polls opened for the 2222 presidential election, was a "last straw" for President Ipson, who lost in a landslide to Maggot-backed candidate Grant Layton. However, algorithmetrics predicted Layton's victory more than a week prior to the publication of Viskari's photo.

In the hours before polls opened, President Ipson's supporters attempted to repurpose Viskari's photo for their own campaign, recaptioning the image with the slogan, "A vote for Layton is a vote for a monster." This referred to the ghastly, stone-like armor worn by the revolutionary "Rock God" at Newark Bay. Instead of swaying undecided voters, the "vote for a monster" campaign backfired, with many believing President Ipson was mocking the female soldier in the photo. Members of a fringe religious cult—the Maggots, popular in 2222 but nearly gone today—believed the figure in the background was not a soldier at all, but the animated stone statue of Margaret "Maggie" Ottomeyer, the Maggots' spiritual matriarch.

The impact of Viskari's photo on the 2222 Presidential race was sensational, but may not have influenced the election as significantly as once thought. As Prof. Burke notes, "President Ipson lost the election when she won the Battle of Newark Bay." Viskari's photo, however, continued to make an impact, as it does to this day.

*The Memes:* The Snowball Monster photo was first used as a meme during Ipson's unsuccessful "Vote For A Monster" campaign, less than 24 hours after its initial release. Since then, the Snowball Monster has been used in a variety of notable ways.

*Caption*: Spray Her With Your Massive Load!

*Note*: Image altered to show the male soldier with an oversized, ejaculating penis.

*Intent*: Image used by Morningstar Products to sell male sexual enhancement products, 2224-2227.

*Caption*: Throw A Strike With Lucky Strike!

*Intent*: Used by Phillip Morris Inc. to promote a line of transdermal nicotine cream, 2231.

*Caption*: Baseball Rocks!

*Intent*: Used as a promotional poster for the International Baseball League Inaugural Season, 2236.

(*Note*: The IBL used this image again a decade later on a commemorative collector's cup to promote its interdivisional playoffs, with the caption, "Stone Cold Warriors, 2246.")

*Caption*: Bring On A Snow Day!

*Intent*: Scholastic digital poster, grades K-12, 2245.

*Caption*: Eat My Balls!

*Intent*: Promotional campaign for Organic Vegiballs, 2249.

*Caption*: War Has Many Faces

*Intent*: United States Army recruitment poster, 2252.

*Caption*: Monsters Are Real!

*Intent*: Entrance poster to ConspiraCon 2255, Exxon Arena, Little Rock, AR.

*Caption*: It's Funny Until Someone Gets Hurt!

*Intent*: Advertisement for Sparta's Winter Funland, Nome, AK, 2256.

*Caption*: Precision Performance

*Intent*: Advertisement, Precision Impact Equipment, Akron, OH / Seoul, Korea, 2265-2271.

*Caption*: American-Made Monsters

*Intent*: Image accompanying Washington Kindle editorial criticizing embargo policies in the Middle East, 2279.

*Caption*: Don't Be A Bully! Intimidating others just isn't cool!

*Intent*: Public dormitory signs at Exmont Prep School, Hartford, ME, 2284.

*Caption*: Chill! Frosty Max 2-Fers All Summer Long!

*Intent*: Max Convenience Store Promotion, 2290.

*Caption*: Revenge Is Best Served Cold

*Intent*: Marketing campaign, Johnson & Sons HVAC, Bonita Springs, FL, 2292.

*Caption*: My Hero!

*Note*: Image altered to show male soldier crushing a cockroach with a wooden mallet instead of throwing a snowball.

*Intent*: Digital advertisement, PTK Pest Control, Ottowa, Canda, 2293.

*Caption*: Sluts Love Hard Ballers!

*Intent*: Image used by Ramco Corp to promote a line of male sexual enhancement supplements, 2294.

# 11

## *Mudspeak V*

Fuck Iceland.

Sure, it's a beautiful little country, but our brief stay there was a nightmare. Admittedly, I made a dumb mistake. I should have kept east and walked through the Greenland Rift Basin. Stayed low, deep. Instead I led Maggie along the Mid-Atlantic Ridge all the way to the Barents Shelf. Stupid, thinking we could slip between Iceland and the Faroe Islands without being noticed.

Let's be honest, I *wanted* to be noticed. I wanted to see human faces and look at the sun one last time. Maybe it was staring at those strange starfish faces, but I longed to see a real human being again before Maggie and I took our last dive into the deep dark.

But I was careless. I knew we were getting close to shore. The currents grew stronger; and, before I knew it, my head broke the waterline, battered by wind and waves.

Maggie and I emerged on Diamond Beach, Iceland, in the dark and snow. The sand was gritty and jet-black, direct-deposited from volcanoes a few miles inland. Hunks of ice, some the size of boulders, rode the violent surf alongside

Maggie and I. One shattered against the back of my head and I saw stars. Frozen chunks dotted the beach, polished smooth by saltwater, glittering diamonds among patches of snow, glass sculptures against black sand and howling wind, surreal and beautiful.

Reykivik lay to the east, so we stayed west, crossing Road One into Vatnajokull National Park. I figured we'd climb the glacier and walk northwest across Iceland. It couldn't be more than a couple hundred miles, and staying inland would keep us out of sight.

But climbing a glacier is a bitch in the best of conditions. Doing it during a blizzard is impossible. Maggie and I were too heavy; we kept sinking into snow drifts and Maggie's lack of hands made it hard to climb out. We were literally freezing, too. I felt my insides crystalizing. If we stopped moving for more than a moment, we might never move again. We'd frack apart and lie in pieces until the glacial ice melted and carried us away, which might be never. Tempting as it sounded, that wasn't our end.

We made better time underwater—it was warmer too—so we returned to Diamond Beach, walking out past the breakers where the footing was better.

A pod of orca circled us as we walked, the lead bull curious enough to nudge Maggie with its snout. They kept their distance but traveled alongside us for several miles before heading off to deeper waters. The harp seals, sea lions, and penguins followed a similar pattern; investigate but don't get too close.

Narwhals were the exception. A pod circled Maggie and I, bumping and nudging us. We tried to shoo them way, but they became increasingly curious…and aggressive. One charged me, its spear bouncing off my neck, and suddenly they all charged, more than a dozen adults, spikes breaking against our bodies as Maggie and I held each other. They didn't stop until the last narwhal snapped its tusk on Maggie's back and swam off. Thanks for the warm welcome, assholes. Fuck narwhals.

It snowed for three days, a storm of biblical proportions. The wind died down after Day Two, but it snowed heavily for another 26 hours. By then Maggie and I had made it to the harbor town of Hofn.

The ground rose quickly beneath our feet—I think we hit a sandbar—and both Maggie and I poked our heads above water. We stood 50 yards from the mouth of a marina, wooden fishing boats from another generation bobbed gently in their slips, knocking against the dock with the creak of ropes and the squeal of rubber bumpers. The sun rose behind us, the first rays of the day touching my shoulder like the hand of an old friend, casting the fishing village in a haze of gold, turning the glacier behind it a dazzling shade of blue. But what struck me most were the trees on the hillside. The blazing shades of orange, red, and brown looked so much like the autumn hills of Northern New Jersey, so much like the woods around our townhouse, the one Sarah and I'd shared all too briefly, the sight would've taken my breath away if I had any to give. Maggie seemed equally affected; she'd grown up in woods like these. She put her arm around my back and we stared at the sunlit foliage until we heard a gasp behind us.

Two fishermen in a small wooden sailboat had drifted up. Both men had beards, one gray, one black, and wore wool caps and heavy coats. They gazed at us, eyes wide. When I turned and waved, they both screamed, and I feared they'd fall off their boat.

"Hello!" I called out, but it sounded like a bag of sandpaper and bricks clacking around. Maggie and I had been underwater for nearly six months, and my public speaking voice, shitty at the best of times, was completely shot.

Black Beard shouted back in a language I couldn't understand. Icelandic? Finnish? Russian? Who knows? I kept waving like an idiot and Maggie joined me. Gray Beard grabbed his arm at the wrist, said something to Black Beard, and pointed to Maggie. Black Beard snapped our picture with his camera-phone as they floated past us into the marina.

Neither of us wanted to duck back underwater, even though we knew we should. The sun rose bright and the shoreline looked magnificent, the blazing trees, the glorious glacier; Iceland was heaven fallen to earth, especially after six months walking the ocean floor. When we saw a strip of black sand beach a mile north of the marina, we couldn't resist going ashore.

Three feet of fresh snow blanketed the beach, except for where the surf had washed it away. We walked north along the ocean's edge, where the black sand packed dense enough to support our footsteps, the sun on our faces, drying us, warming us for the first time in forever. I tried to hold Maggie's hand while we walked, forgetting she didn't have any. We locked arms at the elbows instead.

Road One ran close to the ocean, less than a dozen yards away. Snow plows rumbled past, honking long and loud. We waved. A while later a truck passed and beeped at us. We waved again. More trucks, more beeping. By afternoon, pockets of people stood along Road One, perched precariously atop the mountains of roadside snow, shouting, waving, and taking video. Maggie and I waved back. Iceland was friendly!

Day turned to night and the sky filled with swirling streaks of green and blue, shocking wisps of red, like the universe was cut and bleeding. It felt like the celestial fireworks were just for Maggie and I, though, of course, the aurora borealis was for anyone who ventured this close to the arctic circle.

We walked all night, the stars so bright, my heart ached. I'd forgotten how much I'd missed stars.

The sun rose even more brilliantly the following morning, and it looked like another fine day for travel until a military jet circled overhead. I couldn't tell what country it belonged to, but it really didn't matter. Bad news either way. It followed us for about ten minutes and flew south.

People lined Road One. It looked like an outdoor music festival: campfires, applause, and a mix of American and Icelandic flags. I saw a sign that read, "Welcome Blessed Mother!" Maggie waved to the people along the road and they roared back their approval and adoration. Maggie was a hit in Iceland. I should have expected as much. She was a hit everywhere, even places she'd never been and would never go.

But the crowds made me nervous, the fanatic energy reminiscent of the maniacs who had followed Ghee and I to Newark, eyes wide and wild with the madness of worship. I might be a savior, but Maggie was a god, the Blessed Mother. She waved her stumps and the people on shore cried out with undying love and devotion. It was creepy.

Road One swept out over the beach and the crowd was right on top of us, reaching down from above, hands outstretched, craving our touch. Maggie obliged as many as she could. I high-fived a few kids and ignored the adults. There were too many, too close. It seemed like every living soul in Iceland had come out to see us. A half-dozen fishing boats sailed beside us, but at least they kept a respectful distance beyond the breakers.

Finally, Road One hooked inland and the beach gave way to rocky bluffs, cutting Maggie off from her adoring fans. We waved good-bye and the crowd cheered as we slipped beneath the waves again.

We walked arm-in-arm. Maggie seemed happy and that

made me happy. Maybe I overreacted. People loved Maggie and I shouldn't begrudge her that adoration, even if it frightened me. I simply wasn't used to that much love.

Black boulders cluttered the seabed, slowing our progress. We hooked back toward the shore, seeking better footing. We followed a cliff face, finally emerging in the early afternoon near a grassy patch of shore. The grass felt good beneath our feet, so good that Maggie laid down and stretched out in the sunshine, her body sinking several inches into the soggy earth. I stretched out beside her, sinking into mud like a feather bed, sunspots dancing before my eyes. Maggie touched my arm. I don't think I'd ever felt more at peace, lying in the sun, feeling one with grass and earth, listening to the ocean lap against stone. It sounded like a faucet was running in the distance, someone drawing a bath in the world's biggest tub. It was a waterfall, probably more than one. There were waterfalls all over Iceland, though Maggie and I had yet to see any.

Heavy footsteps disrupted our peaceful afternoon. Two jackasses bundled in parkas, one carrying a video camera and tripod, tramped downhill through the snow and trees. Maggie waved to the two figures and the one without the camera waved back. But the motion caused the waving figure to fall and slide down the hillside, landing hard against the base of a skinny tree. The force of the impact shook the upper tree branches, tumbling snow down on Maggie and I, burying us up to our waists. We looked at each other with surprise and burst out laughing. Sea and sky, grass and snow—today was a feast for the senses! Maggie tossed an armful of snow in my face and I did the same to her.

The cameraman—it was surely a man, I saw a wooly mustache—set up his tripod twenty feet away and started filming. I waved, but the cameraman didn't wave back. I mugged for the camera, making elephant ears with my hands beside my head. The cameraman had no reaction. His partner (a woman maybe) extracted herself from the base of the tree and came limping down the hillside toward her partner.

Maggie waved too, but the photographers just stared at us like we were a Monkey House exhibit at the zoo. So rude. I made a snowball and lobbed it at the camera. I missed the camera but hit the cameraman. I must have thrown it harder than I intended, because the cameraman dropped to the ground and started screaming, clutching his shoulder. *Come on, man! It was just a snowball!* It took several minutes for his partner to help him to his feet and several more for the pair to retreat, leaving their expensive camera behind. I tossed another snowball and successfully knocked the tripod over. Then Maggie and I climbed back into the sea.

We resurfaced a couple of hours later, less than a hundred yards from Road One. The crowds were gone. Only a lone police cruiser remained, lights twirling, siren off. Maggie waved. An officer got out and fired two shots at us with a rifle, but missed both times. He got back in his truck and drove south.

That night was quiet. Maggie and I strolled the beach below the aurora borealis again, arm-in-arm. But by morning there was a military boat following us. I recognized the cannons and gun turrets from a mile away.

Maggie and I slipped back beneath the waves.

Explosions started behind us, but before long they were all around, an underwater thunderstorm. Maggie and I took cover in a deep ravine. The charges were set to explode very close to the sea bottom and the shockwave shredded the seafloor…not even clams were safe. The explosions moved north and we followed the path of destruction. When the explosions returned, we hid again. It only appeared to be one ship attacking us, but it certainly didn't lack for munitions. The depth charge barrage lasted throughout the day and well into the night. It would have continued if we hadn't come ashore in Gerpir.

The barren strip of beach ran along a stretch of tall cliffs on the easternmost point of Iceland, so far east, in fact, Maggie and I couldn't avoid running into it as we circled the island. The sun was high when we took the beach. We had a couple of hours before the warship found us. Once it did, it didn't waste any time using the .50-caliber gun mounted on its stern. The shells stung like hell, but I knew we were in big trouble when Stinger missiles exploded against the cliffs, leaving smoking craters in the ancient stone. Maggie and I didn't stand a chance against that kind of firepower. We found a path leading up into the forest. We startled a couple of hikers—they screamed and ran the other way when they saw us—but we were able to get out of firing range.

Damn. I'd wanted to round the tip of Gerpir and head out to the open sea, dodge depth charges until we made the Arctic. Nansen Basin was closest and had good depth. Now we were trapped on land. We'd be lucky to make it off Iceland in one piece.

We continued west into the foothills of Neskaupstadur, climbing through forest so dense and desolate, it could've been prehistoric. It rained, but I didn't mind. The water dripping through the leafy canopy washed us clean, and ground runoff pointed the quickest route up the mountain.

We climbed for a day and a half. The mountain finally leveled off into a surprisingly lush meadow surrounding a long, thin lake. We followed the lake shore north for miles. The sound of helicopters chased us back beneath the tree cover. I didn't want to get back in the water because we were making good progress on land, but a herd of elk felt otherwise.

The herd tracked us for miles, two males with antlers four feet wide, and four females. Maggie shooed them away, but the males took an aggressive stance, stomping their feet. I shouted and ran at the herd. The elk bolted into the forest as one. I turned triumphantly to Maggie, but the two males suddenly burst from the trees, charging at full speed. Maggie and I braced for impact, but the elk lifted us off our feet with their massive antlers and tossed us into the lake. Maggie and I stood in knee-deep water, watching in disbelief as the two stags snorted and huffed on the shore. We laughed. First the narwhal, now this. Fuck you, Iceland! I flipped the elk my middle finger and Maggie doubled over. Whatever. If we could walk the bottom of the ocean, we could walk the bottom of a lake. No big deal.

But something big and hungry lived at the bottom of the lake. We didn't encounter it until we traveled out to the deep water in the middle. I sensed something following us, but didn't see anything, even though the water was remarkably clear. A shadow moved among the grasses. An eel? A crocodile? Did crocs live this far north? I tapped Maggie's shoulder and pointed; we should walk closer to shore.

We didn't get far before the creature struck, biting my waist and crushing me in its jaws. I couldn't tell you what it was. Neither could Maggie, and she watched the whole thing happen. The creature had a croc's head and the body of a massive eel. I couldn't see the end of its tail. It picked me up in its jaws and shook me until my teeth rattled. Damn, it was strong! I'm no lightweight, even underwater. The creature dropped me to the mucky lake bottom and turned on Maggie, knocking her flat.

Enough of this bullshit. I punched the creature's scaly side. It spun and lashed out, mouth opened as wide as a tunnel, all pale pink and yellow teeth. I grabbed it by the jaws as it lunged, snapped my wrists, and folded its head backwards on itself. Even underwater I heard the crackle of breaking bones. Blood clouded the water and I let the dead thing sink to the lake bottom to rot. Sorry, dead thing. I helped Maggie out of the muck and we continued north.

I lost track of how long we traveled. The lake emptied into a shallow river, which grew deeper and swifter the farther we walked. We rode the current over a waterfall, laughing and tumbling until we landed in a clear, cold pool of water. We swam for a while in the secluded pond, tall pines towering over us, making us feel small and safe. Perhaps we should have stayed, laid down beneath the waterfall and let the pounding water erode our features, wash us away a grain at a time. Instead we dug deep and found the strength to carry on. So stupid.

Our river walk was peaceful, except for hiding from helicopters several times a day. Sometimes we kept our heads above water, other times we completely submerged and let the river currents quicken our pace. Five days, many miles, several forks, and two waterfalls later, we reached the sea. The river's final push ran through a thin gorge in the Langanges peninsula, terminating at a bay near a fishing village…if a dozen homes, a general store, and a boat dock qualifies as a village.

The warship waited just off shore. Maybe they saw us coming, tracked us as we walked arm-in-arm downriver, or tumbled over a waterfall. Did they spy on us while we swam in the pond? I felt violated, like something secret and sacred was stolen from Maggie and I. I marched into the bay, determined to kick some ass, Maggie by my side.

The ship fired into the hill behind us, blowing apart a copse of trees we had stood in thirty minutes earlier. Guess they hadn't spotted us yet. The missiles didn't stop; the assault continued for fifteen minutes, hundreds of Stingers whistling overhead, exploding against the hillside in bursts of flame, earth, and smoke. One of the missiles sailed off course and took out half of the homes in the fishing village.

When the assault stopped, thick clouds of black smoke drifted through the burning village like wraiths. The ship moved north and attacked a cliff a mile up the coast, firing Stingers into the stone until the cliff face crumbled into the sea. Christ, their intel was shit! Did they think we were hiding in a cave? How could we even reach that location? My initial anger gave way to fear, an unease akin to watching a toddler waving a loaded handgun around. Somebody was bound to get hurt.

Maggie and I ran for open water. The bay was only as deep as our shoulders and our exposed heads felt like easy targets. Maybe we should crawl out to sea. The eastern sky swirled gray-black, and I hoped we'd get lucky and weather would cancel the attack.

A fighter jet swooped low overhead, the roar deafening, the pressure wave left in its wake powerful enough to knock Maggie and I off our feet. We landed on our butts on the bottom of the bay. We'd been found. I expected depth charges to turn the bay into a fiery cauldron at any moment. But the jet flew north and joined the warship attacking the stone cliffs. Dangerous morons…innocent cliffs.

Maggie and I tried to slip past the attack and follow the magnetic pull north. But the ocean currents beyond Fontur point were unexpectedly swift, picking Maggie and I up and tossing us like rag dolls, sweeping us north toward the attack. We dug our heels into the soft ocean bottom, fighting for every step we took. Despite the currents, we made progress… until the bombing started.

Depth charges churned the water to steaming foam filled with dead fish. Maggie and I took cover beneath a rocky ledge, chasing away a frightened eel, burying ourselves in the sand like flounder. Two charges exploded nearby, driving us deeper into the earth and blanketing us with a fresh layer of sand and stone. Maggie and I held each other close. When the bombing moved north, we dug ourselves out.

Grit and sand clouded the water, limiting our visibility to a few feet. I couldn't see the ship but heard explosions behind us. The rocky ground rose steeply beneath us, forcing us to climb hand over hand (or stump over stump for Maggie).

Even when my head broke the surface it took me a minute to realize I was above water. The black sky poured rain down in a solid sheet. A wave covered me, and when it passed, Maggie and I stood in the swell, looking around for the ship.

It found us first, firing red tracer streaks over our heads, less than a thousand yards behind us. Fifty-cal slugs pelted my chest. That shit hurt!

Maggie and I dove beneath the waves, sinking to the bottom of the ridge. Stone blew apart above our heads. The ship bottom loomed over us like a black cloud, apparently unaware of the reef below. A wave swelled and the ship bottom nearly touched the seabed.

When the sea lifted the ship, Maggie and I walked beneath it. Maggie stood on my shoulders and I grabbed her ankles for support. She couldn't quite reach the ship's bottom, so I stood on a rock, and when the waves brought the vessel close, Maggie shoved it toward the reef. It wasn't much, but the storm helped. The captain sensed the danger and fired the ship's engines, but I carried Maggie to a higher rock and she gave the ship another shove. The big vessel scrapped against jagged stone with a screech of metal.

Some total asshat, maybe the ship's captain, deployed two depth charges near the bow. Maybe they wanted to flush Maggie and I out, but all they did was blow a hole the size of a garage door in the side of the ship. Underwater explosions have a water hammer effect that hits like a bulldozer, and Maggie and I sailed a thousand yards through open water and half that again sliding to a stop on the ocean floor. We wound up buried under a ton of sand and stone, digging out of our own graves again. Maggie's front was charred black, though her back remained stark white. Same for me, though I'm gray to begin with.

The ship exploded again, this time from within. The depth charges must have ignited ammunition in the ship's hold. Christ, how could they have anything left? The entire hull blew apart, causing the ship to tilt crazily in the water. Wreckage spilled off the deck, sinking to the sea bottom. The burnt bodies sunk slower than the metal guns, and I was reminded once again of the wonderful power of aquatic buoyancy.

My ears rung. My whole body rung, vibrating with the subsonic frequency of the blast. The shockwave must have killed everything in the sea for miles. My first instinct was to help the survivors. Maggie took two steps toward the wreck before I laid my hand on her shoulder and waved her back.

We walked north, constantly looking over our shoulders for ships and submarines. Blasted fish carcasses filled the water for the first couple of miles. After that, the ocean was eerily lifeless. We didn't see anything but bait fish and harp seals until the next day. The arctic basins were at least two days away, probably more like three. They'd send more ships, more bombs. The attacks wouldn't stop until we were destroyed. Why couldn't they leave us alone? Because I wrecked their stupid warehouse and ocean cables? Because I refused to let them lock up Maggie? Did they hate Maggie because of who she was, what she represented, or some combination of the two? Did they *really* hate her (and me), or were we simply loose ends that needed to be tied up, question marks to be erased, anomalies that didn't fit their story? Maggie and I just wanted to die like normal people, not martyrs.

We scrubbed each other with sea sponges until the blackened char washed away. Maggie was so dazzling white, so beautiful, she was hard to look at. I heard boat engines, but they were far behind us. On the third day we hitched a ride on the backs of baleen whales and crossed into the Arctic.

# 12

## *Second Final Report VI*

*GeoTalk Today,* "Do Stones Dream of Sand?" *Professor Seth Watson, Chemloco Annex Lecture Series, September 2242.*

Stones dream of metamorphosis. All rocks are born igneous, spit out by the molten core of the earth like a wad of phlegm or chewing tobacco. They cool to basalt and slowly weather away. That's the life of igneous rock…slowly disappearing, bit by bit, molecule by molecule, until you're nothing but dust, a pile of sand at best. Then you lie around with the rest of the sediment and wait for heat and pressure—the weight of death and rot pressing down from above—to make you whole again.

The only hope rock has is metamorphosis.

Metamorphosis offers change on a molecular level, an entire structural transformation from the inside out. Heat and pressure, sure, but this is chemical too, the black market exchange of protons and electrons, swapping magnetic polarity, mixing it up in inconceivable ways, forever new, always becoming, becoming, becoming.

They all dream of changing. They want to be different from what they are. In that way, humans and rocks are similar.

*Leave a comment below:*

*Luke W wrote:* With all due respect, your "dreaming stone" theory is total dog shit. I know when people assign human characteristics to animals it's called anthropomorphism. ("The cat is sad…the dog is smiling…") I'm not sure what it's called when people assign human emotions to rocks and stones, but I know it's bullshit. Rocks don't dream… blockhead!

*Too Much Time's* "Cryptid and Chimera Tree Of Life," *hosted by Peter Fallon, speaker Seth Watson, WestaCo University, August 2240.*

**The Man Of Stone: The Evolution of Bigfoot**

Good evening. Thank you all for coming and supporting WestaCo University. I'm Seth Watson (*applause*). Thank you. Please, we've got a packed house tonight and I want everyone to get comfortable. Can you hear me okay in the back? Okay, good.

Tales of super-humans are as old as humans themselves. No doubt, the first man to stand upright likely dreamed of being taller, bigger, faster, stronger. We see who we are and project whom we want to be, whom we wish we were.

That's why we created a cryptid to stand in for our superman desires. Bigfoot. The Yeti. Sasquatch. The Wild Man of Europe. These are our projections of primal superiority.

The Man of Stone is the next evolution of our mythical superman. He's lost his primitive fur. Why? Perhaps as a result of environmental pollution or a reaction to harmful electro-magnetic signals. But maybe the Man of Stone is hairless because he is an *evolved* Bigfoot—hairless and larger-brained like the human hominids that branched off from apes millions of years go. His soft skin has turned to unbreakable stone. He can't be hurt. He doesn't die. He's invincible, powerful, unstoppable…

*Cryptid and Chimera Family Tree Exhibit, Allman Financial Holdings, March 12-31, 2245.*

*Enjoy the exhibit? Please leave a comment below:*

*Ted wrote:* I'd like to personally thank TooMuchTime for creating this cryptid and chimera family tree. It's a very beautiful gramgraph—electric, vivid, and engaging. But, as a molecular biologist, I take umbrage with one small detail in the branch concerning the Stone Man of New Jersey. While I see similarities between the Stone Man and the legends of Frankenstein's monster and Bigfoot, I don't see a direct link like the one depicted on your cryptid tree. Instead, I see this creature as a clear descendant of the Jewish golem. It's made from river clay to protect and avenge. These are essential elements of the Stone Man mythos that are missing from Frankenstein and Yeti stories. The Stone Man is an avenger, a spiritual hero…at least he started out that way.

Respectfully,

Theodore Schimtz

*Allan wrote*: More like TheoBORE SHITS! This guy is a pretentious ass…TooMuchTime rules!

*Rebecca wrote*: Duh! It's all FAKE, dude! The Stone Man isn't a descendant of Frankenstein and Bigfoot because NONE OF THAT SHIT IS REAL! Christ, this board pisses me off! I get so goddamn angry at people that I want to kick my dog…and I love my dog! I should kick people! Fucking fucktards!

*MSU wrote:* There's an alien space ship under the North Pole that controls everything. That much is true.

*Music gram review, Mamma Kaiju's "Sea Walk," Musicologist Arnie Moore, December 2239.*

In Mamma Kaiju's latest viral gram, singer Mojo Lansdale emerges from an underwater sand dune. He is joined by bandmates Brian Ob and Roach Clip, trekking through sand and sediment as high as their chests. They kick their feet, sending up enormous plumes of sand and grit that, at times, obscure the band's journey across the sea floor. The sand is filled with bones; skeletons and skulls float in erratic orbits around the band members. Mojo impatiently brushes the floating bones away. He's in a hurry. Indeed, the entire band appears late for a meeting or performance, hustling across the sea floor, plowing through the past, literally, scattering old bones, fossils, and relics. (Mid-way through the gram, Roach Clip kicks over an old wooden chest, scattering gold coins across the sea floor.) The calm, settled past is churned into a state of upheaval by Mamma Kaiju's passing. Things will settle back down, but will never be the same again, the natural order forever disrupted.

*Please leave a comment below!*

*Mary wrote:* This gram reminds of my friend Petra's Lunar Quince. We danced to this song all night long, waiting for Earthrise, but Petra got into a fight with somebody so the party broke up early. I like Mamma Kaiju. I had such a crush on Mojo!

*Pat wrote:* Brian Ob is the shit! G.O.A.T guitarist!

*Manny ED wrote:* Mamma Kaiju sucked then and they suck now. I'm glad Roach OD'd. This band was cursed for making shitty music and stupid grams.

*Geoff wrote:* Somebody needs anger management! Chill out, bro. It's just a band. Agree to disagree.

*Manny ED wrote:* I agree…to skull-fuck your corpse.

*Geoff wrote:* Mamma Kaiju isn't for you. You need smooth jazz.

*Manny ED wrote:* I need to fuck your asshole to death, scumbag!

*Holly Y wrote:* As an archeology student, I find this Mamma Kaiju video interesting because it's semi-accurate. See how the bones down near their feet are like, super old fossils, while the ones up by their chests look fresh? That's called geologic strata.

*Mark Z wrote:* Uh, Holly…were you home-schooled?

*BRB wrote:* …by monkeys?

*Gail F wrote:* Everybody's missing the point…where was Mamma Kaiju going in that video? North. To meet the spaceship. Just like Mother Maggie and The Man of Stone. Clearly, Mamma Kaiju were prophets.

*HR Grease wrote:* I was Brian Ob's guitar tech on the Mercy's For Fools tour. Trust me, those guys were NOT prophets…just mean drunks.

*Interview with Senator Cara Lewis by NewsMakers, March 2242.*

NM: We're coming up on the twenty year anniversary of the Battle Of Newark Bay. You claim you were there.

LEWIS: I *was* there. I know everybody *says* they were there, but I really was. I saw Ghee Dorfhouse's murder. I saw the fences fall. I didn't stand and fight with the Maggots. I was there with other students from Chemolco College.

NM: You didn't fight in the Battle Of Newark Bay?

LEWIS: No. Absolutely not. I was there to protest peacefully. I think most people were. But once Ghee was killed all hell broke loose.

NM: Did you know Ghee Dorfhouse personally?

LEWIS: We went to Franz Rock High School together.

NM: Which of the many artistic interpretations of historic events—the Sixty Mile March and the Battle of Newark Bay—do you most enjoy and which is the most accurate?

LEWIS: Oh, gosh…none of them are accurate! Well, I shouldn't say that. Mae Marcenti's docugram was very good. But even that…it's one person's interpretation of events, one person's vision of history. Even if it's well-researched like Marcenti's work, it's still not the whole story. It can't be. The truth is just too vast to be contained by historians, or filmmakers, or anyone else.

NM: Even elected officials?

LEWIS: Especially elected officials! We see politicians write themselves into history every election year, don't we? They tie themselves to nostalgia to get votes. It's…gross!

NM: So you don't like any of the films, plays, poems, pictograms…

LEWIS: You see, the problem, quite honestly, is that people see *me* as that person. Sometimes I think people like the fake Cara Lewis more than the real thing. It's…well, let's say it makes working with certain members of congress difficult at times.

NM: Are you familiar with the film, "Cara and Ghee: A Love Story," currently in production?

LEWIS: Yes, but I can't…I don't want to talk about it. I don't want to give these false perceptions any more credence.

NM: Even if you don't like the way you're depicted, you have to admit the film has increased your Q-rating tremendously and that can't be a bad thing for your election campaign.

LEWIS: Yes, but I want people to know they're voting for me—the real me—and not the fictional person.

NM: What's the difference?

LEWIS: Uh…pardon?

NM: How is the real Cara Lewis different from the one depicted in "Cara and Ghee" and other artistic representations?

LEWIS: My record speaks for itself.

NM: Did you love Ghee Dorfhouse?

LEWIS: I think we all loved Ghee Dorfhouse for standing up to the establishment the way she did, for sacrificing herself, for sparking the changes this country so desperately needed at the time.

NM: But did you love her personally…physically?

LEWIS: I don't talk about my romantic life and I'm not about to start now. But…look, I'll say this. I *did* love Ghee Dorfhouse personally. I still do and always will. She shaped who I am today and knowing her…knowing her was a gift that I will cherish forever.

*Excerpt from* CARA & GHEE: A LOVE STORY, *written and directed by Oliver Jones, LoveStream Networks Inc, January, 2243.*

Cara grieves as Ghee's casket is lowered into the ground. Tasha tries awkwardly to comfort Cara. When Cara lifts her head, her cheeks are wet, but her jaw is set. She has the same fierce look in her eye that Ghee had during the Sixty Mile March.

*MONTAGE: Cara transforms from student activist to public servant.*

CUT: Cara wearing a Layton/Vanhoven t-shirt, cheering in the student center with other supporters as President-Elect Grant Layton gives his acceptance speech.

CUT: Shot of President Loren Ipson hanging her head in a roomful of dejected supporters.

CUT: Cara in cap and gown, giving a speech at her college graduation.

CUT: Cara in a business suit, entering a boardroom and shaking hands with people around a conference table.

CUT: Cara in a courtroom, wearing glasses, hair in a bun, taking notes.

CUT: Cara holding a golden shovel, surrounded by people in suits, during a groundbreaking photo op.

CUT: Cara behind a mound of paperwork in a cluttered office.

CUT: Cara marching along protesters with "Clean Air, Clean Water 4 All!" banner.

CUT: Cara speaking before the House of Reps.

CUT: Cara smiling and talking with a group of people at a park, giving a speech and gesturing emphatically.

CUT: Cara beneath an umbrella in the same park, in the pouring rain, fewer people, giving a speech and gesturing emphatically.

CUT: Cara speaking before the Senate.

CUT: Cara, older, speaks before an auditorium full of people. She makes a point, steps back from the podium, and the crowd cheers. Several people hold digital signs that say Lewis for Senate.

CUT: Cara smiling, speaking at podium covered in balloons.

CUT: Cara questioning executive at Senate hearing.

CUT: Perp walk of executives.

CUT: Cara planting trees with enviro-group.

CUT: Cara scooping plastic from ocean with ocean cleanup group.

CUT: Cara questioning more men in suits at Senate hearing.

CUT: Perp walk of men in suits.

CUT: (*slo-mo*): Political rally. People holding signs "Lewis/ Waksbloom 2242" and "Lewis for President." Cara steps up to the podium (lens flare). Crowd cheering.

*Professor Randolph Pääskysaari, Human Studies, "Cara & Ghee: A Truthful Lecture" TARGMart Notable Speaker Series, May 2299.*

It's true Ghee Dorfhouse and Cara Lewis were both students at Franz Rock High School during the year 2217, but there is no evidence they were friends or that they even knew each other. Cara Lewis was a senior when Ghee Dorfhouse was an incoming freshman. The student population of Franz Rock High School at the time was 1,489 students. There is no reason to believe, considering their social backgrounds and educational histories, that Lewis and Dorfhouse would have had much opportunity to interact. Cara Lewis was an honor student taking AP classes. The second half of her senior year, Cara secured an internship at the Sussex County Clerk's Office to study municipal and county law—a job which undoubtedly influenced her decision to later pursue a law degree. Cara Lewis' senior internship took her out of Franz Rock High School from January through June 2218, the rest of the school term, further decreasing her chances of interacting with Ghee Dorfhouse.

Ghee Dorfhouse was a troubled student. Her freshman year at Franz Rock High School was her first in a public educational facility. Prior to that, Ghee Dorfhouse was home-schooled by her parents, Jasmine Stickler-Dorfhouse and Lucas Dorfhouse, both of whom were strict Stone Earthers, a faction of the Maggot religious sect. Ghee Dorfhouse and her mother were direct descendants of Maggie Ottomeyer, the inspiration for the famous statue. Or, depending on which version of the statue's origin you believe, they may be *actual relatives* of the Maggie statue.

(*Pause for laughter.*)

Ghee, as you may know, is a truncation of the name Maggie, which, of course, is itself an abbreviated version of the name Margaret. At the very least Ghee Dorfhouse shared her great, great grandmother's name if not her DNA.

(*Pause for laughter.*)

Like many Stone Earthers at the time, the Dorfhouses lived "off the grid." Jasmine and Lucas moved to a rural section of New Jersey supposedly to be closer to the Maggie statue, which, at the time, stood in Franz Rock Memorial Gardens. The region was home to many Stone Earthers as well as as other Maggot followers. The different Maggot religious sects clashed, sometimes violently, prompting government-regulated religious safe zones in and around Franz Rock and throughout the Targmart territories. But the safe zones were often disregarded and terrorist attacks—including the Walmart Bombing of 2184, the Lyn Awakening of 2192, and the 2195 Fly Swarm—sadly became the norm. Some called Franz Rock a (*air quotes*) "modern Jerusalem" because so many different religious sects claimed the area as the birthplace of their religion, but few agreed on its governance.

This was the world Ghee Dorfhouse grew up in, a region rife with religious tension and violence. Her parents were both devout Stone Earthers, each arrested twice for protesting at Maggot community rallies and worship services. In 2221, Jasmine and Lucas Dorfhouse were arrested for vandalizing Maggie, chipping away the stone infant Maggie held in her arms for more than 100 years. The Dorfhouses believed the baby was "unclean," according to their interpretation of Stone Earth scripture. The vandalization of Maggie caused additional violence among the Maggot factions and President Loren Ipson was forced to confiscate the statue in the interest of public safety in December 2221.

In a way, Ghee Dorfhouse was a (*air quotes*) "born rebel." In addition to her parents' extreme religious beliefs, Ghee was also raised by her grandmother Aria Trotman, who is best known for her clean air activism, including the 2161 march on Trenton. This undoubtedly influenced Ghee's decision to lead the Sixty Mile March. The blueprint was there from the beginning. Revolution was in her blood. Ghee grew up in an environment of unrest and upheaval. You had to fight—sometimes physically—for what you believed in.

In addition to being raised a Stone Earther, Ghee Dorfhouse was allegedly highly allergic to Sukodon-Bethryl-ring products, which also influenced her parents' decision to raise her in a rural environment, away from urban air and water filtration centers. It is impossible to know, since Stone Earthers don't share medical information, if Ghee was ever officially diagnosed with B-ring titters, though anecdotal evidence supports this theory. Many religious, political, and private groups at that time questioned the widespread use of socio-pharmaceutical chemicals in air, water, and food prep. These public health fears, coupled with ongoing religious clashes, eventually led to the American Revolution of 2222, specifically, The Sixty Mile March and The Battle Of Newark Bay.

I'm sure you've all seen the film, "Cara and Ghee: A Love Story." The actresses who play Cara Lewis and Ghee Dorfhouse—Hilja Carlson and Sharon Milling—are quite beautiful, as is the romantic relationship between them. But I assure you, it's all fictional. It's simply not true. Little evidence exists that Cara and Ghee knew each other prior to the Battle of Newark Bay.

The films portrays Cara Lewis falling in love with the "ugly duckling" Ghee Dorfhouse on the set of their high school musical. It's true Cara Lewis played Gabriella in Franz Rock High's 2218 production of "High School Musical." Her name is listed on the playbill and Lewis herself confirmed this...though, as we know, we can't always believe things politicians say!

(*Pause for laughter.*)

Ghee Dorfhouse, however, attended one, perhaps two, meetings of the stage crew, but did not participate in the 2218 Franz Rock High School Theater production. She is not listed in the playbill. School records show Dorfhouse's school attendance was spotty in both 2217 and 2218. Records stop altogether after 2219, when Ghee Dorfhouse returned to home schooling.

It is realistic to assume that when Ghee Dorfhouse turned up on national television on May 2, 2222 at the head of the Sixty Mile March, she was probably only vaguely familiar to Cara Lewis at best. Maybe when Ghee was identified as a former Franz Rock High School student, Cara recognized her, but probably not even then. Cara Lewis did not run to the Battle Of Newark Bay to stand by Ghee's side, as film fiction implies. She was there as part of the Chemloco College Student Activities Union, one of many student-led groups attending the Newark protests.

Keep in mind, I don't think anyone anticipated the protest march becoming the Battle Of Newark. The violence took everyone by surprise, even though it was simmering all along, just below the surface. The military came armed and was not about to let the public break into a government facility.

But once Ghee Dorfhouse climbed that security fence, the die was cast. Unit Commander Sgt. Ethan Reed issued two verbal warnings for Ghee to stop. Ghee did not stop. Even if you haven't seen the film, you've surely seen the iconic photograph of Ghee Dorfhouse standing on the upraised palms of what appears to be a stone giant, preparing to swing her leg over the barbed wire fence. The photo captures Ghee framed against a patch of blue sky, fellow protesters packed in tight against the fence behind her, while, right on the other side of the chain link, a tank cannon juts into frame like an angry black spike. That picture, taken by *New York Times* photographer Martin Bey, became a central image used by the American revolutionists of 2222. Martin Bey would have won the Pulitzer Prize for photojournalism in 2222 if Raimo Viskari and Olivia Lyy hadn't snapped a picture of two soldiers having a snowball fight in Iceland later that same year!

(*Chuckles.*)

Speaking of which, I should take a moment here to mention Ghee Dorfhouse's "stone companion." Is this the Rock God of legend gone to rescue his stone bride? Is this the same figure seen in November 2222 in Iceland? And again, twenty years later, on the Aleutian Islands? Is that Maggie herself standing behind him during the snowball fight?

You can decide for yourself. I have neither the time nor desire to turn this lecture in a dissection of folklore and fairy tales. I'm having a hard enough time deciphering Hollywood fact from fiction. We know tech-driven camouflage combat body armor was used by the military and law enforcement at the time, as well as private security firms. So, while it's likely Ghee Dorfhouse's stone companion was a person in Talos combat armor, we still don't know to this day who that person was.

[*Shout from the audience: "Clap Sapperstein!" followed by laughter.*]

Yes, well, as I said, we don't know *who* was in that combat armor during the Battle Of Newark Bay, but I assure you, however, it was most certainly *not* Clap Sapperstein! Why the producers of "Cara and Ghee" chose to cast a buffoonish former athlete in such a pivotal role remains an eternal Hollywood mystery. But we're not here to discuss the legend of the Rock God, nor the thespian skills of Clap Sapperstein, but to separate fact from fiction regarding the relationship between Cara Lewis and Ghee Dorfhouse.

Cara Lewis, the Great Unifier, the 108th President Of The United States, was there on McLester Street on May 3, 2222, watching Ghee Dorfhouse climb the security fence. She probably cheered Ghee on, like so many other protesters. After all, Ghee represented a new hope, a new American freedom. Here was a citizen—a young woman…a little girl—tired of oppression, who was *doing* something, taking back a lost innocence, seizing not only her own empowerment, but empowering a nation.

Cara Lewis saw Ghee Dorfhouse climb that fence. We all saw her, yellow braid hanging over her shoulder, the sun and sky behind her. She looks frail, tired, delicate…yet she looks like a warrior, too, breaching the walls of an enemy fortress.

In Bey's photo, she looks like a goddess, her legion of faithful followers behind her as she faces off against her greatest and final—adversary. Cara Lewis saw her. We all saw Ghee Dorfhouse climb that fence. And we all saw what happened next.

(*Pause.*)

Every powerful tragedy has horrific moments that humanize the event. When President John F. Kennedy was assassinated, it was his wife, Jackie, climbing backwards out of the convertible to recover her husband's brains. When the World Trade Center was attacked, it was the image of doomed souls jumping from the top of burning skyscrapers.

At the Battle of Newark Bay, the moment of humanizing horror comes in the form of a .50 caliber bullet fired from one of the tanks. The shot blows Ghee Dorfhouse's head off. One moment Ghee is swinging her leg over the barbed wire fence, and the next, her head disappears in a red cloud, and she's a headless torso, no longer little Ghee Dorfhouse, no longer the nation's sweetheart, its darling, its hope, but a headless corpse balancing atop a fence for an agonizingly long moment before tumbling over and falling a dozen feet to the asphalt on the other side.

Even before Ghee's body hit the ground, the crowd surged, the fences fell, and the tanks opened fire. One hundred and fifty-four civilians died that day, including Ghee Dorfhouse, who is sometimes called the first casualty of the 2222 Revolution. She is certainly the most visible and, dare I say, the most important victim of the Battle of Newark Bay. She not only changed the hearts and minds of the American people in 2222, she changed the heart and mind of Cara Lewis.

You see, the day Ghee Dorfhouse died was the day Cara Lewis, public servant, was born. While the whole world mourned the murder of Ghee Dorfhouse, Cara Lewis made avenging her death a personal mission. Cara and Ghee were no more than passing acquaintances prior to the Battle of Newark. Maybe not even that. But something important, something vital, passed between them that day nonetheless. The torch of freedom dropped by Ghee's corpse was picked up by Cara Lewis, who carried it throughout the Maggot Revolutionary Force attacks, the Philadelphia Protests, the Miami Uprising, and the election of President Grant Layton in November 2222. Cara Lewis carried the torch of truth when she was elected to Congress in 2235 and when she was elected president in 2242. She carried it for the rest of her life.

Ghee Dorfhouse was not Cara Lewis' (*air quotes*) "bestie." They weren't friends, they weren't rivals, and they weren't lovers. Ghee Dorfhouse was Cara Lewis' revolutionary mentor, her spirit guide. Cara Lewis comes from a long line of public servants—police and firemen populate her family tree, going all the way back to her great-great-great grandfather Walter Lewis, the police officer who discovered the body of Maggie sculptor George Ottomeyer. There are connections that bridge time, but none the girls could have been aware of. Most importantly, Ghee Dorfhouse inspired Cara Lewis to become one of the most powerful and influential women in the history of American government. And so, from the bleeding heart of American tragedy, shines the eternal light of freedom.

Good night and God Bless America!

*Comment on Professor Randolph Pääskysaari, Human Studies, "Cara & Ghee: A Truthful Lecture."*

*BeefheartWIS wrote:* It's too damn hot in the Targmartorium! I'm canceling my subscription to the Speaker Series next year unless TU coughs up some dough for central air conditioning!

*99probs66 wrote:* Check out this clip of President Lewis on the campaign trail in 2242 claiming she and Ghee Dorfhouse were childhood friends who "grew up together." Such bullshit! [Att:Mov8794.M]

*BAterUP wrote:* Another lying politician. There's a surprise. (Sarcasm.)

*FRGirlInJerz wrote:* Ghee and Cara got friendly in high school, even though Cara was a couple of grades above Ghee. They were in a theater production together.

*Lickr wrote:* They were dykes together. Scissor sisters. Lesbos.

*BonnieNeumann wrote:* Cara and Ghee hated each other in high school. They were, like, mortal enemies…until they became friends.

*PodChatter wrote:* Cara and Ghee didn't even know each other in high school. I don't think they even went to the same school.

*MarkNoseStuff wrote:* Prof P's "truthful lecture" is a lie! Ghee and Cara were both secret Stone Earthers of the highest rank. That's how Ghee got the Rock God to free Maggie in 2222, and why the Rock God and Maggie showed up in 2242 to help Cara Lewis win the presidential election. Maggots are still around. Ancient aliens who live under the North Pole control everything!

*AllisonM4tr wrote:* I love Gabby in High School Musical! HSM forever!

*Video-to-text transcript, KnowNet Learning Module:* What Happened To The Maggots?, *produced March 21, 2302.*

In April 2040, a statue by the name of "Maggie" was placed upon a grave in Franz Rock Memorial Gardens. A decade later, the statue was the focal point of a growing religious movement whose followers claimed the statue performed miracles. By 2100, Maggie's followers had spread to every corner of the globe, and by 2200 the Maggots were the world's largest religious group, outnumbering Muslims,

Christian, and Jews combined.

Yet by 2250 the movement was on the decline, and by 2300 Maggot numbers had dwindled to a handful of disparate sects scattered about the globe. Today, the Maggots, and its contentious branches, are gone.

What happened to the Maggots? How could an organization rise to a position of prominence so quickly, only to fall from grace twice as fast? Where did the Maggots go?

There are three primary factors that resulted in the decline of the Maggots:

**Reliance On Concrete Iconography**

It is a general belief among academics and laymen alike that meaningful and lasting religions are based on group behavior and belief in a core value system. The Maggots ideology is literally idolatry—belief in a magical statue. A literal concrete object—the sculpture of Maggie Ottomeyer—drove the movement rather than a shared belief system. Once the object was removed—the destruction of the Maggie statue during the Battle of Newark Bay—the movement could not sustain itself.

**Division Within The Maggot Movement**

While many religions fracture into specialized sects, the Maggots splintered too often and too quickly to support a centralized structure. Maggot factions violently clashed. This may stem from the concrete iconography of the movement: each group sought to claim Maggie as their own. The Stone Earthers saw Maggie as a call to rural, simplistic living, while the statue awakened sacred rites and "house feasts" dormant since the early days of the Roman Empire for the Mithraists. Sisters of The Fist used Maggie's alleged "miracles" as a rallying point for radical social reform, while the Flies considered themselves "evolved Maggots" committed to "willful acts of peace." Such acts included "Flash Fly-Ins," where thousands of Flies would "peacefully" congregate at target locations, causing a disruption of public service and safety, as seen at the 2230 Freedom Convention and the World Cup Riot of 2239. Simply put, there were too many different kinds of Maggots and they did not always play well together.

**The Battle of Newark Bay / Murder Of Ghee Dorfhouse**

While historians argue Maggot numbers were already dwindling prior to 2222, the Battle of Newark Bay was unquestionably a major turning point for the movement. The confiscation of the Maggie statue and its impoundment at a warehouse in Newark brought many Maggot factions together. It's estimated more than 90-percent of the Sixty Mile Marchers were practicing Maggots. Those numbers are reflected in the civilian casualties suffered at the Battle of Newark Bay, the march's ultimate endpoint.

Ghee Dorfhouse, a direct descendant of Maggie Ottomeyer, led the march, along with an unknown—possibility robotic—solider in camouflage combat armor. Ghee's horrific public execution during the Battle of Newark Bay dealt a disastrous blow not only to President Loren Ipson and the Patriot Party, but to the Maggot movement as well. The Maggot Revolutionary Force was blamed for sabotaging the power and communications grid later the same year (an incident later attributed to natural causes). Even though Cara Lewis won the White House on a mixed Maggot ticket two decades later, the movement was already on the backslide, losing numbers year-after-year as followers returned to traditional religions. The destruction of the Maggie Statue in the Battle Of Newark Bay was the ultimate deathblow to the movement. Without its central figure, Maggot unity could not hold.

*Comments (please, keep it kind!)*

*Sally7 wrote:* What happened to the Maggots? We're still here! Underground, asshole!

*55GHEE4EVR wrote:* You forgot: Reason #4—The

quadrupling of Sukod-Bezrene-ring AIR AND H2O POISONING following the Newark Bay Slaughter! The Dept of Human Affairs and the Bilderberg Board began pumping 4x-5x the amount. They just changed the name.

*ProfGeek wrote:* Technically they changed the chemical composition (slightly) along with the name. Either way, that shit still clouds your mind and turns your teeth gray.

*GeoffFDPD wrote:* You're a fucking idiot! The Stone Earth lives! And we know where YOU live, douchebag!

*OneGodMithras wrote:* Mithras emerged whole from stone, like Maggie and the Rock God. Mithras slay the sacred bull. Mother Maggie and The Rock God slay the shadow institutions that imprisoned us. The parallels are clear. Zoroasts unite! The Mysteries have spoken! Prepare your feast-house and welcome in Covenant, Light, and Oath! Let them come! Let them come! Let them come!

*Excerpt from* CARA & GHEE: A LOVE STORY, *written and directed by Oliver Jones, LoveStream Networks, Inc., January 2243.*

*Scene: Campaign Trail, May 2242. Cara Lewis walking through a parking lot. She looks at her cell phone. Several reporters follow her.*

REPORTER 1: Ms. Lewis, do you have any comment on the photos of the Rock God and Maggie taken this morning on the Aleutian Islands?

CARA: T-This is the first I'm seeing them.

REPORTER 1: Do you think this could be the same assailant that stood alongside Ghee Dorfhouse at the Battle Of Newark?

CARA: (*looking closer at her phone, squinting, and then putting the device away and focusing on the news crew*) These photos are astonishing. But they may not be real. I need more information about the authenticity of these photos.

REPORTER 2: Senator Lewis, is there any link between

these photos and the military exercises being conducted around the Arctic Circle and Bering Strait over the last several weeks?

CARA: I don't know anything about that. The Senate approved Captain Poole's request to conduct training exercises in the region in advance of the Martian subsurface ocean exploration campaign planned for 2248. The topography and water temperatures of the Arctic may be similar to the underground oceans of Mars. It's a perfect training ground.

REPORTER 2: Is it possible the two soldiers in these Aleutian Island photos are the same two soldiers photographed during the Iceland Incident of 2222?

CARA: Gosh, that was so long ago…how could it be? Plus, as I stated, the veracity of these images is unconfirmed.

REPORTER 1: They were taken from a secure military stream and time-stamped at 3:30 pm this afternoon.

CARA: It's only been a few hours. I need to know more before I comment. I'll say this, even if they *are* legitimate military photographs, there could be several explanations other than…(*chuckles*)…Maggie and the Rock God. Please, you have to excuse me, I'm late for a lunch meeting here in Harrisburg.

REPORTER 1: The female soldier in the photos is missing her hands. Did you notice that, Senator Lewis?

CARA: (*shaking her head*) I did not. But, as you know, we love the people of Pennsylvania, and we'll be traveling all over the state today talking with people and listening to what they have to say about their state, their country, and who they want in the White House for the next four years. Please, excuse me. I have to run. Thank you.

*Cara and her campaign manager, an older MARTIN MORRIS, break away from the pack. Martin opens a metal service door and Cara steps inside. Martin follows, clicking the door closed behind him. Martin and Cara are alone in a small service kitchen in what looks like a banquet hall.*

*CLOSE-UP of Cara. She looks frightened. CLOSE-UP of Martin. He smiles reassuringly and nods his head in approval.*

*Interview with Cara Lewis by Pamela Milnar on HOPECAST Live, May 5, 2242.*

PAMELA: In addition to running for president, you're also having a film made about your life that's set to debut early next year called "Cara and Ghee: A Love Story." Can you tell us anything about the film?

CARA: No, Pam, I am not involved with that movie in any way.

PAMELA: You disagree with how you're being portrayed in the film?

CARA: Yes…well, again, I'm not involved in that production, but I was asked to consult on a very early version of the script. Once I saw the direction they were taking the film, I stepped away from the project. To me, the film-makers took a very pivotal moment in American history and trivialized it, turned it into something salacious, which may be standard practice for Hollywood movies, but it wasn't something I wanted to get behind.

PAMELA: Are you saying the love story in "Cara & Ghee: A Love Story" isn't real?

CARA: I'm saying, I knew Ghee Dorfhouse in high school, and I was there the day she died…I *did* love Ghee Dorfhouse, but not in the way it's portrayed in the movie. I had great love, respect, and admiration for her, and those feelings grew even more after what happened to her at the Battle of Newark Bay. Ghee Dorfhouse's path to freedom left big footprints—enormous footprints—that I've been trying to fill since 2222. In fact, I can honestly say, following Ghee's footsteps has led us to the campaign trail we're on today.

PAMELA: Have you seen the drone footage from the Aleutian Islands?

CARA: I have. It's remarkable.

PAMELA: Care to remark on it? Do you believe it's Mother Maggie and the Rock God?

CARA: (*smiles, shrugs*) I can't really comment, Pam. President Fuentes says they're Russian soldiers in Talos suits. I believe the President. Don't you?

PAMELA: Are you being sarcastic? I know you don't agree with Vice President Smith-Ledger.

CARA: No comment. I'll ask the Vice President myself during the debates next month.

*HOPECAST Comments:*

*MarkCal wrote:* Cara Lewis is a liar! I went to Franz Rock High School back in the 'teens, when both girls were in school there. Cara and Ghee were constantly lezzing out right in the middle of the school hallways. Ghee got suspended for a week during her sophomore year because the gym teacher caught her licking Cara's box in the girls' locker room. I'm surprised the dyke gym teacher didn't join in! That's what I heard. I ran track in high school.

*McMuffin wrote:* You, sir, are a moron. Cara Lewis had already graduated and moved on to college when Ghee Dorfhouse was a sophomore at Franz Rock High.

*SuzieQE3 wrote:* If the power cuts out during the June debate the way it did back in 2222, I'm going to shit!

*XxLobsteroo wrote:* You'll probably shit anyway, but the suspense is killing me.

*AzurePlane wrote:* Maggot Pride! Maggot Power!

*LiveStream, Candidate Cara Lewis Acceptance Speech, 2242 Presidential Election, November 4, 2242.*

CARA: ...and, finally, I would be remiss if I failed to mention someone very special...someone who is here in spirit only, but without whom I don't think any of us would be here tonight. I know I wouldn't. That person is Ghee Dorfhouse. (*Pauses for applause. A chant of "Ghee, Ghee, Ghee" rises above the room. Cara wipes away tears and approaches the microphone again.*) Ghee Dorfhouse showed me how to be brave, how to stand up and fight for causes worth dying for. Because of Ghee's sacrifice, we are able to breathe clean air again and drink clean water. We've elected leaders not beholden to private agendas but the public good. Thank you for putting your trust in me and I look forward to being your president for the next four years. Thank you, good night, and God Bless America.

*BiblioFriend Search: Books by Captain William Poole, SERP / summaries / excerpts / sample chapters.*

*Excerpt,* The Rock God Beside Me: How A Lost Limb Became A Life's Blessing, *non-fiction, November, 2237.*

Like many wounded veterans, I self-medicated during my convalescence and never stopped. Even with all of the resources available to wounded warriors, many of us feel we can handle our psychological injuries alone.

We can't. At least I couldn't.

Alcohol numbed the pain and fogged the memories. Jack Daniels was my medicine of choice and I got to a point where I'd start drinking each morning and continue all day until I passed out. This was my life for fifteen years, see-sawing between functional alcoholism and falling-down drunk.

Bitterness consumed me. I was a freak with a metal arm. I took longer and longer assignments, further and further from home. I hated being around my wife and kids—they reminded me of how far I'd fallen. I didn't want them to see me pickling myself daily, so I drank on the sly, which wasn't very sly at all when I'd puke in the kitchen sink and piss my pants, passed out on the living room couch. It was easier, less shameful, to stay away and stay drunk on the far fringes of the world, hide away with a bottle in some frozen wasteland or a tropical hell, or the middle of the ocean. It didn't matter. As long as I was away from the people who loved me, I could continue to hurt myself.

Rock bottom came two years ago, on the edge of the Laptev Sea, about 100 nautical miles west of the north pole, aboard a BM-45 navy ice-cutter, *The Spurhead,* on deck, watching the aurora borealis, swirling green, pink, and purple above me like God spilled his paint pallet on the sky's glass ceiling.

I passed out and dreamed of Mother Maggie and the Rock God. This wasn't uncommon; I dreamed of them often, sometimes entire undersea adventures. But this wasn't the re-occurring nightmare of losing my arm or surreal visions of five-faced starfish. This dream was sharp, crystal clear, more like a memory than a dream. I stood on an ice floe before Maggie and the Rock God, no more than a couple of meters away, our tiny island of ice drifting in a lazy circle. I wasn't cold until I thought about being cold, so I figured I was dreaming. But then the Rock God reached out and gripped my shoulder with his stone fingers and it felt real. Not painful, but not comfortable either. The power in the Rock God's grip was terrifying. He could snap his fingers and tear me apart. I couldn't help but tense up, even though I felt the Rock God meant me no harm. His gesture was avuncular, friendly, reassuring...maybe this was his apology for crippling me back in 2222.

Mother Maggie reached out and I jumped back. She held a shining, squirming ball of light in her arms. She handed it to me but I wanted no part of it. The glowing ball terrified me. Bands of energy writhed around inside like translucent worms. I didn't want to touch it; couldn't touch it. I wasn't worthy, wasn't ready to accept what Mother Maggie offered. I put my hands up against my chest, palms out, a hard no on the energy ball. But the Rock God's grip tightened, not so friendly after all. I couldn't go anywhere until I took what they were offering.

That's when I woke up. I'd puked on myself and spilled half-a-bottle of Jack in my lap. I stripped down to my skivvies and tossed my vomit-and-alcohol-covered uniform overboard. I took a swig from the Jack Daniels bottle and tossed it overboard too. That was the last drink I ever had, or will ever have. There were no answers at the bottom of a bottle, only more problems.

I stood, nearly naked, my hands on the railing. I thought about tossing myself overboard too. My wife and daughters would be better off. But I lacked courage...plus the residual dream floss clinging to my mind made me think twice about Mother Maggie. What was the glowing ball? An energy source? A life form?

Responsibility. Responsibility for myself and my actions. That's what Maggie and the Rock God wanted me to have, what I felt unworthy to accept. I'd avoided it for so long. I had to get ready, get worthy.

When Art White found me out on the deck of *The Spurhead,* I was nearly hypothermic, but I was no longer suicidal. I had a renewed mission, a renewed purpose...and it started with mending fences back home.

*Summary,* Stone Eyes *(writing as BP Haas), novel, August, 2240.*

Undersea superheroes face off against an army of angry squid and irritable octopi in this wild ride on the bottom of the ocean!

*Summary,* Stone Hands *(writing as BP Haas), novel, August, 2241.*

Stoneman and Martha are back to save the world from an

uncanny underwater threat in this thrill-a-minute aquatic adventure!

*Excerpt,* Stone Heart *(writing as BP Haas), novel, September, 2243.*

"Ouch!" Stoneman grabbed his foot, searching the sea floor beneath him. A spiky, purple anemone twinkled in the filtered sunlight. How could its spines puncture his stone foot? Stoneman didn't know, but his foot throbbed. Liquid warmth flowed up his leg and through his torso. Cold hands gripped his heart and the ocean swirled around him. He fell, but never hit the ground.

Instead he kept falling. Not fast, like a free fall. He wasn't plummeting. He was gliding through open space, down and away.

*I'm flying!*

*Stupid! Stones can't fly!*

But here he was, drifting through vast space, the cosmos an endless tapestry of eternal night, countless stars, infinite worlds. He tumbled toward a blue marble, burst into flames as he rocketed toward the planet's surface. He spun around the planet three times, the final orbit low enough to yield views of vast forests and jagged mountains, massive lumbering beasts and trees as tall as skyscrapers. He skimmed the surface of icy waters before plunging into a northern sea, cold so intense, his non-heart skipped a non-beat, plunging through the water, down, down, down, toward a glowing ship on the bottom of the ocean floor.

*That's me! That's Martha and I standing next to a space ship!*

The craft glowed dim green around the edge, soft and florescent, like a forty-foot-wide clock radio. Stoneman hovered above the scene like a voyeuristic ghost, an ethereal peeping tom. An opening filled with aquamarine light appeared on the side of the space ship, and a trio of thin, bald, naked beings emerged, surrounding Stoneman and Martha on the ocean floor. The beings carried glowing balls of light that grew brighter and brighter until the scene on the ocean floor was swallowed in glare and Peeping Tom Stoneman was forced to cover his eyes and looked away. When the light faded, everything was gone; himself, Martha, the aliens…even the space ship. Gone, like it had never been there at all.

*Did I imagine it? Was this a dream?*

It'd been so long since he'd slept, he'd forgotten what dreaming was like. But he didn't think his foot would hurt this much if it were only a dream.

*Was it a hallucination? A visitation? What did these beings from beyond the stars want?*

Stoneman shook his head and rubbed his foot but nothing came any clearer or hurt any less.

*Excerpt,* From Stone To Stone: My Life with the Mobile Stone Entities, *spiritual/self-help, February, 2245.*

I took my last drink aboard the deck of *The Spurhead* in 2237. And on New Year's Day 2239. And after spending the night passed out and puke-covered in a Days Inn bathroom after Wizards & Warlocks Weekend 2241. I'm almost as good at quitting drinking as I am at falling off the wagon. Alcoholism is a disease that never lets you go. It's always waiting there for you to screw up. I'd like to tell you I'll never drink again, but all I can promise is that I'll always fight the temptation. I'll resist the call to throw myself into the black abyss of drunken forgetfulness. That's all I can do.

The last time I quit drinking was April 2242. I drank a beer with my crew following our successful mission guiding the Mobile Stone Entities through the Bering Strait. It was worth falling off the wagon for—it felt good to celebrate. But I stopped after one beer…frankly, the taste of alcohol makes me nauseous now.

Guiding the MSEs through the Strait wasn't easy. We lost a good soldier—Commander Meriellen Whiting. Whiting accidentally launched a positioning anchor that the MSEs perceived as a threat. They responded accordingly. The MSE_Male attacked Whiting's Vassik vessel, breeching the view-port with his fist. The pressure differential caused the Vassik to implode. Whiting was killed instantly.

After attacking Whiting's Vassik, the MSE_Male turned on the rest of our crew. I ordered McClunkey and DaVolt to lock and load but I didn't give the order to fire. How could I, after following these beings my whole adult life, after sacrificing my flesh, blood, and bone, after dedicating my life so completely to these statues that they inhabited my dreams and waking moments alike? How could I destroy my gods?

I needed a miracle…and I got one.

MSE_Female stepped forward, a glowing ball of radiant white energy in her upraised arms. DaVolt screamed in my headset for me to back away or engage. I couldn't do either. I couldn't do anything except watch the MSE_Female pass a pulsating white medicine ball of love, hope, and power *through* the view-port plastiglass. The cabin of my Vassik filled with light, but it wasn't blinding or frightening. Just the opposite. The light calmed me. The light was love.

The light was love.

The light *is* love.

How many years had I searched for this answer? Since a monster stole my arm twenty years ago, certainly, but probably much longer than that. Why did I need to journey to the bottom of the sea and beg an answer from ambulatory statues? It was so simple, there in front of me all along, the difference between night and day.

Light is love.

The light inside the Vassik cabin faded as it flowed into my body, like steeping tea in reverse. The dissipated became concentrated inside me. Heat. Strength. Confidence. Was this how the disciples felt when they received the Holy Spirt, tongues of fire dancing like sugar plums above their heads? Was this my baptism?

It was a blessing, the fulfillment of a dream. The walking stones. The ambulatory statues. The MSEs. Maggie and the Rock God. The mud man and mud woman. Whatever their names, whatever they were, the creatures who tore me apart were the same that made me whole again.

*Synopsis,* Touched by Stone, *stream series, 8 episodes, writer, 2255-6.*

Hosts Brenda Mosely and Brian Nott talk to former Maggots about converting to Old Religions and how Mother Maggie's teachings may—or may not—still apply to their daily lives.

*Synopsis,* Stone Heart Diaries, *stream series, 144 episodes, writer, executive producer, 2258-2265.*

Walking/talking statues, Betty and Bob, travel through time and solve mysteries in this CGI-based world of wild characters and outlandish plot twists. But, no matter how crazy things get for Betty and Bob, they can always count on sound educational principles and their devotion to one another to save the day! Nominated for four Excellence In Educational Programming Awards!

*From Knownet,* Aleutian Islands Sightings of 2242, *last updated December 2301.*

On the afternoon of May 6, 2242, two figures were spotted by military drones sitting atop an unnamed Aleutian Island outcrop (now called Stoneman's Pike off Knob Point). The sightings followed several weeks of intensive military training exercises in and around the Bering Strait, leading most to assume the figures were soldiers, possibly robotic naval divers, testing new Talos equipment. Then-President Fernando Fuentes reported they were lost Russian divers, but later rescinded those statements.

*Overview*

The two figures, seen walking and sitting along the barren peak, were first spotted at 3:33 pm and were gone by 10 pm, 6.5 hours after they arrived. The figures were not spotted again after 10:01 pm on May 6, 2242.

Prevailing theories suggest the figures were lost soldiers who returned to the waters of the North Pacific and were rescued by military personnel, though neither the United States nor Russian military have claimed responsibility for the incident.

*Campaign Hoax Theory*

The figures seen on Stoneman's Pike strongly resembled figures spotted along the shores of Iceland two decades earlier (See "The Iceland Incident"). The "Iceland soldiers" themselves appeared to be fashioned after Maggot religious icons Mother Maggie and the Man Of Stone (See "Maggie-Statue" and "Legend Of The Mud Man-North Jersey"). The 2222 appearance of these iconic religious figures in Iceland occurred during a chaotic year in American history when many believed "stone soldiers" in modified Talos combat armor, combined with the Maggot Revolutionary Force (MRF), played an active role in The Sixty Mile March, Battle of Newark Bay, and the Transatlantic Cable Failure.

The appearance of the stone figures in Iceland was considered by some to be part of an elaborate campaign hoax by Maggot-backed Freedom Party candidate Grant Layton to influence voters in the 2222 Presidential elections, which Layton won by a large margin. Both Cara Lewis' 2242 campaign and Layton's 2222 campaign were successfully managed by Martin Morris, further suggesting the Aleutian Island sightings were part of a planned campaign tactic.

However, the lack of an official military statement on the Aleutian Island sightings by either US or Russian military fueled rumors the Rock God and Maggie had returned.

*Other Theories:*

- Russian Spies—In the 2270 streamcast, *Water Blue, Danger Red,* historian J. Walter Smartz suggests the two "stone soldiers" were Russian military divers assigned to infiltrate Arctic Sea US military exercises in April/May 2242, but found themselves trapped and forced to surface due to a logistical error. [*Read more…*]
- Geological Formations—Earth science Professor Hans Päivänurmi Ph.D suggests the sightings on the Aleutian Island outcrop were neither organic nor robotic but shifting rock formations on the outcrop erroneously identified as humanoid beings by the limited imaging technology of 2242 drones. [*Read more…*]
- Sun Spots—Author and solar physicist Chandra Lovell also pins the blame on poor drone imaging software in her book, *Sunlight On Stone: How Sunspots Won The 2242 Presidential Election* (Fuct The Dog Press, 2294). [*Read more…*]
- Maggie and the Rock God—Though mostly relegated to folklore, some believe the figures atop the Aleutian Island outcrop were Mother Maggie and the Rock God (living figures made of mud and river clay—see "Golem-Jewish Folklore"). The stone duo are part of 21st-century Maggot mysticism and feature frequently in 22-23rd-century art, music, and pop culture.

(See "Living Stones: Cultural References")

(See "60MM: Interpretive Dance")

(See "Heidi In The Tippy-Top Wayback")

*Classified transcript, live drone monitor, USS Youseff, Amchitka Pass, North Pacific, CPL. LANCE ERRIKS, MJR. NORM WASANI, 2:45 pm, May 6, 2242.*

CPL. LANCE ERRIKS: The drones don't detect a heat signature, sir. There are no people inside those suits.

MJR. NORM WASANI: Robots then.

CPL. LANCE ERRIKS: No machine signatures either, sir. Scans make them appear like they're made of solid rock.

MJR. NORM WASANI: How is it possible?

CPL. LANCE ERRICKS: A cloaking device, perhaps? How should we proceed, Major?

MJR. NORM WASANI: Buzz them with the drone. See if you can chase them back into the water.

CPL. LANCE ERRICKS: No attempt at capture?

MJR. NORM WASANI: That would be a major can of worms, Corporal. Let those two monsters crawl back into the sea.

CPL. LANCE ERRICKS: Your call, sir, but I think we might be able to drop a gravity net on them.

MJR. NORM WASANI: No. Let them go.

CPL. LANCE ERRICKS: What do you think they're doing?

MJR. NORM WASANI: Don't know, don't care. If they don't return to the water in thirty minutes, blow them to dust.

CPR. LANCE ERRICKS: Sir, the drone images are automatically relayed to headquarters. Filing a report is standard protocol.

MJR. NORM WASANI: You run this up the ladder, Erricks, it'll go all the way to the top. You know that, don't you?

CPL. LANCE ERRICKS: I suppose so, sir.

MJR. NORM WASANI: Is that what you want? The President breathing down our necks?

CPL. LANCE ERRICKS: It's…protocol, sir.

MJR. NORM WASANI: Fuck me running, Lance! Okay. Okay, send it up. I'll give it an hour, see who responds. In the meantime, buzz those fucking freaks. Maybe they'll go away.

*Classified transcript, private meeting of Major Aleksanteri Garwood and President Fernando Fuentes, 5:15pm, EST, May 6, 2242.*

PRESIDENT FUENTES: What the hell am I looking at?

MAJOR GARWOOD: We believe they may be Mobile Stone Entities, Mr. President.

PRESIDENT FUENTES: You mispronounced Talos troops, Major Garwood.

MAJOR GARWOOD: Uh…Mr. President?

PRESIDENT FUENTES: That other shit is classified. Deep classified. Like, on a need-to-know basis. I don't need to know. Understood, Major?

MAJOR GARWOOD: I think so, Mr. President.

PRESIDENT FUENTES: So I'm looking at Talos soldiers stranded on a rock somewhere. Where and when was this image taken?

MAJOR GARWOOD: This afternoon by drones over the Aleutian Islands. The…they're sitting on an outcrop off Knob Point.

PRESIDENT FUENTES: Are these Americans? Are they in need of rescue?

MAJOR GARWOOD: No, Mr. President.

PRESIDENT FUENTES: Then why do I care, Major Garwood?

MAJOR GARWOOD: Well…these images have hit the streams, sir. People have seen them and there's a portion of the public that believes this is Maggie and the Rock God, or some reincarnation thereof.

PRESIDENT FUENTES: Come on! Nobody believes the

streams! You're telling me we can't spin out of this? Paint it as a falsehood? I mean, these pictures could be anything... plastic bags caught in the breeze.

MAJOR GARWOOD: The female is missing her hands, Mr. President.

PRESIDENT FUENTES: Shit. Still, people will believe it's a hoax. It's an election year. Cara Lewis is slumping in the polls, so somebody drummed up a Rock God and Maggie publicity stunt...probably that asshole, Martin Morris. Didn't Morris do the same thing during the '22 elections?

MAJOR GARWOOD: The country was falling apart in '22, and Ipson didn't know her ass from her elbow, if I may speak frankly, sir. Killing Ghee Dorfhouse lost her that election. I'd hate to see something silly like this hurt our party.

PRESIDENT FUENTES: I'm at the end of my second term. This is a problem for Vice President Smith-Ledger's campaign manager. Not me.

MAJOR GARWOOD: The vice president can't give military orders, Mr. President.

PRESIDENT FUENTES: What are you asking, Major?

MAJOR GARWOOD: Let me take the MS...these things out. After nightfall. Poof...they're gone. Nobody needs to know.

PRESIDENT FUENTES: Without getting into details, what do you think is going on, Alek?

MAJOR GARWOOD: I think...William Poole. You're aware of Captain Poole's recent undersea arctic operations?

PRESIDENT FUENTES: Yes, yes, I'm aware, but again, I *do not want details* about this, Alek. The less I know the better.

MAJOR GARWOOD: Of course, Mr. President. I think... perhaps Captain Poole's mission needs to be reevaluated with a new end in mind. I mean, Poole promised we'd never see these two again. Yet here they are.

PRESIDENT FUENTES: There they are.

MAJOR GARWOOD: They need to be gone, Mr. President.

PRESIDENT FUENTES: I appreciate what you're saying, Major. But we need to learn from our mistakes. Learn from history. The Sixty Mile March taught us the consequence of handling these things on live stream. Everything's streaming everywhere, all the time. You won't be able to get near those things without someone seeing, even at night.

MAJOR GARWOOD: I think I can, Mr. President. They're in the middle of nowhere.

PRESIDENT FUENTES: There *is* no middle of nowhere. Not anymore. Eyes everywhere. A military action lends these things credence. If we care enough to destroy them, they must be real, right? No, let's sit on this. Stay mum. Let them crawl back into the sea.

MAJOR GARWOOD: What if they don't, sir?

PRESIDENT FUENTES: We'll see what tomorrow brings. In the meantime, I'll contact Bill Poole and see what he has to say.

MAJOR GARWOOD: I'd be curious to hear his excuse as well, Mr. President. I warned him against…against these Bering Strait exercises, sir. I feared this would happen.

PRESIDENT FUENTES: We need to sit tight and let this resolve itself. At least until all of the facts are in.

MAJOR GARWOOD: With all due respect, we've followed Bill Poole's…*mission* for the last month, and these…these *things* are not right, sir. Not right at all. They're an abomination. An abomination in the eyes of God and man. I don't know why they've been allowed to roam free for decades—

PRESIDENT FUENTES: Hey! Hey! Hey! What did I tell you? Those are stranded Talos soldiers. That's all. Nothing else. I'm not taking any action until I get more information on this, Alek.

MAJOR GARWOOD: I've given you the information.

You're making a mistake, Fernando.

PRESIDENT FUENTES: You're displaying disturbing anti-Maggot sentiment, Major. Its concerning. Keep your personal beliefs out of this, Alek.

MAJOR GARWOOD: Perhaps you should contact Alexandra Hall in addition to Captain Poole. She's had a lot of experience dealing with…this.

PRESIDENT FUENTES: Damn, Hall's a scary bitch. But I'll contact her.

*Live drone monitor, based on USS Youseff, CRPL. LANCE ERRIKS, MJR. NORM WASANI, 10:01 pm, EST, May 6, 2242.*

ERRIKS: Nothing on the drone, sir. They're gone.

WASANI: Back into the sea. Good riddance.

ERRIKS: I guess you were right. My apologies for earlier, Major.

WASANI: All's well that ends well, Lance. Good night.

*From* The Bob and Joe StreamCast, Topic: Aleutian Island Sightings, *May 8, 2242.*

BOB: Look! That is *totally* Maggie and the Rock God! It *has* to be!

JOE: Calm down, Bob. Those are Talos combat suits. We've seen them a million times before. There's no reason to get excited.

BOB: Those are *not* traditional Talos suits, Joe. Maggie's missing her hands! Come on, tell me those don't look like the same two soldiers who showed up in Iceland twenty years ago!

JOE: Yeah, they *look* like them, Bob, but that doesn't mean they *are* them! Besides, the soldiers that showed up in Iceland were a hoax to get President Ipson out of office. There's no reason to believe these two characters aren't doing the same thing.

BOB: For what reason?

JOE: To get Cara Lewis elected president.

BOB: Oh, come on! Now who sounds crazy?

JOE: People still believe that Maggot shit. It still has pull with the public.

BOB: Twenty years ago Maggots had political pull, but not anymore. Cara Lewis has distanced herself from the movement for years. I think being associated with the Maggots, especially a violent fringe group like the Maggot Revolutionary Force, hurt Lewis more than helped her.

JOE: Don't be so sure, especially if gullible assholes believe those are actually the Rock God and Maggie sitting atop those rocks.

BOB: Well, it really *does* look like the Rock God and Maggie.

JOE: See, Bob. You're one of those gullible assholes. This makes me question your judgment about everything.

BOB: Give me a break, Joe. You're not going to bully me into your viewpoint. I know what I'm looking at.

JOE: What do you think you're seeing, Bob? The Rock God and Maggie sitting on a rock in the middle of the goddamn Pacific Ocean? You think those are actual *stone beings* who walked along the seafloor, through the Bering Strait, and then climbed atop an uninhabited Aleutian outcrop just to have a look around? That makes sense to you? You don't think soldiers in Talos suits is a more logical explanation?

BOB: I didn't say it makes sense, but that doesn't mean it's not possible.

JOE: You know the United States has been conducting military exercises in the Arctic for months. Don't you think it's more likely the appearance of these soldiers is connected to *known military exercises* rather than *mythic stone beings* crawling out of the sea?

BOB: I'd feel more comfortable if the government was

more transparent about the nature of these military exercises. What are they *doing* in the Arctic?

JOE: They're preparing for the Martian Deep Ocean Expedition! Congress voted to fund it three years ago!

BOB: I'm not sure I believe the "official" story, Joe. Who's to say it's not all a ruse to clear a safe path for Maggie and the Rock God to pass through the Bering Strait?

JOE: Well, let me be the first to say that sounds fucking ridiculous and I think you're an idiot.

BOB: Great, Joe. Vulgarities and name-calling. Your debating skills are world-class.

JOE: Sorry, Bob, but you sound really stupid right now.

BOB: What if the entire military operation is a coverup so Maggie and the Rock God could be brought out of the Arctic Circle? Everyone knows that's where they've been hiding since the Iceland Incident.

JOE: Everyone knows…what? They've been hiding under the North Pole for the last twenty years?

BOB: Yes.

JOE: Did they visit the alien spaceship while they were there?

BOB: Now you're just being a jerk, Joe. It's not cool to make a mockery of other people's beliefs.

JOE: You're a moron.

BOB: Okay. I think we're done here.

JOE: Idiot.

BOB: Nice. Real nice.

JOE: Fool.

*From* NewsFlash: with Former President Loren Ipson, *May 13, 2242.*

IPSON: We've seen this before, people. This election is shaping up like a re-run of 2222. Mystical beings are spotted half a world away and our nation goes into a panic. Don't let it happen again. Don't let Martin Morris steal this election the way he did in 2222. Don't believe it!

Allow me to paraphrase a parable here: Truth and Lie bathe in a well together. Lie jumps out, steals Truth's clothing, and runs off. Truth gets out of the well and asks people to help find Lie and her missing clothes. But people couldn't stand the naked Truth. No one helped her. So Truth returned to the well, and ever since then Lie travels the world, dressed in the clothes of Truth.

Don't believe the lies, people. Embrace the naked truth!

*From Military.Mail.Box, private account, General X____X, November 5, 2301.*

To: General X___X

From: Brigadier General Jayden Gamble

RE: MSE: Final Classified Report

Dear General X___X,

This concludes the report you requested on the Mobile Stone Entities. You'll find narrative gaps following the Iceland Incident, but I went as deep as my security clearance would allow. I feel I delivered a clearer picture of how MSEs are perceived, both by civilians and military insiders. In a nutshell, MSEs are near-mythical creatures, falling somewhere between white whales and unicorns. Any grain of truth that may have once existed has been lost in a sea of nonsense, gibberish, and "original works of art." On that level, mission accomplished.

Please do not hesitate to contact me if you have any additional questions.

Sincerely,

Brigadier General Jayden Gamble

# 13

## *Third Final Report I*

*From Military.Mail.Box, private account, General X____X, March 15, 2302.*

To: General X____X

From: Alexandra Hall

RE: Final MSE Report

Dear General X____X,

As per your request, here is the information missing from Lampu and Gamble's MSE reports. My condolences on the unexpected passing of Brigadier General Gamble. Damn helicopters—I never feel safe around one. Brigadier Gamble put a lot of work into her report and her contributions will not be forgotten.

As I'm sure you understand, security is of the utmost importance. Receipt of this classified report means you yourself may be included in future reports on this subject. Knowledge is power, as well as membership. Being in the know makes you part of an elite group of individuals. Welcome to the club, General X_____X. Enjoy!

Alexandra Hall

PS: Grapevine says you scored a beachfront at the MRC! I

was in Oahu last month and the facilities are breathtaking. Hope to retire there one day myself. But, you know…miles to go before I sleep! Good luck, General!

AH

*Redacted information from private debriefing, President Loren Ipson and Vice President Taru Burnett, August 22, 2222.*

…BURNETT: Of course. But…the stones are, like, walking around the ocean now?

IPSON: What the hell do I know, Taru? They shouldn't be walking around at all!

BURNETT: We should take them out. Especially if they're vandalizing our infrastructure. It should be easy on the open sea. Less eyes.

IPSON: Hall says no. Military wants to track them.

BURNETT: Christ, they sat back and tracked them during the Sixty Mile March and look how that turned out! We should eradicate this problem now, before it rears its ugly, rocky head again.

IPSON: You're right, Taru. But that's not the way it's going to go.

BURNETT: You're Commander-In-Chief, Loren. The military does what you say.

IPSON: The armed forces aren't my personal hit squad, Taru. We've been told to give the walking stones a pass, so we give them a pass.

BURNETT: Who's giving the order? PharmCo? Metaceuticals?

IPSON: You'd think so, right? If you believe the legend, the Rock God was built to bring down Big Pharm. But the Pharm Hands are quiet. I think it comes from higher.

BURNETT: What's higher than Pharm? Fuel and Utilities doesn't have that kind of clout. Tech? Med? They want to study the stones for…weapons? Didn't we do that already with the Talos armor?

IPSON: It's not our place to ask questions, Taru. We do our jobs and we do them right, understood?...

*Special Forces Classified Report form NATO Naval Station, Gohli, Denmark. Sgt. Matthew Marks / Corporal Andrea Tessier / Headquarters: (Dispatcher unidentified), 5:22 am, December 30, 2222.*

MARKS: HQ, this is Marks. Targets, Mud Boy and Mud Girl are tracking toward Stranger. Advise?

HQ: ETA for Mud meets Stranger?

MARKS: ETA 88.3 hours.

HQ: Standby, Marks.

*(Transcription of in-room audio recording, Sgt.Marks/ Cpl.Tessier)*

MARKS: They're going to blow them up.

TESSIER: Nah. If they were going to blow them up they would have done it in Iceland.

MARKS: They tried and fucked it up. But they're out in the open now...and getting too close.

TESSIER: How close will they let them get?

MARKS: Don't know. Back in '75 a Russian sub got lost and drifted within 14 miles before they sunk it. Five years ago they scuttled a research vessel that tried anchoring right over top. But that's rare. Most of the time they don't bother surface vessels.

TESSIER: When is the last time The Stranger made contact?

MARKS: Damned if I know! Ten years? A hundred? Maybe The Stranger chatters 24/7 down there. Ain't our jobs to listen. We watch. Somebody else listens.

TESSIER: Has anyone, you know, *met*...whatever's down there?

MARKS: No trespassing. They even have a sonar perimeter to keep critters away. That's why the future looks bleak for

Mr. and Mrs. Mud here…unless they change course and walk another way.

TESSIER: Have…have you ever heard that The Stranger speaks in angels' voices, whispering the secrets of life and death?

MARKS: Oh, come on, man. That's black 'net bullshit! Don't tell me you believe them fairy tales?

TESSIER: Then what are we looking at? Who is The Stranger? Who are Mud Boy and Mud Girl? What are they doing here? Where did they come from?

MARKS: Listen, Tess. Our job isn't to ask questions. We're not even supposed to be talking about this shit—

(*Unidentified in-room sounds*)

TESSIER: Hey! Hey!

(*Four loud reports. Gun shots?*)

TRANSCRIPT ENDS

*Classified Transmission, North Pole Agency, (StrangerCom), multi-language translation, 11:59 pm. December 31, 2222.*

Let them come. Let them come. Let them come. Let them come. Let them come. Let them come. Let them come. Let them come. Let them come. Let them come. Let them come. Let them come. Let them come. Let them come. Let them come. Let them come. Let them come. Let them come. Let them come. Let them come. Let them come. Let them come.

*Transcription of in-room audio, Major Daniel Kitula's office. Present: Major Kitula, Major J. Davies-Hussain, Ensign Allison Jacobs, Cpl. Harold Patz, Under Secretary Roy Streat, Admin. Ass. Manuel Martinez, 1:01am, January 1, 2223.*

MAJOR KITULA: Fuck me blind! These fuckers are quiet for eighty-five years and suddenly they want to meet the walking stones?

MAJOR DAVIES-HUSSAIN: The current belief is that

David Lawrence and Maggie Ottomeyer represent a heretofore unseen life-form, which may explain the Stranger's interest in them.

UNIDENTIFIED SPEAKER/(*Possibly Ensign Allison Jacobs*): (*inaudible*) ... represent black magic! Devil shit!

(*Inaudible argument*)

UNIDENTIFIED SPEAKER/(*Possibly Admin. Ass. Manuel Martinez or Under Secretary Roy Streat*): That's the Blessed Mother you're talking about!

UNIDENTIFIED SPEAKER/(*Possibly Cpl. Harold Patz or Under Secretary Roy Streat*): Blasphemy!

MAJOR KITULA: Okay! Cut the shit! We're not here to argue superstitious mumbo jumbo. We're here to figure this situation out. We got two stone freaks approaching the Stranger on foot. We can't be certain this isn't an attack. My inclination is to err on the side of caution. Eliminate the walking stones to preserve the safety of The Stranger.

MAJOR DAVIES-HUSSAIN: With all due respect, Major, the Stranger's message couldn't be more clear. It came through in twenty-two different earth languages, including Morse Code. They all translated the same. 'Let them come.' Clearly, the Stranger is interested in meeting the ambulatory stones, sir.

MAJOR KITULA: Why does there have to be a fucking freak-show on my watch? Stranger duty's easy duty. They sit on the ocean bottom and we watch. It's a cake job. I'm eighteen months away from an MRC end-unit! Why this shit now?

MAJOR DAVIES-HUSSAIN: History happens when it happens, Major. Chance chooses its witnesses. We've been chosen...everyone in this room. We're witnesses to history. Earth history...interplanetary history...we've been chosen.

UNIDENTIFIED SPEAKER/(*Possibly Cpl. Harold Patz*): We are the *very few* chosen to witness history. Sometimes I worry they keep the witness pool small in case history needs to be re-written or ignored.

MAJOR KITULA: It's not our job to ask questions or worry about things beyond our scope, people. We follow orders. If the brass tells us to sit back and let this unfold, that's what we do. Say your prayers for a successful mission in private.

UNIDENTIFIED SPEAKER: The Stranger is the true God!

MAJOR KITULA: I told you to knock that shit off! Anyone who can't separate their personal beliefs from the mission at hand will be dismissed from this advisory board. Is that clear? Fuck your personal beliefs. You put them aside when you're in uniform...even when you're out of it. Understood?

(*General affirmation*)

MAJOR DAVIES-HUSSAIN: We understand the gravity of this situation and how it touches many of us on a deeply personal level. But I concur with Major Kitula. Every decision we make is in the interest of protecting the American people. We are the nation's sworn defenders. We must put ourselves aside and act as one.

CPL. PATZ: How are we protecting the interests of the American people by withholding information from them? The Stranger was here *before* mankind—why keep it a secret? Why haven't we hauled that tin can up to the surface already and taken a look inside? Scientists should be—

MAJOR KITULA: You're out of line, Patz! Stick to the job at hand. See it through. File your report. End of story.

CPL. PATZ: (*inaudible*) ...part of a global mission at this point. The United Nations and World Congress should be notified... (*inaudible*).

MAJOR KITULA: Enough! Let's do this bullshit and do it right, people. No fuck-ups. This meeting is adjourned... except for you, Patz. Have a seat. We need a word.

*Classified transcription of in-room audio recording, Naval Station,*

*Gohli, Denmark, Prvt Aleksanteri Garwood / Prvt Tracey Mutz / Headquarters (dispatcher[s] unidentified), 10:33 am, January 2, 2223.*

MUTZ: Shit! Shit! Shit! This is the death seat, man! This is where Tessier and Marks got it!

GARWOOD: Tessier and Marks were reassigned, Mutz. You need to take a chill pill.

MUTZ: Fuck that! Look! Those are bullet holes down by the floorboards! They aced Marks and Tessier right here, man! In this room!

GARWOOD: You're getting hysterical. I'm going to have to ask you again to sit down and perform your duties—

MUTZ: Ah! It's lighting up! It's lighting up!

GARWOOD: (*into mic*): Headquarters, confirm vessel illumination. Over.

HQ: Vessel illumination confirmed, Denmark.

MUTZ: Oh, God! Oh, God! Look how the light hits Mother Maggie! Look at her glow!

GARWOOD: Final warning, Mutz. Take your post.

MUTZ: The Stranger is emerging! Stop them! Don't let them touch Mother Maggie!

GARWOOD: Sit down and be quiet!

MUTZ: Don't let them touch her! Don't let them touch her!

(*Loud report. Gunshot?*)

GARWOOD: Headquarters, confirm physical contact. Over.

HQ: Physical contact confirmed. Uh, everything okay over there? You left your com on.

GARWOOD: No problems. Private Mutz temporarily jeopardized the mission but I was able to neutralize the situation.

HQ: Okay, Denmark. Hey! Confirm visual. Do they have a flare down there?

GARWOOD: Confirm increased illumination,

Headquarters. The energy source appears to be…possibly electrical…maybe fusion-based. It's hard to tell. The light has swallowed them all.

HQ: Confirm last statement, Denmark? 'The light has swallowed them all'?

GARWOOD: The…the lens flare is blinding. I've lost visual on both targets and the Stranger. Confirm?

HQ: Roger that, Denmark. We have your back. The brilliance is blinding. Switching to infra-red camera to confirm…holy shit!

GARWOOD: What's going on?

HQ: There's only one figure standing in the middle of the ball of light.

GARWOOD: Confirm that last, Headquarters.

HQ: There's only one being inside the light…and it…it looks like…a giant starfish.

GARWOOD: A starfish?

HQ: Okay. Okay, it's gone. They're all gone. The MSEs and the Stranger…the ball of light is empty and dimming.

GARWOOD: Confirm the light is dimming, Headquarters. Still no visual on the targets.

HQ: That's because they're gone, Denmark. They're not in there. It's like a magic trick. The ball of light is as empty as Christ's tomb.

GARWOOD: Uh, I need a confirm on this, Headquarters. The glow has faded, but I still have no visual on the MSEs nor the Stranger. It appears the vessel has gone cold. It's totally dark. You sure you didn't see the parties enter the vessel?

HQ: I'm not sure what I saw, Denmark. Four went into the light and became one. Now there's none. Hey, I'm a poet and I didn't even know it! (*Laughs*)

GARWOOD: Headquarters, are you recording this? My cameras are rolling, but I don't have infrared.

HQ: Of course. We've got it all, Denmark.

GARWOOD: You're saying all of the targets simply... disappeared into thin air?

HQ: Thin water! (*Laughs*) Oh, blessed be!

GARWOOD: Headquarters, I need to speak to your unit commander, please.

HQ: Go fuck yourself, Denmark! This changes everything. Mother Maggie and the Stranger have become one! One! Holy shit! Holy fucking shit! (*Loud report. Gunshot?*)

GARWOOD: Headquarters, you still with me?

HQ: (*new voice*) Yeah, Denmark. We've got your back. Slight equipment malfunction. Must be going around today, you know?

GARWOOD: Understood. Confirm visual. The Stranger's vessel is cold and dark. No sign of mission targets.

HQ: Confirmed, Denmark. All quiet at the North Pole.

*Classified transcript of Major Daniel Kitula and Major James Davies-Hussain private video chat, 11:04 am, January 2, 2223.*

MAJOR KITULA: Where the hell did they go?

MAJOR DAVIES-HUSSAIN: Our best guess is they were taken aboard the vessel, though we're not sure how that was accomplished.

MAJOR KITULA: What about the idea they blew themselves up?

MAJOR DAVIES-HUSSAIN: It's possible, but we haven't gotten any elevated radiation readings from the site. No debris, no blast pattern. No damage to the vessel and they were standing right beside it.

MAJOR KITULA: Could it have been some type of low-radius, cold fusion device? We still don't know how the vessel is even powered.

MAJOR DAVIES-HUSSAIN: We probably never will. We've done all we can with the remotes, but we're not authorized to go further.

MAJOR KITULA: Fucking Patz is right. They should send the bots down to take that vessel apart. Or blow it up. Thing gives me the creeps.

MAJOR DAVIES-HUSSAIN: Things we're unsure of are always a bit intimidating.

MAJOR KITULA: Hell, I'm not sure about anything anymore, Jim.

MAJOR DAVIES-HUSSAIN: We live in confusing times, Daniel. Not our job to question. We watch, record, and file reports. Job well done. Let some other asshole figure it out.

MAJOR KITULA: This was supposed to be a world changer, Jim. Two great mysterious forces coming together! The Stranger and the walking stones! Instead it was a big fucking dud.

MAJOR DAVIES-HUSSAIN: Time will tell what it was, Daniel. It's not our place to know.

MAJOR KITULA: Fucking bullshit.

MAJOR DAVIES-HUSSAIN: Absolutely.

*Classified transcription of in-room audio. Major Aleksanteri Garwood's office. Present: A. Garwood, Cpl. Peter Modgill, Denmark Station, 2:07 pm, August 2232.*

MAJOR GARWOOD: Can you tell me what I'm looking at, Pete?

MODGILL: These images were captured last week from a bathyscaphe in the Amerasian Basin of the Arctic Ocean at the base of the Chukchi Plateau.

MAJOR GARWOOD: Great. Now can you tell me what I'm looking at?

MODGILL: This image appears to show a pair of arms sticking out of an accumulation of sediment at the base of a cliff.

MAJOR GARWOOD: Seriously? That could be anything!

MODGILL: Here's an image from another angle. You can

see the arms appear to be missing hands.

MAJOR GARWOOD: Dear God. Christ on a pony.

MODGILL: This image was taken approximately half a nautical mile from the first. The photo analysts are split fifty-fifty on whether these are feet sticking out of the sand or a symmetrical rock formation.

MAJOR GARWOOD: Fuck me…who else is aware of this? Major Downes? Davies-Hussain?

MODGILL: No. Sgt. Knowles at our Russian post was alerted to the anomaly and put his scientists on it. He passed it off to us, but I haven't sent it up yet, sir. I thought you might have a…personal interest.

MAJOR GARWOOD: Thank you, Pete. (*Pause*) How long have they been down there?

MODGILL: Based on the depth of sediment and annual accumulation rates, it could be upwards of a decade, sir.

MAJOR GARWOOD: Fuck! How is that possible? Were they *teleported* to this location from the vessel back in '22?

MODGILL: It appears they've been buried for quite some time, sir.

MAJOR GARWOOD: How…? Okay. Okay. You've got exact coordinates on these…feet and arms?

MODGILL: Drawing it up now, sir. We should be accurate to within 1.5 meters.

MAJOR GARWOOD: Good…good… (*Pause*)

MODGILL: What would you like to do, sir?

MAJOR GARWOOD: I'm not going to do anything, Pete. Pass it down the line…up the ladder…wherever the hell the chain goes. Let some other asshole figure it out. If they've been asleep down there for the last ten years, maybe we'll get lucky and they'll never wake up.

*Classified transcript of third emergency meeting of Military Counsel On Mobile Stone Entities, February 27, 2242.*

LT. WILLIAM POOLE: I've read your proposal thoroughly, Major Garwood. Depth charges. A trench filled with explosives in the middle of the Chukchi Sea. It's quite a welcome party you have planned for the MSEs, Major.

MAJOR GARWOOD: With all due respect, Lieutenant, it's the welcome these two abominations deserve. We're well aware of the havoc they caused twenty years ago. Because they've been dormant, we left them alone. But now that they're moving again, I don't see we have any choice.

LT. WILLIAM POOLE: I've been studying other choices since the MSEs were relocated in 2232. I've written extensively about it. I don't think meeting these beings with violence is the way to go, Alek. It's been tried before—most notably in Newark Bay and Iceland—and the results were disastrous. The MSEs are not prone to violence unless provoked. I think we should approach them the same way.

MAJOR GARWOOD: We've all read your science fiction series concerning the walking stones, Bill. I'll admit, it's a thrilling story, and I'm glad you're having such success with it. I'd like to (*inaudible* ) Anika Palmer (*chuckles*). [*Transcriber note: Anika Palmer is an actress appearing in 'Stone Heart Diaries,' a multimedia adaptation of Lt. Poole's work.*] But your fantasy novels have no place in a fact-based military tribunal. Look what the MSEs have done in the past. Look what they're capable of. These things *must* be stopped. Now. Today. We can't let them get closer to land.

LT. WILLIAM POOLE: (*arm raised*) Does this hunk of metal look like fiction to you, Alek? I gave my *arm* to the MSEs at Newark Bay. I've spent every day of my life since then studying them, trying to figure what makes them tick. And I'm not alone, Alek. The late Major James Davies-Hussain wrote extensively on the MSEs. The common perception is wrong. David Lawrence and Maggie Ottomeyer are not monsters. They're people...at least they were. They've become something more than human at this point. They've evolved. Don't you see?

MAJOR GARWOOD: I see your arm, Bill, and I see a miracle of modern science. I see you, Bill, and I see a warrior, someone who has sacrificed for his country. But what I don't see is how you can forgive those stone monsters for what they did to you, for what they *took* from you. You of all people should want revenge.

LT. WILLIAM POOLE: It's not personal, Alek. It's not about revenge. I think David Lawrence's lust for revenge fueled his early choices and got this whole ball rolling. But his mission has changed. I believe David and Maggie are... going home.

MAJOR GARWOOD: To Atlantis? Bikini Bottom? (*chuckles*)

LT. WILLIAM POOLE: We'll never know if we destroy them. Monitor David and Maggie all you want. Tag them with trackers if they make you nervous, but let them go where they want to go. They're not bothering anyone on the bottom of the ocean! I think they may be looking for a volcano or a fault line in the Pacific that they can disappear into.

MAJOR GARWOOD: (*inaudible*) ...one-armed freak... (*inaudible*)

LT. WILLIAM POOLE: What did you call me?

MAJOR GARWOOD: I didn't call you anything. I said Herald's Peak. It's a location off Herald Canyon. There's a natural bottleneck there. Perfect place for an ordnance trench. It's in my report...you said you read it thoroughly.

LT. WILLIAM POOLE: Yeah, I did. It says, "Blow them up." Your report could have been reduced to a fortune cookie message, Alek.

MAJOR GARWOOD: I outlined several scenarios where the MSEs could be captured, but they all pose too great a risk. Elimination is the best plan, Bill.

LT. WILLIAM POOLE: I disagree with you, Alek. I think others do, too. Let's put it to a vote.

MAJOR GARWOOD: Fair enough. Let's vote.

# 14

## *Mudspeak VI*

When the whale bumped me from behind, I assumed it was an attack. I spun around with my fists up. Maggie and I were jumpy after the ship sank, expecting torpedos to come flying out of the dark at any moment. But the whale circled around and nuzzled its snout between my legs—*climb aboard, let's ride*. Maggie was already on the back of a gray beluga, her forearms pressed tight against the whale's body. I climbed on the back of the whale next to me, grabbed its pectoral fins and we were off.

Unlike the giant ray Maggie and I had tried riding in the Atlantic, the whales didn't buck us off. The belugas moved fast and gracefully through the water despite our weight on their backs. They traveled in a pod of six, each taking turns carrying Maggie and I. When the lead whale tired, it tipped me off, and I'd tumble through the water until a new whale slid beneath me and caught me on its back.

We traveled like that for days, racing across the surface, falling, then rocketing forward through the water again. I expected the whales to drop us off somewhere north of Norway, but they kept going, slipping through the Fram

Strait between Svalbard and Greenland, taking us deep into the Arctic Ocean. The belugas handed us off to a pod of four orcas, which carried us north. When the orcas tired, they passed us off to a pod of a dozen big blue whales. Perhaps our free ride wasn't entirely altruistic; I got the feeling the whales didn't want us walking through the Nansen Basin any more than the giant starfish wanted us exploring the Mid-Atlantic Ridge. Did the whales have a secret city at the bottom of the sea too? They couldn't dive that deep; maybe they protected something else living on the bottom of the Nansen Basin, an ally, or a food source...maybe more giant starfish.

The whales carried us hundreds of miles. I expected another attack, but it never came. Maybe the military couldn't track us while we rode the whales. Maybe they lost interest. Either way, after several days of whale travel, I began to relax. They carried us past the Barents Shelf and out over deep water, switching out whale pods as needed.

The whales finally dropped us off beneath a thick layer of ice in the middle of the arctic. I realized the ride was over when I fell for over an hour and another whale never came to pick me up.

We landed on top of a jagged black seamount. Gakkel Ridge? Probably, based on the deep trench running down the middle. Another seam in the earth. Fortunately, we landed on the north side of the trench. We found a path etched by a landslide and slowly descended into Amundsen Basin.

The climb down Gakkel Ridge took us the better part of a week. It felt like climbing down a mountain of hard, black marshmallow, old lava pillowed on top of ancient lava, atop prehistoric lava.

The bottom of the Arctic Ocean was fairly clean and garbage-free. One notable exception was a pile of rusty metal barrels marked with faded hazardous waste symbols.

Someone had aimed for the Gakkel Trench but missed. Four of the containers were cracked open, but temperature and pressure kept the contents confined to a greenish cloud that hovered like an aura around the damaged cans. Maggie and I gave the barrels a wide berth.

We walked past a shipwreck, nothing more than a few wooden boards and a brass plaque that read *SS Baychimo*. We'd found the final resting place of the ghost ship of the arctic. Whoop-dee-do.

Life at the bottom of the arctic was surprisingly dynamic. We walked through a forest of jellyfish tentacles, the creatures' bodies hovering hundreds of feet above us, the poison tips of their appendages sliding harmlessly over our stone skin like party streamers. We worked our way around giant clams as tall as our chests and glowing green sea spiders twice as high. Why was everything so gigantic down here at the bottom of the arctic? Elevated oxygen in the water? Maybe the cold slowed the aging process and allowed cells to reach their maximum size.

We got eaten once. Swallowed whole by something invisible, thin-skinned, and immense. We walked for an hour without realizing we were inside of something until I stumbled over the bony ridge of the creature's jaw. Maggie and I took advantage of the free ride for a time, lying against the creature's thin, slatted rib cage while our devourer carried us farther north.

Once the creature veered east, I pried its jaws apart and held them open for Maggie like she was a boxer exiting the ring. We stepped out onto bedrock and silt. The creature moved off with nothing more than a flutter in the darkness, an unseen, unstoppable force of nature, huge, invisible. Why not remain inside the beast, allow it to digest us and shit us out? What did it matter?

It mattered. Maggie and I belonged to the earth and to the

earth we would return, swallowed by a subduction zone trench, not an invisible sea monster.

We carried on into the deepest part of the Eurasian Basin. The iron ore in my body tingled. The north pole was close, a few miles away. The plain leveled out to a gentle downward slope.

A vessel sat on the ocean floor ahead of us, flat black and half buried in black sand. I mistook it for a shadow. But as we walked closer, I saw its outline was too refined, too uniform. This was a man-made vessel.

But I was wrong about that, too. The vessel looked and felt plastic, a fiberglass car bumper or PVC pipe, except it clanked like hollow metal when I rapped my knuckles against it. Maggie and I walked the periphery of the vessel twice. It was the size of a small house and perfectly round. No windows, no doors, no markings except for an indented groove running along the outer edge. Maybe it was a storage container packed with more hazardous waste, stashed away like a dirty secret.

I knocked twice; shave and a haircut, two bits. Nothing. We walked around the vessel again. Its design was aerodynamic; it didn't *look* like a storage container.

The ridge around the edge of the vessel began to glow, blue dissolving to green, growing brighter until it was a solid beam sweeping over our bodies. It scanned us from head to toe, like an MRI, except completely silent.

I wasn't afraid. Maggie didn't seem to be either. A fish swam past, the soft green light making its fins glow like a neon beer sign.

The beam shut off and the vessel went dark. I looked at Maggie, my eyes readjusting to the murk. *Show over?*

Not yet. The groove glowed again, brighter this time. An opening appeared and blinding light spilled out, making the bottom of the Arctic as bright as a sunny day. Maggie covered her eyes and I squinted through my fingers.

Two figures emerged from the vessel. The door closed behind them, plunging the ocean bottom back into darkness. But the figures continued glowing green, as if lit from within. They stood no taller than our chests, their bodies thin, almost scrawny. Pencil necks struggled to keep their bald, bulbous heads balanced between their shoulders. *Were they wearing diving suits?* That would explain the big, unblinking eyes. *But why so short? Were they children? Dwarves?*

The soldiers I'd fought in Newark looked like me, but they were only men in plastic suits. We're all trapped in our armor. George made new bodies for Maggie and I—swapped our blood and bone for sand and stone—but we're no less trapped.

Maggie and I weren't wearing plastic suits and neither were the figures standing before us. Everything was as it appeared. Maggie and I were walking statues and these were little green men from outer space.

I extended my arm to shake hands. The creatures ignored my offer. Instead, one of them held up a three-fingered hand, colors swirling in its palm like a cosmic kaleidoscope. I tensed, remembering the palm blasters the stone soldier used in Newark. This looked more like a magic trick than a weapon.

The creature on the left stretched its glowing palms toward Maggie and she reached out to meet its touch. Bad idea. I stepped forward to stop her, but the figure in front of me placed its palm against my chest.

Memories of Ghee flooded my mind, making my knees buckle. How many times had Ghee placed her hands against me in the same way? Once to call me to action. Again to stop me from killing. A final time before I lifted her to her death. Every time Ghee laid her soft skin against my rough stone, I felt Sarah's touch traveling through time, spanning generations. Maggie looked like Sarah, but Ghee *felt* like her, the beat of her heart, the rise and fall of her lungs, and sparkling vivacity of her lifeforce. I don't know if I believe in reincarnation, but Ghee's touch was like catching a whiff of Sarah's perfume, or hearing the clack of her heels on the floor above me.

I felt Ghee and Sarah beside me as the little green alien pressed its trio of multi-knuckled, reptilian fingers flat against my chest. Tingling warmth radiated through my body, not unpleasant, but…strange. In addition to Sarah and Ghee, I felt my father-in-law George's presence, too. But, unlike in life, George bore no malice toward me. When the parade of souls I'd murdered at Cashman and Clarke showed up, they passed only as interested spectators with no judgment or apparent ill will. All mistakes bygones, all sins forgiven. All's well that ends dead.

I turned to look at Maggie. The alien creature held Maggie's stumps, a glowing orb of energy growing between them like a rapidly inflating balloon…

…and then I fainted.

Yeah, I passed out like a two-ton stone paperweight. It's embarrassing. I'd never passed out before, either as a fleshy man or a stone one.

The next thing I remembered was Maggie shaking me awake. *Awake*! How could that be? I hadn't slept in over two hundred years! I didn't need sleep. But something in that creature's touch shut down my head and sent me off to LaLa Land. Maggie looked equally disoriented. A cluster of mussels hung from her chin, giving her an odd black beard. We must have been out for quite a while.

We lay at the base of a cliff. There are so many different mountain ranges under the sea it was impossible to know which one this was. There are no streets signs in the deep down. We probably should have brought a GPS.

The metal in my body told me we were on the far side of the north pole, hundreds of miles away from the feel of it. How could we have traveled so far? Had another mule team of whales carried us here, or had those beings tossed us into their space ship and dumped us off on the far side of the arctic like drunken prom dates?

Maggie helped me to my feet and I plucked the mussels off her face. She scraped several handfuls off my back.

Land lie somewhere above us; Canada off to the left, Russia to the right. Maggie and I followed the mountainous cliff east, looking for a good spot to climb.

We walked for weeks before the cliffs suddenly banked left and the ground began a slow, steady incline. The slope grew steeper and steeper, until Maggie and I were crawling, climbing. If either of us fell, we'd be finished, shattered on the rocks below.

When the grade grew too steep, I carried Maggie piggy-back. She couldn't climb without hands, and, honestly, I enjoyed the feel of her arms and legs wrapped around me. I carried her often, even when I didn't have to.

The climb took more than a month. Instead of pain or fatigue I felt a constant pressure building inside, turning to heat. Every fiber of my being burned by the time Maggie and I reached the top of the black mountain. When we did, I lay in the soft sand for a long while until my body temperature returned to stone cold. Maggie walked on my back and that helped loosen my knotted muscles. She had good feet.

A long, empty plain stretched before us, broken only by the occasional coral colony or a field of seagrass. Was this the Siberian Sea? The Chukchi? As long as we kept south, we'd eventually hit a coastline and could work our way to the Bering Strait.

The only excitement during an otherwise long, uneventful walk was when a weird-mouthed goblin shark shot out from beneath a stone and bit my leg. I shook it loose and pushed the fish away, but it kept coming back, more aggressive each time. It locked its jaws around my head and tore savagely until Maggie grabbed it by the tail and pulled it off. I finally had to tear the shark in half, which produced a whole cloud of other sharks. A feeding frenzy whipped up and Maggie and I couldn't get out of there fast enough. We're slow as turtles and the sharks wouldn't stop biting us, even when all their teeth broke. Stupid sharks.

We didn't see a thing for days. The ocean above us was still covered with thick ice, but the underside of the floes were fuzzy with phosphorescent green growth like springtime moss. It's amazing how life not only survives but thrives in these torturous environments.

As the ice broke up, I saw patches of black open water overhead. A herd of walruses investigated us. Two bulls dive-bombed Maggie and I, but I bitch-slapped them and they left us alone. *Coo-coo, ka-choo, douchebag*. Polar bears dove above us, but we were still too deep for them to reach. Good. I didn't want to wrestle a polar bear. They're mean.

We spotted two battleships anchored off the Russian coast. We gave them a wide berth, but we saw two more the closer we got to the Bering Strait. They were funneling us toward land, penning us in.

Fuck it. If the military wanted us, we couldn't stop them. We walked on. Schools of herring followed, wrapping around us like a cloud of smoke. Sea life grew plentiful the closer we got to the coast. So did the ships. These weren't fishing vessels. Fishing vessels don't have torpedo tubes. I saw two points of land in the distance—the tip of Russia and the tip of Alaska—separated by a matter of miles. A line of ships blocked the Bering Strait, like dark storm clouds on the horizon.

Four underwater vessels approached us near Herald

Island. These were small, individual submersibles, but, like the warships, these tiny subs were outfitted with torpedo tubes and gun turrets. Maggie and I stood shoulder-to-shoulder. The vessels approached slowly, cautiously, creeping to within twenty feet and fanning around us until Maggie and I were nearly surrounded.

The submarines were flat black, similar to the strange vessel we'd encountered near the North Pole. But the mirrored glass front of the lead vehicle cleared like smoke inside a crystal ball, revealing a man inside. The captain of the vessel smiled and waved a metal arm. Was that a weapon, or did he really have a robotic limb? Maggie returned the captain's wave.

A bullet struck Maggie in the back of the head, snapping her neck forward, a cloud of dust and grit swirling around her shoulders.

*Christ, they've blown her head off!* I thought of Ghee's headless body tumbling out of my grasp. *No. Not again.*

I spun and leapt on the attacking sub. My speed surprised both the sub captain and myself. I drove my fist through the vessel's mirrored black glass. The next half-second unfolded in slow motion. The glass shattered around my fist and brilliant white light burst from the interior of the vessel. A soldier's shocked, slack-jawed face flashed by so quickly I couldn't identify race nor gender before the soldier's skull collapsed under the sudden pressure change, body imploding on itself in a red mist. Water flooded the vessel and the sub surged forward, knocking me to the ground, belching black smoke until it flipped over and came to rest on the sea bottom.

I stood and shook my fists. One down, three to go. I'd never survive, but I'd go down fighting.

I didn't have to.

Maggie emerged from a cloud of bubbles like a vision,

Venus rising from a clamshell. A chunk of her head, including her left ear, was gone, and a crack ran down the center of her skull like a part in her hair. She raised her arms and shook her head.

*No. No more violence. No more fighting.*

The captain with the metal arm was white as a sheet, hands over his head like he was being mugged. He shook like a leaf; I swear I could smell his fear and sweat through the glass and water. I didn't trust him—the raised hands might be a ploy—but Maggie approached the vessel. I followed behind, not wanting her to get too close. But Maggie kept going until her stumps touched the vessel's glass front. The captain gazed into Maggie's face. He slowly lowered his hands—one metal, one flesh and bone—until they rested against the glass opposite Maggie's stone stumps.

An orb of energy grew between them, no bigger than a pea at first, swirling green, pink, and blue, growing and expanding until it was the size of a beach ball, glowing brilliant white, covering both Maggie and the captain's forearms. The ball of light appeared on both sides of the glass —both underwater and inside the vessel—until Maggie pulled away and the light drifted entirely inside with the captain. He held it in his hands until it expanded to fill the interior of the vessel, dissipating into a shimmering essence that never completely faded.

The captain smiled at Maggie. He nodded and spoke into his headset. A moment later the remaining subs circled around and lined up before us like a firing squad. This was it. I slipped my arm around Maggie's waist.

But, to my surprise (probably not Maggie's, because she's smarter), the submarines turned in unison. Something popped out of the back of the lead vessel and I jumped in front of Maggie, thinking it might be a torpedo. But it was a tow line, two of them, made of thick nylon rope, and a pile of metal pipes that clanged on the ocean floor. Maggie turned to me and winked.

The two subs on either side of the leader slowly backed up, emitting the same chirping backup beep garbage trucks used. Robotic arms popped out, reminding me of spider legs. Each sub had three arms and they worked as a team, nine spindly limbs quickly assembling the pipes and ropes. When they were done, the arms retracted into the black bulbous bodies. The tiny subs moved back in line with the lead vessel.

They'd built a bench, a love seat some might call it, the kind you find on a front porch glider. White containers that looked like giant pills were placed under the arms for buoyancy, allowing the seat to float several feet off the ocean floor. The long tow ropes connected it to the lead sub. Our underwater chariot was complete.

*Holy shit! Was this really happening?* Maggie smiled and took my arm, leading me to the bench and sitting me down like I was a child. She sat beside me. The chair sank to the ocean floor beneath our weight, but then the white containers hissed with compressed air and we lifted up like an amusement park ride, a Ferris wheel taking off, stomach dropping, fear and exhilaration blending together. The lead sub moved forward, picking up speed. Maggie and I rose higher in the water, parasailing behind the sub, watching our shadows race over the ocean floor.

Maggie put her hands over her head and howled like a teenager on a rollercoaster. She *looked* like a teenager, her smile broad and carefree, mouth opened wide with unbridled joy. I couldn't stop laughing. Flying through the water behind a military escort was so sudden and surreal. We were finally on the fast track to…what? Our death? Our future? Whatever lie next. If it's nothingness, we'd welcome it. We had to know. Even stones dream of becoming. It's all we dream of.

We sailed through the Bering Strait like royalty, the sea

above us clogged with military vessels: cruisers, cutters, carriers. We passed several full-size submarines. Some were miles away, dim shadows lurking in the murky water. Others were close enough to touch, torpedo tubes gaping black holes.

But none fired. We passed unmolested into the Bering Sea. The ships overhead shrank in number the further south we traveled, until it was just us and our trio of mini-subs. Our escort slowed considerably once we crossed the continental shelf. The seafloor fell away in a sudden series of cascading cliffs. The sensation of sailing over vast nothingness was disorienting and scary. I slipped my arm around Maggie's shoulders, pulling her close, and gripped the metal frame of our seat. It felt puny and weak, like the whole thing might rattle apart at any moment. Our chariot wasn't made for an extended stay in the deep ocean and neither were the mini-subs. They took us pretty deep—a slow descent that lasted nearly a day—and then the tow ropes unlatched from the lead vessel with a soft metallic clink and floated away. The submarines stopped but Maggie and I continued our downward trajectory, falling down and out into the darkness. Air hissed from the floaters beneath our chair, turning our underwater free-fall into a controlled descent to the sea floor. About a hundred feet from the bottom, our chair finally collapsed under the ocean pressure, and we tumbled the rest of the way. Fortunately, the landing was soft.

They dropped us in the Aleutian Basin, in a flat gap between two mountains; Bowers Ridge and Shirnov Ridge, I think. The trench was less than a hundred miles from here, just beyond the Aleutian Islands.

# 15

## *Third Final Report II*

*Excerpt from* "Arctic Flight, A Spiritual Journey" *by Sgt. William Poole, spiritual/self help, September 2246.*

They looked like a couple of kids sitting in an oversized swing, a chariot of sorts, laughing like children, giggling, arms held above their heads like rollercoaster riders. The Cyroscope zeroed in on their faces—carefree, lit with a joy that made them glow. I couldn't help but smile, too. If they were children on a hayride, what did that make me? The farmer driving the tractor? Their father?

Just the opposite. In truth, they were both my parents. The day I lost my right arm was the day I was reborn as a product of my attackers. For a long time I sought revenge for my violated body. But once I let go of that anger, I realized how profoundly these two had altered my mind and soul. An arm was a small price to pay for the gift of enlightenment they gave me, a gift that guides me like a holy light through the darkest of times.

I am a product of Maggie and the Rock God, a lowly disciple made of soft flesh and meager bones. Yet I was their protector too, leading them to safety through the tight confines of the Bering Strait.

Military ships of every nation lined our path. Most of the sailors on board believed they were part of an elaborate military exercise, but a few were aware of the majestic event happening in the waters beneath them. They knelt and wept as the Stone Saviors passed, offering thanks and praise, as was just and right. We owe the world to stone.

I pulled back on the throttle. The Vassick was fast for a submersible, capable of top underwater speeds close to thirty-five knots. I couldn't get the needle past twenty towing two tons of stone, but it was fast enough. Maggie and the Rock God seemed to enjoy themselves.

The only glitch had been Commander Whiting firing on Maggie. Was it an accident? Surely, Meriellen didn't think she could stop Mother Maggie with standard weaponry. What had gone wrong? Whatever happened, it cost Whiting her life (and the Navy a $3.2 billion Vassick). I shudder as I recall how quickly the Rock God moved, how he tore Whiting's sub apart like paper.

It could have easily ended there. McClunkey screamed and sobbed in my headset, but DaVolt was pissed. She cursed and opened her torpedo ports. I shouted at her to hold her fire and she told me to fuck myself, screaming, "Whiting is out! Whiting is out!" over and over. I pulled rank on DaVolt and she cursed me again. I couldn't stop her from firing on the Rock God…unless I took her out first.

Dear God, history echoed in my head in the most sinister of ways. Ghee Dorfhouse was killed by an accidental bullet. Whiting's accidental shot got her killed. Now I might need to take out DaVolt the same way I had Baxter two decades earlier. Maybe this was God's will. Or the Rock God's. Or just bad circumstances. Either way, I locked my battle cannon on DaVolt's Vassick and gave her a final warning.

Mother Maggie saved the day…my life…the world. She

certainly saved Valerie DaVolt's life. I would have killed her in order to protect Maggie and the Rock God. But Maggie stepped forward and gave me her gift of light and love, passed it from her soul, through water and glass, and into my heart and mind. Maggie's light illuminated the cabin of my Vassick so brightly, I imagined DaVolt and McClunkey could see me through fifty yards of murky sea water. (Both later confirmed they could. DaVolt said I looked "orgasmic." Weirdo. At least it got her to close her torpedo tubes.)

Maggie's light spoke with a voice like an angel and told me exactly where to pilot the Vassick. I dropped my tow rope and DaVolt suggested the suspension swing. McClunkey and DaVolt built the swing and Maggie helped the Rock God climb aboard.

I turned the Vassick south and opened the throttle halfway. The vessel lurched forward and the swing lifted along with its stony cargo. Maggie smiled and that's when I was reborn again. It was her smile that led me like a beacon through all those dark years, the reward I'd sought all along. A smile of hope and forgiveness, a smile of reason and mad artistry, a smile that could cure the world.

*From Books4U Comments on* "Arctic Flight, A Spiritual Journey by Sgt. William Poole," *December 31, 2246.*

*Charlotte R wrote:* Did this really happen?

*Herbert M wrote:* I think Bill Poole thinks it really happened.

*Alpi G wrote:* It really happened. This is not a novel.

*Anne H wrote:* It's spiritual/self help. I believe this story is Mr. Poole's metaphor for alcoholism.

*The Fonz wrote:* If you look at *Arctic Flight* in relation to the rest of Poole's literary works, it's clear this is all part of his "Beneath the Arctic" series. *Arctic Flight* is like a very boring climax to *Terror Under The Sea.*

*Hillevi B wrote:* I liked this book, but I didn't understand it.

*Tamika K wrote: Jaws* was better.

*Carey J wrote:* Is there still a spaceship under the North Pole?

*Nina M-C wrote:* The spaceship IS the North Pole. It's a giant magnet that controls everything.

*Travis C wrote:* This book sucked.

*Justin S wrote:* Total shitfest.

# 16

## *Mudspeak VII*

We rise and fall, rise and fall, success and failure its own tide, forever ebbing. It took a long while to climb the Aleutian Ridge. It was all points and crags, a slow go for stone feet. But we climbed until we broke the surface on a stoney spit of land covered with sand and green-brown brush. The island was tiny and uninhabited, barely more than a couple of acres of exposed rock peeking out of the sea. It probably disappeared completely come high tide.

But Maggie and I sat a while, enjoying the sunshine and fresh air. I slipped my arm around her waist and she rested her head on my shoulder. This tiny rock sticking out of the sea might be the most beautiful place on Earth. Maybe the subduction zone would chew us up and spit us out and we'd be reborn as a little volcanic island like this.

The sun warmed us, the wind caressed us, and, just before sunset, a soft rain fell and washed us clean. A rock could really live life full measure in a place like this. Maybe we should stay, spend the rest of our time here, eroding away together.

A drone buzzed overhead, killing our vibe. It only stayed a

few minutes, circling high in the sky before taking off east. It returned an hour later, buzzing so low over Maggie and I that I tried to swat it out of the air. Way to ruin the moment, assholes. We took the hint and left, climbing down into the sea.

The shelf dropped off into deep water almost immediately. Maggie and I spent a lot of time on our butts, letting gravity drag us down, a sleigh ride into the cold, dark deep. The water pressure increased around us, first like a blanket, then like a blood-pressure cuff, a giant fist trying to grind us into sand.

Down, down, down, into the belly of the earth we climbed. The undersea mountain teemed with life. We passed dark caves filled with yellow eyes. We walked through a field of undulating seagrass as tall as our shoulders. Crabs—always crabs, forever crabs— followed in our footsteps, while squid and jellyfish dangled overhead like tacky decorations at a middle-school dance.

A sloping ledge ended at a cliff. Maggie hung over the edge while I climbed down her body until I hung from her ankles. I dropped and counted to one hundred before landing on a slope of loose rocks. I stood, planted my feet, and turned to catch Maggie. We did this for the next five cliffs we encountered, until my knees buckled on the sixth catch and we tumbled downhill for half-a-mile. After that we jumped together, arm-in-arm.

We fell farther each time, free-falling for two minutes, then five, then fifteen, thirty. Sea life dwindled the further we descended, until it seemed there was only us and other stones. We journeyed deeper and the sea life returned, swarms of small, glowing fish at first, followed by bigger and bigger creatures, until we were down among the deep sea giants again.

The denizens of the North Pacific treated us with distinct

indifference. Nothing attacked us, but nothing helped us either. The fish in the deep trench were nervous and jumpy. The water vibrated almost imperceptibly and the ground trembled beneath our feet. This was a place where the Earth itself couldn't be trusted, where the ground might change shape at any moment.

As if to re-enforce the idea, the seamount began to quake, forcing Maggie and I to hold each other for support. The quakes came so often, Maggie and I quickly learned to walk and climb through the tremors. They usually didn't last for more than a minute. Once, we were forced to hide inside a cave while stones the size of bowling balls cascaded down the mountainside. I didn't want us to get buried in there, so we left before the tremors died down. We were too close for stupid mistakes.

The bottom of the world was near. The pressure from above made every footstep a Herculean labor. How much deeper could the trench go?

We came to another cliff. Standing on the edge and peering over felt different. This abyss seemed deeper, blacker, more final. Maggie and I locked arms and jumped.

We fell for hours and hours, miles and miles. We fell forever, our final fall, tumbling head over heels, clacking together like billiard balls, falling through clouds of fish that darted away as we rocketed past, yet were caught in the swirling chaos of our turbulent wake. We cut through the water like a meteor, holding each other for dear life and blessed death.

But the ocean is cruel. Twisting currents hammered us the further we fell, smashing us against the sides of the trench. My knee cracked like a clap of summer thunder against stone harder than I, and my right foot floated away into the darkness along with my ankle and most of my calf. Then Maggie was gone too, pulled from my grasp by the bully sea, whisked away like Dorothy in a hurricane. I was alone, falling fast and hopeless.

I landed in a pile of garbage, of course. The grossest thing I encountered was a set of false teeth fused to a plastic water bottle. Maybe this was the next evolution of sea-life. It took hours, but I clawed my way up through a hundred feet of rot and waste to free myself

The trench was as wide as a soccer field and filled side-to-side with garbage: decaying plastic, rusted metal, tile shards gone green with furry algae. Ragged plastic bags waved like battlefield flags, while hard plastic formed jagged, angular heaps. I tried to stand, forgot my foot was missing, and fell. I crawled with the crabs (fucking crabs) until I found a length of metal pipe to use as a walking stick. It didn't help much. The pipe kept getting stuck in the garbage. The ground shifted beneath me, trash chasms opening and closing like hungry graves looking to swallow me whole. My balance was shot and I fell often.

The trench ran east-west, but I didn't know which direction Maggie had fallen. I could be walking away from her. I could be walking *over* her, not knowing if she lay buried in trash. Some end for my beloved queen.

I walked west for several hours, then decided she'd probably landed east of me and turned around. Microscopic creatures glowed like clouds of green fire…enormous beasts moved fast and invisible in the darkness. I started to panic. (Okay, I *did* panic.) What if I never found Maggie? What if I spent the rest of eternity wandering the bottom of the Aleutian Trench looking for my lost love? Such a romantic notion!

It sucked.

I found my foot atop a pile of PVC elbow couplings repurposed as a habitat for mussels, eels, and crabs. I left it there. What was I going to do with it? Mix up a batch of concrete and glue it back on? Masonry supplies were hard to find at the bottom of the ocean. Maybe coral, calcium, and plankton could fuse it back together, but I didn't have time to waste. I left my broken foot to the crabs and carried on.

Holes pitted the garbage at the bottom of the trench. Any of them could be Maggie's impact crater. I poked my walking stick deep into several holes, but didn't strike anything solid. What if she fell beyond my reach and couldn't get out? I replayed our separation over and over in my mind; my broken leg floating away and Maggie slipping out of my grasp. How much longer had I fallen after that? Long enough that she could have landed anywhere.

I paced the sea bottom, my thoughts scattered. I tried to come up with a logical plan for locating Maggie and couldn't think of any. The idea of spending eternity alone down here at the bottom of the sea filled me with dread. I hadn't felt fear —real terror—since being reborn as stone. But the thought of never seeing Maggie again gripped me with cold terror and raw, open-wound sadness. I'd convinced myself I'd never love again after Sarah, and I was able to beat those emotions down for two hundred years. But being with Maggie, basking in the positive energy she radiated, the beauty of her smile, turned my stone heart to mud once more.

I walked east toward Alaska and the trench grew wider, the water cloudier. The earth trembled constantly, stirring the sand, trash, and sediment. Three figures swam toward me out of the murk. They had tubular arms that ended in webbed fingers, veiny breasts that hung in triple rows on their chests, and powerful tails covered with iridescent scales. Kelp grew around their genitals. These mermaids weren't the beautiful, Daryl Hannah-type. Their faces were more fishy than feminine, with thick, purple lips like a grouper, bulging eyes, and thick necks that flexed pink, frilly gills. They stopped in front of me.

*Man of stone seeks woman of stone.*

*The lady of light.*

*The rock with tits.*

They'd seen Maggie! Was she with them?

*She's not here.*

*She's gone.*

*West.*

But *was* she here? How long ago had she left?

*Go away, rock head.*

*The boulder bitch isn't here.*

*She's gone. She's gone.*

Yeah, yeah, she's gone west. That's pretty fucking vague. Can you give me another hint?

*Follow the light.*

*Follow the light.*

*Follow the light, stone boy.*

I hobbled away, but every time I looked over my shoulder the mermaids were still there, watching me. Unfriendly bitches. Maybe they were protecting something back there. The ocean was filled with private places off limit to visitors. I understood. I would have happily stayed hidden in the backwoods of New Jersey, covered in vines and dirt, sinking into the earth, if Ghee and Maggie hadn't needed my help. But surely the mermaids saw I was desperate, out of my element. Couldn't they help a dumb rock out?

Follow the light is bad advice in total darkness. I headed west as fast as one leg and a rusty metal walking stick would carry me. According to the mermaids, I'd been traveling in the wrong direction all along. Stupid, stupid, stupid. But how did the mermaids know about Maggie (*"the lady of light…the boulder bitch…"*) unless she'd been there? Maybe there was a deep sea communication system I wasn't aware of.

Fear crept in again, a new-old feeling. I didn't try to stop it, reveling in the majesty of terror, its overwhelming power.

Fear took me on a thrill ride, a log flume of adrenaline. No, I wasn't afraid of the nasty mermaids or anything else that swam out of the dark. I could fight those things and I hit hard. What frightened me—perhaps what frightens us all—isn't what swims out of the dark, but the darkness itself, the veil that separates worlds, the hidden, the invisible, never seen but always there, right on the other side. The dark goes on forever. But I go on, too, staggering one-legged into the nothingness, the fear in my heart affirmation of my existence. I live and I'm scared shitless, but I'm not stopping for nothing, not for anything.

Except Maggie.

Her light, a glowing medicine ball twirling above her head, illuminated the sea floor for miles. All the creatures of the deep were drawn to it, as was I, just another ocean dweller now, a moving hunk of earth no different than the tectonic plates that shift and grind atop the planet's surface, buckling up and swallowing one another. She sits atop a throne of neon coral, surrounded by fish and fanfare, oysters spitting pearls that mound around her feet like a bubble bath, bright red sea lilies waving like adoring fans, shocking pink sea cucumbers moving in the currents, hard to differentiate from the plastic trash bags drifting along the bottom. Maggie smiled and she *was* the light, it came from her smile, her brilliance, her love. I dropped my walking stick and fell to my knees. I could crawl faster than I could walk, a child frustrated by the learning curve of toddlerhood. Maggie met me halfway, scooped me up in her strong arms as I swooned. We knelt among the piles of trash and pearls, her inner power recharging my own.

I wanted more. I guess everyone does. I'd hoped we'd make it to the Marianas Trench, the deepest point on earth, but the Aleutian suited our needs just as well. It's a solid choice as far as subduction zones, swallowing two- to three-inches per year of the Pacific plate. At that rate we'd be gone completely in fifteen years, hardly any time at all. Sometime after that we'd turn back to magma.

We laid down before the mouth of the great beast, the beginning and end of the world, the alpha and the omega, the ass and the mouth, like the uni-orifice our starfish guide used to eat and shit itself out. The pressure of the plates above and below us was divine, infernal, heat like an electric blanket on a cold winter morning, a comforting barrier against the outside world.

We go in, our bodies pressed together until the heat and pressure of the world fuses us into one.

There is no death, only rebirth.

May we be reborn as diamonds.

# 17

## *Final Note*

*From DaScoop aggregator, February 1, 2313.*

Hello! Because you enjoyed _*Final Report: Mobile Stone Entities*_, you might also enjoy these related articles.

*From* American Military Today, *May 15, 2303.*

It is with great sadness and deep regret that we announce the unexpected passing of General X____X. The general was traveling to a retirement celebration last night when authorities lost contact with his helicopter shortly after takeoff. A debris field was found near Oahu Beach… [*Read More*]

*From* Modern Sculpting Artstream, *"What's New?" April 2305.*

The Newark City Arts Council, in conjunction with the Chemloco College Endowment Grant Foundation, hosted the installation of artist Sven Bjorgensen's statue, "Ghee," in the city's historic Waterfront Park this week.

The installation ceremony, hosted by the mayor and council, also marked the opening of a luxury condominium complex at Waterfront Park, once home to shipping and storage facilities as well as the site of the Battle Of Newark Bay.

Ghee Dorfhouse, the revolutionary leader who spearheaded the Battle of Newark Bay, is a controversial historical figure, and Bjorgensen's statue—featuring a young woman climbing over a fence—has garnered mixed reviews among both politicians and the public (though many art critics have spoken favorably of Bjorgensen's use of tone and texture).

A bronze plaque beneath the statue reads:

*Magaret "Ghee" Dorfhouse, an American patriot and leader of the Maggot Revolutionary Force, sacrificed herself for the sake of her nation—and the world—on this spot, May 3, 2222. May the gift of freedom be eternally cherished and the light of truth burn forever bright.*

The Waterfront Park Condo Association thanked the... [*Read More*]

*From* Global Geo News, *October 2313.*

Subduction slippage and crust consumption in the Aleutian Trench is blamed for the magnitude 7.7 undersea quake that wiped out all but the highest peaks of the Hawaiian Islands last month. The ensuing tsunami rendered the Hawaiian Islands all but uninhabitable, washing away miles and miles of homes, businesses, and military facilities, including the 10,000-unit Oahu Military Retirement Center.

Donations can be sent to Maggie's Smile Foundation... [*Read More*]

[*Related articles of interest*]

"An Introduction to Clay Pottery" - *KnowNet Learning Module*

"Folklore and Myth in Modern America" - *Chemloco College Online*

"Untold Military Secrets Revealed!" - *Hoobah Stream*

"North Pole Vacation Excursions" - *Go4ItTravel*

"'Let them cum! Let them cum! Let them cum!'" - *Adult XXX Playland*

"Personal Self Defense Strategies" - *BXHome*

"Home Security Made Easy" - *BXHome*

"How To Change Your Identity And Disappear" - [*anonymous*]

**END**

## Also by Rob Errera

Fiction

*Hangman's Jam, Volume 1*
*The Dunwich Horrors Die Tonight, Hangman's Jam II*
*Kiss The Sky Goodbye, Hangman's Jam III*
*Songs In the Key Of Madness, New Variations On Hangman's Jam*
*Sensual Nightmares*
*Eight Strange Stories*
*The Mud Man*

Non-Fiction

*Autism Dad, Volume 1*
*Autism Dad, Volume 2*
*Autism Dad, Volume 3*
*Fake News and Real Bullshit*
*Rock 'n' Roll and Comic Books Taught Me All I Know*
*Santa's Little Helper Wants to Eat Your Children*

## About the Author

Rob Errera is a writer, editor, musician, and literary critic. He is the author of **The Mud Man** and the **Hangman's Jam** series of stories as well as the non-fiction **Autism Dad** book series. He lives in New Jersey with his wife, two kids, and a bunch of rescued pets. Follow the fun at ***roberrera.com***.

www.ingramcontent.com/pod-product-compliance
Lightning Source LLC
LaVergne TN
LVHW091038080826
845145LV00002B/543

* 9 7 8 1 9 4 9 0 4 3 3 4 1 *